Calum McSwiggan

UNION SQUARE & CO.

NEW YORK

For anyone who's ever wanted to wish away the
thing that makes them different.

UNION
SQUARE
&CO.
NEW YORK

UNION SQUARE & CO. and the distinctive Union Square & Co. logo are
trademarks of Sterling Publishing Co., Inc.

Union Square & Co., LLC, is a subsidiary of Sterling Publishing Co., Inc.

This edition first published in 2023 by Union Square & Co., LLC.
First published in Great Britain by Penguin Random House UK in 2023.

ISBN 978-1-4549-5165-0 (hardcover)
ISBN 978-1-4549-5167-4 (e-book)
ISBN 978-1-4549-5166-7 (paperback)

Library of Congress Control Number: 2022055567

For information about custom editions, special sales, and premium purchases,
please contact specialsales@unionsquareandco.com.

Printed in the United States of America
2 4 6 8 10 9 7 5 3 1

unionsquareandco.com

Cover and interior design by Liam Donnelly
Cover art by Kevin Wada

Chapter One

"Wishing for world peace is a *terrible* idea," I say, dropping the Play-Station controller down on Dean's bed as our *Fortnite* avatars do their victory dance. "Because that would last for what? One day before humanity found something else to fight about? What you need to do is wish away the cause of conflict instead. You need to wish away . . . toxic masculinity."

Dean laughs. "Oh, come on, Max. That would be your one genie wish? Not for infinite cash . . . or boys? But to rid the world of *toxic masculinity*?"

"You're telling me it wouldn't be a better place for it?" I grin, lying back on Dean's bed and cozying myself into his extravagantly colored cushions. "There'd be no prejudice, no conflict," I continue. "And boys could paint their nails without worrying that it makes them gay."

I hold my sparkling nails up to the window. "You did a good job," I say, admiring the silky sheen as it catches in the streetlights of Brimbsy Road.

Dean has been expertly painting my nails ever since the day I came out to him. He keeps telling me I need to learn to do it myself, but no matter how much I practice, I just don't have the steady hand or the patience to get it right.

"Some of your best work, I reckon. Just wait until Mr. Johnson gets a load of these."

"Don't," he says, laughing again. "*Maxwell Baker, what the devil is that on your nails?*" he mimics the PE teacher's voice impeccably.

"Please, sir," I plead with puppy-dog eyes, "it's just a little nail polish."

Dean beams. "He's gonna lose it for sure. Total meltdown guaranteed."

"Let him," I say just as Dean's mum pushes open the door with two steaming mugs of hot chocolate topped with whipped cream and marshmallows.

"Here we are, then," she says, setting the mugs down on the desk, exchanging them for a pair of Dean's dirty socks with a barely audible *tut*.

"Thanks, Marcy," I say, looking at Dean to remind him to say it too.

"Oh yeah, thanks, Mum," he adds, amping up the sweetness.

"How was the meeting?" I ask, and she shrugs.

"Same old," she says. "They're applying for planning permission again. They don't take no for an answer, these white men." She turns to Dean then. "Good for nothin', the lot of them. Especially your father. No offense there, Max."

"None taken." I get up and grab one of the hot chocolates. "They're idiots if they think they're going to win against you."

Marcy smirks at that. "Well, they're free to waste their energy tryin'."

For the past five years, a property-development company has been trying to tear down the Brimsby Road townhouses to replace them with some fancy new apartments. Marcy has stopped them three times already, rallying the community to save the place that so many of them have lived their whole lives. It's pretty amazing she finds the time really, what with being a single working mum and all. She's a force to be reckoned with: you don't mess with Dean's mum.

"Well, we'll see anyway," she continues. "We're trying to bury them in paperwork, but I'll chain myself to their bulldozers if I have to."

"Don't get yourself arrested, Mum," Dean says with a grin.

"Well, it wouldn't be the first time . . ." she mutters, and then quickly changes the subject. "It smells like teenage boys in here."

My favorite, I think, but I don't say that out loud. Some things just aren't meant to be said in front of parents, no matter how chill they are.

"Light one of those scented candles or something, would you?" she says, walking across the room to crack the window.

"Max doesn't smell that bad, Mum, jeez," Dean jokes, and she shakes her head with a chuckle.

I do a subtle sniff test, but I swear I'm fresh as a field full of daisies.

"Sexy," Dean adds, catching me with my nose in my armpit.

"All right, well, behave now," Marcy says, turning to go back out again. "No more cutting up your best clothes."

"But we were improving them!" I protest.

"Yes, I'm sure that's what you *thought* you were doing," she says with a decidedly wicked smile, closing the door behind her.

Dean cracks up. "I think my mum just read you to filth, Max!"

"She's always been savage," I say. "I can see where you get it from."

"What can I say?" Dean shrugs and picks up two of the candles on his chest of drawers. "Unicorn Cupcake . . . or Pistachio Mint Dreams?"

"Cupcake," I say, which quite frankly was the obvious answer.

"Cupcake it is." He nods and begins rummaging in his underwear drawer. "*Oh* . . ." He stops in his tracks. "Well, *these* definitely aren't matches."

"Huh?" I say, trying to see what he has in his hand.

"Wanna give it a go?" He holds up the three-pack of Durex.

3

"Oh God," I groan. "Don't even joke. I can't believe those are still in there! You do know they have an expiration date, right?"

"Third of August," Dean says as he squints at the box. "Barely even a year out of date! Maybe they'll still work?"

"Throw them away!" I say in mock horror. "You need to pay more attention in sex ed."

"I'm joking," he says. "I can't toss them, though. Memories and all that?" He drops them back in the drawer and closes it.

The condoms had appeared three years ago while I was staying at Dean's for the summer just after my parents split. Marcy went all out on the food while I was here—jerk chicken, curried goat, and all kinds of other Caribbean food I'd never tried before. I guess it was her way of trying to make me whole again. She told me I was one of the family, and she really meant that—because she was convinced Dean and I were secretly dating. Despite telling her over and over that we were just friends, she'd wink and say, "If you say so." Then, one night, to Dean's absolute horror, we came upstairs to find *them*. They were Marcy's way of offering support, no questions asked, but the way Dean gasped when he opened the drawer will stay with me forever. It was the first time I really laughed that summer—and I laughed till I couldn't breathe.

The joke was on me, though, because I then had to be at the center of the most awkward family discussion in which Dean had to explain once and for all that he hadn't, in fact, been upstairs bumping uglies with me the whole time. I'm still not sure she was convinced, though.

"Another round?" I say, picking up the controller.

"Nah, three victory royales is enough," he replies. "We can't keep beating all these straight boys. Their egos are fragile enough."

"Toxic masculinity," I say with an I-told-you-so shrug. "This is what I'm telling you. It's gotta be the wish."

Straight Expectations

"I don't buy it, Max," Dean says, finally finding the matches and lighting the bright pink candle, the flame illuminating his flawless Black skin and killer cheekbones. He's wearing a subtle face of makeup today, just enough to bring out his most feminine features. "I've known you long enough to know you wouldn't wish for something so selfless. You'd use your wish on something stupid that would come back to bite you in the ass."

"What are you trying to say?" I reply indignantly, sitting back upright.

"You could be stranded on a desert island, and you wouldn't wish for food, shelter, or water. You'd waste your last wish on one stupid thing. And his name is Oliver Cheng."

I wish I could deny it, but Dean is absolutely right. Oliver is exactly how I'd spend my one and only genie wish. In fact, I'd wish for a thousand more wishes and still use them all on him. He's the perfect boy-next-door type, and he's been living in my fantasies rent-free ever since he came to our school a year ago. Dean and I were the only openly queer kids in our whole class before that, and then *BAM!* Oliver Cheng. With messy black hair that sticks up at all angles, dimples stapled into each perfect cheek, and deep brown eyes that make the school corridors appear to narrow around him. I've had many a crush during my time at Woodside Academy, but none of them compare to the way I feel about him.

"I just wish he'd acknowledge my existence," I say, something I've repeated about four thousand times this week alone. "Just a *hey* would be nice."

"Really, Max? This again?" Dean says, exasperated. "You literally never make any effort to talk to him. Why don't you just put on your big-boy pants and ask him out? Honestly, what's the worst thing that could happen?"

"Complete and total humiliation!" I groan, covering my face with a pillow. "I'd rather live in hope than face that rejection. Besides, a boy like me doesn't just go up and ask out a guy like Oliver Cheng. He's a solid ten. An eleven, in fact. I'm barely even a six."

Dean rips the pillow off my face and hits me with it.

"Don't you dare," he says sternly, waving the pillow at me threateningly. "You are not a six. Nor are you a seven, an eight, or a nine. You're a *ten*, Maxine. And if boys like Oliver Cheng can't see that, it's their problem, not yours. Got it?"

"Got it," I say with a nervous laugh. Dean relinquishes his weapon.

"A six?" he scoffs, running one hand over his neatly shaven head. "Honestly, Maxine, we're gonna have to work on that self-confidence."

Dean has always been this way. My biggest cheerleader from day one; even through our regular squabbles, he's always had my back. We became friends back in primary school. The other kids seemed to know I was gay before I did, and it made me a bit of a target. Dean was always out and proud, though. Thomas Mulbridge had been picking on me for weeks until Dean stepped in to defend me. Thomas never dared try it again after that. I didn't come out to Dean until years later, but I think he knew, even back then. Queer people have a way of finding each other, and I don't know what I'd have done if Dean hadn't found me.

"So go on, then," I finally say. "Your turn. If not for boys or world peace, what would you ask for from our ever-so-fabulous genie?"

"Hmm," Dean says, pacing the room as he thinks. He's wearing a cropped yellow hoodie and baggy gray sweatpants, and somehow, even dressed down like this, he still oozes with style.

"Well," he continues, "I think I'd wish for a few more years in the here and now. For senior year to stretch on a bit, you know?"

"What?" I say, dumbfounded. "You have one solitary wish and you're going to waste that on—let me check my notes—ah yes, more school."

He's laughing now, but I don't stop.

"Not the ability to magic up fabulous gowns with the snap of your fingers? Not the leading role in a West End show? But *more school*? Really, Dean? Literally anything would be better than that. You're banned from making wishes! Your wishing card has been revoked!"

"Okay, but hear me out!" he says, falling onto the bed beside me.

"*No. Shan't*," I say. Emily Blunt, *The Devil Wears Prada*.

"What does Chris say every single time I come over to yours?"

"That we should '*make the most of this time because these are the best years of our lives*,'" I say, heavy on the mockery. "And do you know why he says that, Dean? Because he's straight! And it may be true that the straights peak in high school, but I dunno if you've noticed this yet, but *we* are not heterosexuals!"

"We aren't?" He slaps a hand to his mouth, aghast.

"No," I say firmly. "We aren't. And I can't believe you're treating my mum's boyfriend as some font of wisdom. The man can barely even tie his own shoes."

"I don't think that's true, Max," Dean says, laughing.

I shrug. "Well, whatever. You have to pick a better wish. We can't stay stuck here forever. I need to get out of this town and kiss some boys!"

"My God, is that all you think about?" Dean asks. "Despite what you think, Max, there's more to life than boys and kissing."

"Is there, though?" I grin, and he playfully shoves me.

"I'm not saying I want to be seventeen forever," he continues. "It's just that things are pretty great right now, and I don't really wanna mess with that."

"Oh, come on!" I say. "You can wish for *anything*! And you're really gonna throw it away, just like that? For a few more years here with little old me?"

"It's not all about you, Max," he says, rolling his eyes.

"But I mean . . . yeah. It's our last year. This is it. We don't get to go around again."

I suppose he has a point. I still don't know what I want to do when I leave school, so a little extra time to figure that out couldn't hurt. It's easy for Dean: he was born to be on the stage. He practically came pirouetting out of the womb. But me? Sometimes it feels like I was forgotten about when they were handing out talent.

"Maybe you're right," I finally concede. "I guess there is something to be said for the way we run Woodside, annoying Mr. Johnson, using the corridors as our own personal runway. That's definitely something I'll miss."

Dean smiles. "That's the spirit!"

"You better believe that if I found a magic lamp tomorrow, though, I'd still be wishing for a Friday-night sleepover with Oliver Cheng."

"A Friday-night sleepover?" he says. "What are you—nine? Well, I guess anything to get him in his underwear, right?"

"We'd be wearing matching pajamas, actually."

"Matching pajamas?" Dean echoes with utter disbelief. "You're such a doofus, Max."

"That may be true, but I'm *your* doofus, and nothing will ever change that." I pick up the controller. "Come on, let's give these straight boys one last run for their money."

Chapter Two

I always meet Dean outside the drama department on a Wednesday afternoon, but rehearsals must be running over today because the cast is still inside. This year they're doing *Little Shop of Horrors*, and I can hear a female voice expertly carrying the notes of "Somewhere That's Green." It's a song about wishing for something better, and she really sings it like she means it.

I peer awkwardly through the door until Mrs. Ashford notices and waves me inside. She has frizzy ginger hair and deep laugh lines, and although she can be a bit of a stress ball, she's always been my favorite teacher. I haven't taken drama since sophomore year because I can't act to save my life, but she's always run an open-door policy for all of us queer kids regardless. Need advice? A name change? Condoms? Mrs. A has your back.

"She's good, huh?" Mrs. A whispers, scooting down her desk to make space for me next to her. She doesn't take her eyes off the singer for even one moment.

It's Poppy Palmer, or Double P as she's known to most of us, playing the role of Audrey. She's perfect for it actually because they're both so misunderstood. Poppy has built up a bit of a reputation for making

9

out with pretty much every guy on the soccer team. People can be a little judgmental about that, but if she was a guy, people would be celebrating it, so I say more power to her. Make out with every last one of them. I've even thought about going to her for pointers, to help me get Oliver's attention. He's the one soccer player she's never gotten to.

Double P finishes the song to a round of applause. Dean is sitting in the front row, cheering the loudest as his hands thunder above his head. I throw in a little whistle for good measure, which makes Poppy blush.

"Nicely done, Ms. Palmer," Mrs. A says as the class begins to settle down. "You're really nailing those high notes, and you've got the accent down to a T . . ."

"Thanks, but . . . ?"

"But," Mrs. A says, "I want you to really try to sell us on Audrey's innocence. She's young and naive and imagining a future she thinks she may never have. When she sings about wanting a '*big, enormous twelve-inch screen,*' I want you to really exaggerate that. It's something she can only ever dream of. That's what I want to see."

"Got it," says Poppy. "I'll work on it. How big is twelve inches anyway?"

One of the boys snickers. "As if she doesn't know!"

"Well, you certainly don't," Poppy shoots back without missing a beat, and the boy's friends all laugh.

"It's the length of a ruler," Mrs. A says. "It's tiny for a TV by today's standards, but that's the point. Her dreams aren't big, but to her they seem unobtainable. We'll work on it—you've got this."

"All right, thanks," Poppy says, and collects her bag as the students start to get up and filter out of the room.

"See you later, Max," she adds, catching my eye as she lingers in the doorway for a moment.

"Oh, uh . . . okay?" I say, and she gives me a little smile and disappears.

There's always been this awkward energy between us. Dean reckons she has a crush on me, but Dean doesn't know what the hell he's talking about.

"Before you go," Mrs. A says to me as the room empties, "the costumes for the Doo-Wop Girls." She gestures to three mannequins in the corner dressed in pleated blue polka dots. "What do you think?"

Back in sophomore year, once we'd established that *Max Absolutely Cannot Act*, Mrs. A put me in charge of wardrobe, and she still asks for my opinion. She hardly needs my advice, but I appreciate it anyway. It's nice to feel included.

"They're great, but they need accessories," I say, pulling up an image of the original cast on my phone. "Here, look. High seventies glam. Gloves, bows, ribbons, the works. Go big on the makeup too. They need to look so fabulous they seem totally out of place on Skid Row."

Mrs. A smiles at that. "You really pay attention to detail, don't you?"

"What do you mean?"

"Cover your eyes," she says, and I do. Another one of Mrs. A's teaching moments. "What color are my shoes?"

"They're red," I say without even having to think about it.

"And my bracelet?"

"It's yellow, but it doesn't really match your top and—"

"All right, all right, I didn't ask for the commentary," she says with a snort.

I laugh. "Sorry. Can I uncover now?" I peer through my fingers.

"You can uncover," she says. "All right, get out of here. Thanks for the tip on the costumes. I'll see what we can get from the thrift store."

"What would you do without me?" I say as I go catch up with Dean. "Feel free to put me down in the program as fashion consultant, yeah?"

I can hear her chuckling as we head out of earshot.

"I reckon it's gonna be the best show yet," Dean says as we make our way toward the senior class common room. "The perfect one to end on. I'm gonna miss it, you know?"

"You will *not*," I say with a snort. "You'll forget about Woodside faster than you can say *Chenoweth*."

"I guess," he says, but doesn't sound convinced.

I don't know why he's so worried. Dean's future is laid out in front of him: he'll bounce straight from drama school to the West End. Everyone can see that but him.

"Meanwhile, I still don't know what I'm gonna do when *I* leave," I say.

"What are you talking about? You've got your gap year! Do you know how lucky you are? If Mum could afford it, I'd be right there with you, Max."

"Yeah, I know, but—"

"But nothing! Actual sunshine! European boys! Gay bars where you'll be old enough to drink!"

"But then what?" I say, but Dean just shrugs.

"You'll figure it out. At least you don't have to worry about auditions. You still okay to run lines with me tonight?"

"Yeah, I guess," I say, perhaps a little too unenthusiastically. Dean's final auditions for drama school are coming up in a few weeks, and between rehearsing for those and *Little Shop*, I feel like all we ever do is run lines. It's starting to feel as if *I'm* the one who's auditioning. "We could get a few games of *Fortnite* in first, maybe?"

"Yeah, but we've got Queer Club in, like, five minutes," he says.

"*Ohhhh*," I groan. "I completely forgot . . . Do we really have to?"

Dean shoots me a dirty look. "Yes, Maxine, we have to."

"Is Oliver going to be there at least?"

"I'm not even gonna dignify that with a response . . ."

"Yeah, but is he, though?"

"I swear to God," Dean says, laughing as we turn into the common room, "you have either got to get with that boy or get over him."

There's a buzz in the air as we enter. There are only a dozen people here, but the energy is infectious. Dean founded the Queer Club our freshman year, and he's been holding it in the common room ever since. The younger students love it because they're not usually allowed up here, and—you've got to hand it to Woodside—this place *is* pretty cool. There's a little kitchen to make snacks and drinks, loads of bean-bags and comfy sofas with blankets for when it gets colder in the winter. We did almost have those confiscated, though, after Rachel Kwan and Simon Pike were caught up here after hours putting their hands in places they shouldn't.

I do a quick scan of the room to see who's here. There's a couple of younger kids from the lower grades, plus Gabi and Shanna, the insepa-rable couple from junior year.

Shanna has rainbow-colored hair, and Gabi's falls down past her shoulders in gorgeous ombré brunette waves. Shanna is dressed in patch-work double denim with her immaculate blue-and-pink trans Pride Adidas, showing her support for her partner. Gabi is in fiery red overalls with some shiny red vintage Mary Janes. My favorite thing about their outfits, though, is their matching white backpacks, both covered in doz-ens of colorful Pride pins. It's cute that they're so proud of their relation-ship and who they are.

They give us a little wave as they help some of the younger kids hang a string of rainbow bunting from the ceiling. It's nice to know we'll be leaving this group in good hands once we're gone.

Our friend Alicia hurries into the room behind us. "I'm not late, am I?" she says. "I got caught up in the workshop."

She's dressed in camo-print overalls dotted with splashes of paint, a matching headband pushing back her perfect box braids with an HP pencil securing her hair in place. Alicia isn't LGBT+ herself, but she's an honorary member of the group, and she hasn't missed a single session.

I guess she's just come straight from working on the set for *Little Shop* because her arms are full of art supplies. Alicia is an *incredible* artist and insists on helping out the drama kids on every show by designing and building the whole set. Last year she transformed the auditorium into a US courtroom for *Legally Blonde*, papering the walls with newspaper clippings from cases where innocent people had been found guilty. Her mum's American, and a lawyer, so you can see where she took the inspiration from. Once every surface was covered, she used blue and red paint for the stars and stripes.

"You really didn't need to come," Dean says, taking the battered paint can precariously shoved under her arm. "I know how busy you are . . ."

"I'm not *that* busy, Dean. You're the one juggling auditions, Queer Club, *and* the show. I've just got a few teeny-tiny projects."

"You're both ridiculous," I groan, barely concealing an eyeroll. I have absolutely no extracurriculars, and hearing them squabble about who's busier is my least favorite pastime. "Come on, shall we get started?"

I flop on to one of the sofas and tap the space beside me. Alicia sets down the rest of her art supplies and joins me, and Dean heads up to the front. He stands with his back to the fireplace and clears his throat, all official like, but before he can speak the door opens and I turn around to see that all my prayers have been answered.

Oliver Cheng is standing in the doorway. He's wearing a black hoodie with a matching baseball cap, and I just love the way his hair flicks out from underneath it at the sides. He gives a shy little smile, and, although I try to remain cool and collected, I swear the temperature in the room has doubled because suddenly my mouth is dry, and my palms are sweaty, and I've forgotten how to breathe.

"In and out, in and out," Alicia teases because apparently it's *that* obvious.

The moment is quickly ruined, though, because right behind Oliver is the last person I want to see—Thomas Mulbridge. For some reason, he and Oliver became friends shortly after Oliver arrived at Woodside. Now they're almost inseparable. It's concrete proof that the universe hates me.

"Hey, Oliver," Dean says. "Nice of you to join us, Thomas."

"Just here as an ally," Thomas replies with a big stupid grin, and my eyes roll so hard that I think I actually give myself a migraine.

"Yeah, 'cause God forbid anyone should think he's not straight," I whisper to Alicia.

She shrugs. "He's probably just being supportive."

Alicia doesn't dislike Thomas the way I do. She's heard the stories, but she didn't go to the same elementary school as me and Dean, so she didn't see what he used to be like. Neither did Oliver for that matter; there's no way he'd be friends with him if he knew. Once a homophobe, always a homophobe, and now he's sitting here in our club.

"I thought today we could talk about the history curriculum," Dean continues. "Who else is sick and tired of hearing about Franz Ferdinand and Henry VIII? I know Mrs. A teaches us about all the queer greats, but it's like the rest of the teachers are afraid to even say the word *gay*."

Dean carries on talking about the need for more LGBT+ history to be incorporated into our lessons, but I'm barely listening. How can I pay attention with both the man of my dreams and my sworn enemy sitting behind me? I really don't understand what Oliver sees in him anyway. All they have in common is that they're both on the soccer team.

"Why does Oliver never hang out with anyone but Thomas?" I whisper to Alicia. "I mean, what do they even talk about?"

"Huh?" she says, glancing back at them. "I think he's just shy, Max."

What a *ridiculous* thing to say. Straight-up hotties like Oliver don't get shy.

I'm left brooding on the unfairness of it all as Dean continues with the session, starting an activity where we have to say a few words about an LGBT+ person we look up to. Most people pick celebrities, but one of the younger kids mentions Imraan, the school librarian, which I think is really cute. Especially since they're followed by Thomas saying Ian McKellen "because he was really good as Gandalf." What an absolute tool.

Everyone else's answers, though, are really telling about who they are and what they aspire to. Oliver says Joshua Cavallo for "being brave enough to be out in the world of sports," Dean chooses Layton Williams because "no one is more fabulous onstage," and Alicia says Mickalene Thomas because she "isn't afraid to let her identity shine through in everything she creates." It's actually all really inspiring until I realize I have no idea who I'm going to choose. Who *do* I look up to anyway?

"Max?" Dean says, and, shit, it's already my turn, and my mind just goes blank. I can't think of a single LGBT+ person, and suddenly I feel Oliver's eyes on me, which just makes me choke even more. "I hadn't really thought about it," I say. "I mean . . . um . . ."

Dean raises an eyebrow as if deciding whether to let me off the hook. I can tell he's secretly annoyed, and I can't exactly blame him. Even Thomas had a better answer than me.

"Well . . ." I begin just as the door to the common room swings open again.

Thank God, I think, until I turn to see Mr. Johnson standing there. First Thomas, now Johnson—who next? The Westboro Baptist Church?

"Here to join us, Coach?" Thomas teases, but even he doesn't look pleased. Mr. Johnson is about the least popular teacher at Woodside.

"Who's responsible for that?" Mr. Johnson points to the battered paint can on the table beside the door, and that's when I notice the drips leading out into the corridor . . .

"Fuck, that was me, sorry," Alicia says. "Sorry! I mean, uh . . . *fiddlesticks?*"

"*Fiddlesticks* indeed," Johnson grumbles. "You've left a trail all the way back to the auditorium."

"Sorry, sir," Alicia says. "I'll clear it up. Can it wait till after the meeting, though?"

"Of course," he says sarcastically. "I'll just ask the paint not to dry until you've finished with your little club." He looks up at the rainbow bunting and scowls. "I didn't know you were an LGBT anyway, Alicia?"

"Well, I'm not, but—"

"Then I don't see why you need to be here at all. My halls, however, require your immediate attention."

"Yes, sir," she says dejectedly as Mr. Johnson turns to leave.

"Oh, come on, don't be a dick," I say, stopping him in his tracks. Some of the younger kids gasp. I know I shouldn't antagonize him, but I can't help it.

Mr. Johnson's jaw clenches for a moment, but then he forces a tight-lipped smile. "Just for that, you can go and help her. And then detention for both of you straight after. How's that?"

"Max has a right to be here," Dean interjects. "They both do."

"Oh, so you'll be joining them too, Mr. Jackson? Very glad to hear it," he says. "Just make sure you do a thorough job. I want those floors to *sparkle.*"

"He's literally the chair of the group, Coach," Oliver says, and for a moment I think he's going to get detention too. But of course Mr. Johnson would never do that to one of his precious soccer players. Thomas and Oliver apparently have immunity.

"I guess this session has come to an end, then, hasn't it?" Mr. Johnson says smugly, turning to the younger kids. "Which means you lot better clear out since you no longer have permission to be up here."

"Leave them out of this!" Dean says, his voice and anger rising now.

Mr. Johnson just smiles at that. "You really think you run this place, don't you, Jackson? I certainly hope you have a plan for after you leave school. I think you'll find the real world to be quite a different place for the likes of you."

"What's that supposed to mean?"

"Big fish," Mr. Johnson says, staring hard at Dean. "Tiny little pond."

Dean stands there, speechless.

"You've got two minutes to get out before I start handing out more detentions," Mr. Johnson snaps, scanning the room as if he's making a mental note of who's here. "Oh, and boys?" he adds, looking at Thomas and Oliver. "Maybe before the next match you should paint your nails like Max and Dean? I'm sure the opposition would just *love* that."

"Was that a threat?" Alicia jumps up, unable to restrain herself any longer.

"I'm sure I don't know what you mean?" Mr. Johnson says. "I'm just encouraging my team members to be their authentic selves. *Love* the new hair, by the way."

The door clatters shut behind him.

The room is silent for a moment, our collective anger hanging in the air.

"I'm sorry," Oliver says. "That was totally out of order."

"Yeah, he's not usually that bad," Thomas adds, but of course he thinks that. On the field Mr. Johnson is probably all high fives and motivational speeches.

"I'm gonna talk to him," Oliver says, heading through the door. Thomas follows.

"We're not leaving," Gabi says then. All the other kids nod in agreement.

"I appreciate the support," Dean says, "but you should go. There's no point in you all getting into trouble as well. He's honestly not worth it."

"Well, how about we all help out, then?" Shanna offers. "To clean the halls, I mean. We'll just take the meeting out there."

"Actually . . ." Alicia says, "that's not a bad idea."

A smile appears on her lips. She goes over to rummage through her bag and pulls out a giant pot of shimmering iridescent glitter. "He *did* say he wanted the floors to *sparkle*."

"Oh my God, you wouldn't," I say, laughing.

Alicia shrugs. "Watch me," she says, unscrewing the lid and blowing a puff of shimmer into the corridor. "Let's make this a work of art."

Chapter Three

"I still can't believe you glittered the whole school!" Mum is leaning against the breakfast bar, laughing.

"Just doing what we were told," I say with an innocent smile.

I'm glad she had my back on this. Alicia's dad was pretty cool with what we did too, but Marcy grounded Dean for a week, on top of the week of detentions we got from Mr. Johnson. I guess she doesn't want him getting a taste for making trouble with people in authority, and I get that. Sometimes I forget how much I get away with just because I'm white. It's kind of ironic coming from her, though. I guess the difference is that she knows the risks she's taking when she stands up and tells them *no*.

"You must get that rebelliousness from me," Mum says, retrieving a wineglass from the cupboard. "It's certainly not from your father."

"Ah, don't be mean, Mum," I say, perching on one of the stools. "Dad's not always a Goody Two-shoes. He can be a rebel when he wants to be."

"He once literally drove all the way back to the supermarket because he forgot to pay for his plastic shopping bag," she says. "But *sure*, he's a real rebel."

"And you think this one's any different?" I say, nodding to Mum's boyfriend, Chris.

"Oi! I'm practically Han Solo." He turns to Mum. "And I guess that makes you my Princess Leia," he adds, and gently kisses her.

"Okay, gross," I say, but they ignore me, and Mum goes to open a bottle of red. "Wine already? It's not even six o'clock."

"*Now* who's a Goody Two-shoes?" she says cheerfully. "Besides, it's date night."

"I'm not sure an evening at the Woodside Academy theater classifies as a date," I say with a smirk. "Doesn't exactly scream romance, does it? Talk about low standards."

"Low standards?" Chris laughs. "You're joking. With Dean in the cast? It'll be like taking in a West End show."

"You're right about that," I say, but—just for the record—Chris has never *actually* seen a West End show.

His first and only musical was last year's production of *Legally Blonde*, and he didn't stop talking about it for weeks. The lead role was gender flipped, with Dean playing the extravagantly camp Eli Woods. And that casting, combined with some very clever lyric changes from Mrs. A, turned the show into a commentary on the way both Black and queer people are treated unfairly under the law. It was nothing short of brilliant. She drew the line at Dean's request to change the title to *Legally Black*, though. Apparently, that was "taking it too far."

"How's bricklaying anyway, Chris?" I ask.

Chris laughs. "I keep telling you, I work in construction."

"So you don't lay bricks?"

"Well, yeah, sometimes . . ."

"So a bricklayer, then."

"He's got you there," says Mum. "It's okay, though. I think bricklaying is kinda *sexy*. My strapping, bricklaying boy toy."

"I'm not a bricklayer!" Chris protests.

"But you're fine with being a boy toy?" I say, and he rolls his eyes.

I love teasing him about his age. Chris is five years younger than Mum, which is kinda weird because Dad is five years older. Mum says age is just a number, but there's a ten-year age gap between the two men, and it's *really* hard not to notice.

"Anyway, Max," Mum continues, "I was thinking maybe we could see your dad this weekend? The four of us could do something together?"

"He likes soccer, right?" Chris adds. "There's a big match on Sunday, and I know a guy who can get us all cheap tickets—"

"*Soccer?*" I say in disbelief. "I'm sorry, have you *met* me? And you 'know a guy'? That sounds sketchy as hell."

"I told you he wouldn't go for it," says Mum smugly.

"Yeah, hard pass on that one," I say. "But sure, we can do *something*. You look nice, by the way," I add, admiring Mum's outfit. She's wearing a stylish powder-blue romper tied at the middle with a white belt and white flats to match. It's just the right amount of baggy, with two buttons undone at the top.

"Well, we had to make an effort for Dean, didn't we?" she says, shaking her blond hair loosely around her shoulders, her gentle baby blues offset against mother-of-pearl earrings. Everyone says I'm the spitting image of Mum, and I've always taken that as a compliment. She's a hottie—there's no denying that.

"Ahem." Chris loudly clears his throat, gesturing to his own outfit.

"I don't know what you want me to say. Blue jeans and a plain white shirt? I mean, I guess you don't look *bad* . . ."

"The sass!" he says. "I thought I looked pretty fashionable actually."

"You do, sweetie," Mum says, reaching out to fasten one of his buttons. "Ignore Max. He's only teasing."

"At least you ironed your shirt," I say, reaching for the wine bottle just as Mum snatches it out of range. "Just a little?" I say, flashing her an angelic smile. She considers for a moment, as if wondering whether she has the energy to put up a fight, then sighs and gets me a glass.

"Only one," she says firmly. "You're not eighteen yet, Max."

"Thanks, Mummy," I say, grinning, and fill the glass up to the brim. "Are you not having one, Chris?"

"Driving, aren't I, mate?" he says, and there's that word again. *Mate.* Like acrylic nails on a chalkboard and yet a staple of Chris's vocabulary.

It's hard to like him sometimes. I mean, he's not a bad person or anything, but he and Mum started dating during her and Dad's trial separation, and that sort of felt like the last nail in the coffin in terms of their relationship. Sometimes I can't help but wonder if they could have made it work if Chris hadn't appeared on the scene.

"What time are we leaving?" I ask.

"In about five minutes?" Chris says, looking at his watch.

"All right. I'm gonna grab my jacket," I say.

"Don't you dare spill that," Mum calls after me, but I'm already hopping up the stairs two at a time, wine sloshing dangerously around the glass.

My bedroom is a work of art, if I do say so myself. I've decorated the walls with all the cute Netflix heartthrobs you can imagine. All painstakingly cut out from magazines intended for teenage girls. My favorite is the shirtless KJ Apa I've had pinned on the back of my door ever since I went through my *Riverdale* phase. I was so obsessed I even tried to dye my hair to become a stunning copper redhead like Archie Andrews. Obviously, it went wrong, and I ended up walking around for weeks looking like an overly confident tangerine until I finally admitted defeat and let Dean strip me back to blond. *"Honestly, Maxine, all future hair changes need to be run by me first. Do you know what most gay boys would give to be naturally blond?"*

On my desk, there's a photo of the two of us, next to an old, barely functioning computer. It's a class photo and must be ten years old—Dean and I are sitting front and center, arms wrapped around each other, cheesing into the camera. It can't have been taken long after Dean put Thomas in his place because, if you look really closely, you can see him grumpily scowling at the back.

I grimace as I take a gulp of wine. I don't really like the taste, but it's rare Mum lets me have alcohol, so I swallow it all the same before reaching into my wardrobe to pull out a shiny deep red varsity jacket. It's one of my favorites, from the girls' section, and ever so slightly too small, but it's got soft cream sleeves and a shiny rose-gold zipper that perfectly matches the sparkle in my nails. I couple the jacket with bloodred high-tops and tight cream jeans that show off my ass. Oliver will probably be there tonight after all.

I stand in front of the full-length mirror, agonizing over every little detail, twisting the stray curls in my fringe and then spraying them within an inch of their life. It's still missing something, so I roll up the sleeves and finish the look with the rainbow friendship bracelet Dean gave me years ago. I rarely wear it because it clashes with pretty much everything I own, but today is a special occasion so I do it just for him.

"Are you ready, Max?" Mum calls just as I snap a mirror selfie.

"Coming!" I yell back, quickly uploading it to Instagram as my OOTD. I chug the wine and hurriedly go back down the stairs where they're waiting by the front door.

"Now remember—best behavior. No talking to my friends. No gossiping with the teachers. And definitely no PDA. Don't humiliate me."

"Oh, come on, Max," Mum says, laughing, and goes to touch my head affectionately, but I bat her hand away with lightning reflexes before she can ruin my hair. "We don't try to humiliate you."

"No, you do that without trying, don't you?"

"Is that crush of yours going to be there, then?" Chris smiles wickedly. I know he's trying to push my buttons. He loves teasing me about Oliver almost as much as I like annoying him about his age.

"I think so," I say. "But if you speak to him, if you so much as *look* at him, I'll destroy something you love."

"Harsh! Like what?"

"I don't know. Sports?"

"You'll destroy . . . sports?"

I raise an eyebrow as if to say *don't test me*. "Well, since the two of you can't work the TV without me as your own personal tech support, I'll change the sports channel password just before the next cricket match. How's that?"

"You'd actually be doing me a favor," says Mum.

I'm glad she agrees with me on this. If you have to watch sports, at least choose an interesting one!

"Noted," Chris says. "Don't, under any circumstances, speak to Max's boyfriend." He opens the front door.

"He's not my boyfriend," I say, rolling my eyes.

God, I wish he was, though.

There's always something strange about being at school after dark. Like you shouldn't be there, almost as if you're breaking the rules. I ditch Mum and Chris almost immediately, and it doesn't take long to find

Alicia. Her enormous smile reaches out through the darkness, and she practically throws the pair of iced coffees she's holding all over me as she runs up and wraps her arms around me. She's dressed in a silky white dress with bloodred bangles clasping each wrist. I'm glad she agreed to sync up our outfits—she absolutely understood the assignment.

"*Ahhh*, I'm so excited!" she says, letting out a squeal.

"Highlight of the school year, right?"

"Right," she says, beaming at me. "Here," she adds, handing me one of the coffees.

"'Toto'?" I say, reading the name on the side of the cup, and she spins hers around to reveal *Dorothy*. It's a game Dean and I started last summer, and I guess it caught on because now she's doing it too.

Alicia's dad appears behind her. He's a tower of a man who works part-time as a personal trainer. Alicia's mum is always working late so he takes care of things at home. He's quite intimidating at first glance, but, if you look past his rippling muscles and exceptionally strong jawline, you soon see that he's a big softie.

"How's it going, Maximillian?" he says in his soft Zimbabwean accent. He reaches out one of his enormous hands and pulls me into a hug. I can feel his muscles tighten as he squeezes the air out of me with his solid titan grip.

"Good, thanks, Mr. Williams," I say. "How are you?"

"I'll be doing just fine if you call me Darius, Max. How many times do I have to tell you?" He laughs. "How are the boys treating you, anyway? Like nothing short of a prince, I hope? Anyone I need to give a talking-to?"

"No boy troubles at the minute," I say. God, I *wish* I had boy troubles. "But I'll let you know if I need your . . . services."

He chuckles. "You do that. So what's this show about, anyway?" He puzzles over the program, trying to make sense of it.

"I told you a thousand times already," Alicia says, rolling her eyes.

"Well, remind me. I can't remember everything."

"It's about a murderous alien plant that grants wishes," she says, checking her blood-colored nails. "You know, in exchange for being fed human flesh."

"*Ri-ight*," Darius says, looking a little perplexed.

"It's one of my all-time favorites," I add with a grin.

Darius laughs. "Of course it is. Well," he says, clapping his hands together, "I'm sure it's gonna be great. And I can't wait to see this set of yours, Alicia. If it's anything like last year . . ."

"Speaking of which," I say. "Is your mum not coming, Alicia?"

"She's on her way," Darius says. "Wouldn't miss it."

Alicia smiles at that. "Anyway, we should go." She checks the time on her phone. "We promised we'd go backstage to see Dean before the show. We'll see you in there?"

"All right," Darius says. "Tell him I said good luck."

"You're supposed to send broken legs, it's *bad* luck otherwise."

"I'm supposed to do *what?*"

"Never mind," says Alicia, laughing. "Come on, Max," she says, grabbing my arm and dragging me away.

As much as she loves him, she's always terrified that the next word that slips out of her dad's mouth will be something that'll embarrass her. And that's something I can *absolutely* relate to. Sometimes I think adults conspire to make their kids' lives as unbearable as humanly possible.

Backstage before the show is always chaos, and today's no different. Mrs. A is in a frenzy, squawking at various students as she tries to get everyone ready. Her wife, Fiona, is here too. They're a power couple, if ever I saw one. Fiona works as a wedding photographer, but always comes to help out on show night. She takes awesome pictures with her fancy DSLR camera, really capturing the magic onstage, and snaps a few backstage shots as well. She says we'll thank her for the memories when we're older. Really, though, we know the main reason she's here is to talk Mrs. A down when the pressure gets to be too much.

"There's my star set designer!" Mrs. A beams, clocking Alicia as we shoulder our way into the room. "Honestly, how will I cope without you next year? Even professionals can't do what you do!"

Alicia laughs. "Can I put that on my art school applications? Maybe you can pay me to come back one day. If you're lucky, I might even give you a discount."

"If it's not a five-finger discount, I'm not sure we'll be able to afford you," Mrs. A says. "You'll be far too busy for little old Woodside anyhow."

"Never," Alicia says. "Mates rates all the way."

"I'll hold you to that," she says, and winks. "Anyway, the stage is set, I've checked over everything; we've got it all under control."

"Good to know," Alicia says. "But actually we just came to say hi to Dean."

"He's back here somewhere." Mrs. A gestures vaguely behind her. "But curtain's in fifteen. He's the least of my worries right now."

She goes to help one of the Doo-Wop Girls attach her bow as Fiona reads items from a checklist.

"Here, let me," I say, stepping in to fix the sapphire ribbon.

"Thanks, Max," Mrs. A says. "Did you see the program yet?"

"Huh?" I say, grabbing one from a cluttered dressing table.

"Second page," she says as I open it.

There, right at the bottom, is *Max Baker—Fashion Consultant*.

I burst out laughing. "Oh my God, I wasn't serious!"

"I know," she says. "But I thought it might be useful for your university applications. An extracurricular to make you stand out."

"I already stand out," I say, catching some air in my jacket as I give her a little twirl. "I'm not going to uni, though. I'm gonna do the gap-year thing."

She shrugs. "Well, for next year, then."

I look back down at my name and suddenly get a little sad. I don't know why—maybe it feels undeserved? Like I'm a little kid who's been given a present on their sibling's birthday just so they don't feel left out. Sometimes it's hard to be in Dean's and Alicia's shadows. They're the two most talented kids in school, and I'm just sort of . . . here. *Fashion Consultant.* It's nice, but it's not exactly true.

"You couldn't give Thomas a hand, could you?" Mrs. A says, interrupting my train of thought. "He's having a bit of a wardrobe malfunction." She nods over to where he's got himself in a tangle with his bow tie.

I groan. "Do I really have to?"

She doesn't say anything, just gives me one of those looks.

"Fine," I say, rolling my eyes in the most overexaggerated way I can. "But I'm only doing this for you!"

"You're a star, Max," she murmurs, her attention distracted again.

"While you do that, I'm just gonna double-check the lights real quick," Alicia says. "And then we'll find Dean?"

"All right, but don't be long," I say, and I really mean it. The last thing I want is to be stuck talking to Thomas.

"Need a hand?" I say, trying not to sound totally unfriendly.

"Please," he says, his fingers still tangled up in the bow tie.

Close up, it's sort of hard to believe I was ever intimidated by him. He's short, with pale skin and blue eyes, mousy brown hair he doesn't know how to style properly, and a few rogue freckles across each cheek. He's playing the role of Seymour, and, as much as I don't like to admit it, he does actually look kinda cute in his thick-rimmed glasses, messily tucked-in shirt, and very snappable suspenders.

"Sorry about the other week," he says as I fix the tie. "With Mr. Johnson? At gay club? That really wasn't cool."

I frown. "It's Queer Club, and if you thought it wasn't cool, you could have said something," I point out. "That's what being an ally is, Thomas. Stepping up, even when it isn't easy."

"I know," he says. He looks really uncomfortable. "I did go with Oliver to talk to him afterward, but it's hard, you know? He already has me on the bench this season as it is. If I start pissing him off, I'll never get to play."

"Some things are more important than soccer," I reply.

He doesn't say anything to that, just looks at a loss for words. He probably doesn't have the capacity to imagine *anything* more important than soccer. I'm in a good mood, though, so I let him off the hook and change the subject. "You nervous?"

He winces. "A bit. I've never played the lead before. People keep saying I should just picture the audience naked, but I don't see how that'll help. Like, can you imagine how hard it would be to remember your lines if all the hot girls suddenly had their tits out?"

"I'm gay, Thomas . . ." I say, rolling my eyes. As if he needs the reminder.

"Yeah, well . . ." he replies awkwardly, fumbling for words. "For you, it would be hot guys with their dicks out or whatever."

"*'Hot guys with their dicks out'* . . . ?" I reply incredulously. "I've been in the boys' changing room, and I can assure you it's nothing to get flustered about."

"Oh, forget it," he says. "I'm just nervous, is all."

"It'll be fine," I say. "Just chill—it's only a school show. It's not like your whole future is riding on this or anything."

"I guess," Thomas says. "How are you doing, anyway? You managed to pin down a boyfriend yet?" A feeble attempt to redeem himself.

I shrug. "Not many gay guys to choose from around here."

"What?" he says. "There's loads. What about Dean? Or Oliver?"

"That's two," I say. "Not loads. Besides, Dean has been my best friend for, like, ten years. That would just be weird."

"How about Oliver, then?"

I stop fiddling with Thomas's tie for a second and try not to meet his eyes. The last thing I need is him finding out about my crush on his BFF.

"You know," I say, removing the tie and tossing it aside, "I think it'll look better without this actually."

I wonder if I should run this last-minute costume change past Mrs. A, but then remember her encouraging words and know that she'll trust me.

"There's one rule when it comes to accessories," I continue. "'Before you leave the house, look in the mirror and take one thing off.' Do you know who said that?"

"No?" Thomas straightens up and turns obediently to look at himself in one of the mirrors.

"Coco Chanel."

"Is that a drag queen?"

Straight people, honestly.

"Never mind, just go for the open collar," I say, unfastening his top button.

"All right. Thanks, Max."

I nod. "Don't mention it. Now I need to find Dean. Have you seen him?"

"Yeah, he's in the back," Thomas says. "You two are *always* hanging out. Are you sure you shouldn't get together?"

"That's homophobic," I say as I turn on my heel. "Break a leg, Thomas," I add, and mean it just a little bit too much.

I find Alicia obsessively checking and double-checking the lights and have to literally drag her away from them so we can go and see Dean. We find him right at the back of the dressing area, surrounded by people frantically getting into costume, warming up, and doing last-minute run-throughs of their lines. He isn't in costume yet. He's just sitting in front of one of the long vanity mirrors, calmly and carefully gluing down his eyebrows as he prepares to paint a full face of drag. He's already got color on his nails, a glittering emerald green, and his costume is hanging up beside him, a tangle of verdant fabrics.

"More fans?" Dean says, smirking as he catches sight of us in his mirror. "Sorry, no autographs until after the show!"

Alicia leans down to exchange air kisses with him while I beeline for his costume, lifting it up to get a better look.

"Keep those grubby little hands to yourself, Maxine!" Dean says, smacking my fingers away. "You'll ruin the surprise."

I laugh. "Sorry! I thought you'd be ready by now."

"I've got loads of time. I don't come on until the end of the first half."

"So what's the twist this year, then?" I ask.

I know the two of them have been working on it together, but they've kept everything hush-hush, even from me.

"Well," Dean begins, "you already know I'm playing the villain, Audrey II. But I'm playing it in drag because do you know what this show's really about?" He pauses for dramatic effect. "Society's obsession with stomping on anyone who's different. Black people. Queer people. Anyone who sets even one little toe outside the cis-white-hetero mold."

"How do you work that out?" I'm unconvinced.

"Well, all these beige 'normal' people want to come and take a look at the fabulous exotic plant." He gestures to his own body. "But the moment it shows it has a mind of its own? Then they want to chop it down and kill it! It's like all those straight people who just *love* to watch *Drag Race*, but don't actually care about queer people; they just see us as something to be ogled at. The second we want to talk about prejudice or our rights? Suddenly we're being too loud."

"You make a good point," I say. "But the plant is hardly a *victim*, Dean. I mean, it quite literally tries to take over the world!"

"Which is exactly what I'm trying to do," he shoots back. "Maybe the world would be better off with a little more *vegetation*."

"Spoken like a true villain," says Alicia, grinning.

Dean shrugs. "What can I say? I'm a method actor."

"Well, speaking of villains," I say, perching on the edge of the dressing table, "you know Mulbridge reckons we should be a couple?"

"Oh, I don't think so," Dean says, pouting and looking me up and down. "If Thomas had half a brain cell, he'd be setting you up with Oliver. Not fobbing you off on me."

"Ouch! What happened to me being a ten?"

"You *are* a ten, Maxine, but I'm a twelve, and those numbers just don't add up. Besides," he adds, "two bottoms don't make a top."

"What?" I laugh a little awkwardly. "I never said I'm a—"

Dean grins. "You didn't need to, sweetie."

"Well," Alicia says, clapping her hands, "as much as I love hearing you two discuss the intimate details of your fictitious sex lives, we better go grab some seats before all the good ones are taken."

"Right," says Dean. "And that reminds me." He reaches into the dressing table drawer. "Here," he says, handing us a pair of lime-green party poppers. "Grab an aisle seat. Somewhere in the middle of the audience and be ready to set these off."

"Why, what are you planning?" I say, looking back and forth between them. Alicia pretends to zip shut her lips, clearly in on the secret.

"You'll see," Dean murmurs, now busying himself with his makeup. "Just wait for my cue . . ."

The auditorium is full, and there's a hum of excited voices as kids and parents begin to take their seats. The aisles are crammed so I don't even see the person coming toward me until we've already collided.

"Oh my gosh, I'm so sorry," I say, regaining my balance and then losing it again as I look up into the perfect deep brown eyes of Oliver Cheng.

"Don't worry about it," he says with a smile, his cheeks dimpling. He turns sideways and scooches past me. "Hey, Alicia!"

"Hey, Oliver," she replies as if it's no big deal. As if it's perfectly normal to just say *hey* to Oliver Cheng. That's the thing about Alicia: she's friends with absolutely everyone. She's arguably the most popular girl in school, and for some reason still chooses to spend half her time with me and Dean.

"He's so perfect," I say as I watch Oliver take a seat in the front row.

"Really? You never mentioned it," Alicia teases, but I barely even look at her. I literally can't take my eyes off him. He's wearing a baby blue hoodie with tight white jeans and a fresh pair of matching Feiyues. Ten out of ten for coordination.

Alicia sighs. "God, they've literally chosen the worst seats in the house," she says, bringing my attention back to the room. Her mum is here now, sitting with Mum, Chris, Marcy, and Darius. "Why on earth are they second row from the back?"

"Because they're parents and don't know any better," I say, giving them a little wave. *We're gonna sit up here,* I mouth, and pull Alicia into a couple of seats in a middle row, like Dean instructed. I take the aisle and Alicia sits down next to me.

"Great view," I say, nodding toward Oliver.

"I *will* hit you," Alicia says. "I didn't spend weeks working on the set just for you to spend the whole show staring at the back of his head."

"I can look at the set *as well.* I'll split my attention fifty-fifty."

Alicia makes good on her promise and thumps me on the arm.

Suddenly Mrs. A's voice sounds out across the auditorium with a final warning for people to take their seats. The lights go down and the crowd hushes. It's silent for a moment and then, to the unmistakable opening bars of "Little Shop of Horrors," the curtains draw back to reveal the masterpiece within.

It's a Manhattan skyline, caught up in curling, twisting vines, and it's so beautifully put together that it takes me a moment to realize the full brilliance of what Alicia has done. It's not just any skyline: it's a skyline entirely made up of recycled fashion. Old shoeboxes wrapped in denim have been stacked high to make skyscrapers, with twinkling fairy lights shining through delicate lace windows, and lipstick graffiti scrawled across the walls. The vines that consume the cityscape look like they've been plucked from a collection of emerald corsets; a black leather jacket hangs front and center with *Little Shop of Horrors* stitched in bloodred cursive across the back; and a tiny flower shop crammed full of plants sits beneath it with high heels and platform shoes for plant pots. Shoelaces suspend the Brooklyn Bridge over a pleated ballgown river, and an upturned stiletto stands proud for the Empire State Building. It's a stage fit for a drag queen. Alicia can claim all she likes that she did this for "extra credit," but it's obvious she made it for *him*.

"Alicia, it's incredible," I whisper, taking in every detail. "I can't imagine how long it must have taken."

"It's the stage he deserves." She shrugs and shoots me a little smile as the spotlight finds the Doo-Wop Girls and they sashay out to center stage.

The show starts without a hitch. There are a couple of sour notes, and the American accents are all over the place, but otherwise it's pretty good. The Doo-Wop Girls are great; Double P plays a really likeable Audrey; and, although Thomas's singing and acting are both a little bit wobbly, it actually suits Seymour's geeky character, and he gets more laughs than anyone else.

There's no sign of Dean, though—until just before the intermission, when we finally hear his voice for the first time. He doesn't say anything at first; there's just the sound of an unsettlingly evil laugh. Almost inaudible, just loud enough to make the audience stir uncomfortably in their seats. Thomas plays along, lifting up plants from the shelves of the flower shop and putting them back down again in search of the eerie noise.

The laughter grows a little louder, as if reveling in Thomas's confusion, and as the spotlight focuses on the audience, scanning our faces, he peers anxiously out into the crowd. Everything is perfectly still for a moment, and then as the spotlight finds the double doors at the back of the auditorium, Dean loudly kicks them open and strides out from the shadows, cackling maniacally as he does.

He's wearing a green sequined dress adorned with twisting vines of curling ivy that meander down his arms and catch at his wrists. His upper torso is exposed and painted jade, and elaborate emerald earrings dangle from each ear. The gown hugs his muscular body, floating all the way down to a pair of feather lace-up six-inch heels. The shoes lift his body in all the right places, and he dazzles as he catches the light, his silky train giving him the silhouette of a femme fatale. His face is fully beat into a horrific, contorted masterpiece. He doesn't wear a wig, his shaved head working perfectly with the look, only adding to the femininity. He looks beyond fierce. Exactly how you'd imagine a mutant drag queen Venus flytrap to appear. As entrances go, it's hard to beat.

Dean belts out the first line of the song then, his voice effortlessly filling the auditorium as he strides down the aisle. Onstage, Thomas looks like he's about to have a heart attack. The audience is eating it up, their eyes fixed on Dean's each and every move. He stops when he gets to me and seductively reaches down to stroke my face. Thinking this must be the moment he was referring to, I quickly fumble in my lap for the party popper. Dean clamps an emerald-nailed hand around my bicep just in time to stop me.

"Don't pop your load just yet, my boy," he ad-libs, getting a roar of laughter out of the audience, and, with the spotlight hovering above us, I feel Oliver's eyes on me and blush. Dean picks up the song and continues down the aisle and into the plant shop where poor Thomas Mulbridge is waiting for him . . .

Thomas gives it his best shot, but he just can't keep up with Dean. The mismatched pairing adds to the hilarity, so it kind of works, but I'd be lying if I said I didn't take some pleasure in seeing Thomas flounder in Dean's fabulous presence. It feels like karma, as if everything has finally come full circle since elementary school.

From there on, the show is a hit. Dean is transcendent, and his brilliance lifts the rest of the cast, who are clearly having a ball. So much so that when one of the fairy lights from the set comes loose as the audience claps along to the final encore of "Don't Feed the Plants," no one seems to realize.

"That's not supposed to happen, is it?" I whisper to Alicia as the trailing cable wraps around one of Dean's legs and begins to tangle up in his dress.

"Definitely not," Alicia says, her eyes widening in horror as she watches her masterpiece start to wobble. Dean hasn't noticed—he's in his element up there, enjoying every moment—and, as the cable snags one final time, the entire set comes crashing down around him. He stays on his feet, though, styling it out, and the audience only cheers louder.

"Now?" I ask Alicia, not quite believing what just happened.

"Now!" she says, and our party poppers explode into a cloud of green confetti, setting off a domino effect as a succession of preplanted party poppers burst around the room.

Alicia and I are the first on our feet, screaming for Dean at the top of our lungs, and, as the flash from Fiona's camera goes wild, the whole room rises for a standing ovation. Dean looks astonished by the reaction, and as he stands tall in the demolished set, taking graceful bows and blowing kisses, I realize that the whole room is now cheering and shouting his name.

He's the star of Woodside Academy, and the only person who doesn't know it is him.

Chapter Four

"Have you got it?" Dean says, rushing up to me as I open my locker after first period. "Please tell me you remembered?"

It's Monday, and he's wearing tiny white jean shorts and a cropped pink hoodie. He's ripped off the sleeves and cut it unevenly along the bottom to give it a distressed look that I love.

"Got what?" I say, and his face instantly drops. "Of course I've got it," I tease, pulling out the article from the local paper. It's a half page accompanied by a super-artsy-looking photo in black and white. One of Fiona's.

"I can't bear to look," he says melodramatically, pushing the clipping back into my hands. "You're gonna have to read it to me, Max."

"I have to admit it's a bit brutal," I say. "Somebody ought to tell this guy he's reviewing a student production and not a Broadway show."

"Oh God," Dean moans. "It's because I destroyed the set, isn't it?"

"Chill out and listen." I clear my throat for added effect. "'Woodside Academy has become known in recent years for its avant-garde takes on popular musicals, and so expectations were sky-high for *Little Shop of Horrors* on Saturday night, as the curtains opened to reveal an upholstery Manhattan made entirely of recycled clothing . . .'"

"Okay," Dean says. "So far, so good."

"'But as the show went on,'" I continue, "'the audience's excitement started to wane. The show was missing that usual Woodside edge, and I began to wonder if this production might not live up to previous years . . .'"

"Oh God," Dean wheezes, leaning back against his locker. "Okay, stop reading," he says, trying to snatch the review out of my hands.

"'Until the tide was turned by the arrival of the spectacular Dean Jackson,'" I say, and Dean gasps, his hand retreating as he allows me to carry on. "'Breathing new life into the show through his drag portrayal of the carnivorous Audrey II, Jackson was pitch-perfect throughout, and quite literally brought down the house with his big dramatic finish—collapsing the latest of Alicia Williams's magnificent sets around him. A five-star performance from a boy destined for a career on the stage.'"

"Oh—my—God!" Dean says. "This is going straight into my applications!" He snatches the paper out of my hands and reads through it a second time. "Whew," he says, blowing out his cheeks. "For a minute there, I thought my career was over before it had even started."

"I don't think the *Woodside Advertiser* has enough prestige to put an end to your career," I say, laughing.

He doesn't take his eyes away from the article, though, reading it a third, fourth, and fifth time, almost as if to make absolutely sure it's real.

"Have you shown Alicia?"

"Not yet. Do you want to do the honors?" I nod toward her as she appears from the direction of the common room, her arms full of art supplies, doing her usual popular-girl thing as she stops to say hi to absolutely everyone.

"MAGNIFICENT SETS!" Dean shrieks, interrupting her mid-conversation and startling her so much that she drops her supplies all over the floor. A tub of glitter serendipitously bursts open and scatters everywhere, making Mr. Johnson's corridor sparkle once more.

"What?" she says, bewildered, as I rush over to help clean it up.

"Who had magnificent sex?" Some of the freshmen look horrified.

"MAGNIFICENT *SETS!*" Dean repeats, flapping the article in front of her.

"*Ohhh,*" she says, taking the clipping from him and lighting up as she reads it. "Magnificent SETS!"

"You're going to art school, baby!" Dean hollers, throwing his arms around her.

"Let's not get carried away!" She laughs coyly as he releases her. "This is incredible, though. Have you seen what it says about you?"

"*Have I seen what it says about me?* Pitch-perfect. Five-star performance. Big dramatic finish." Dean licks his finger and touches it to his body, making a sizzling sound as he does. "Destined for a career on the stage."

Alicia beams. "Well, we already knew that. Every single drama school is gonna want you, Dean. They'd be idiots not to."

He waves her away. "I've still gotta get through the auditions."

"Yeah, but what more proof do you need?" I say. "*Of course* you're getting in."

"Don't jinx it, Max," he says. "You know they only take, like, a handful of people each year. They don't just accept anyone, you know?"

"But you're not just *anyone!*" Alicia says. "You're Dean Jackson!"

"Pfft," he says. "That might mean something here at Woodside, but out there?" He points to the double doors at the end of the hall. "Big fish, tiny pond."

"You did *not* just quote Mr. Johnson." Alicia frowns, trying to scoop up the glitter but just spreading it around more.

"You're not a fish, Dean Jackson. You're a . . . I don't know . . . what's the biggest thing in the ocean?"

"A giant squid?" I say. "No, a sperm whale!"

"A sperm whale!" Alicia says, laughing. "A great, big, gigantic one."

"Absolutely full of sperm spaghetti!" I add.

Alicia squints at me. "I'm sorry, what did you just say?"

"Sperm spaghetti," I repeat, pulling up Wikipedia. "'Sperm whales' heads are full of a mysterious substance called sperm spaghetti.'"

"It does *not* say that!" Alicia snatches my phone away from me. "*Spermaceti*," she says. "Not *sperm spaghetti*."

"To-may-to, to-mah-to." I shrug. "The point is that Dean's full of sperm."

"That literally could not be further from the point at all," she says. "Or the truth."

"Right, well, as helpful as all this is," Dean says, "it doesn't matter what sperm-filled animal you think I am. I've still gotta nail those auditions, and the big one is next week."

"And you will! Don't even stress about it," Alicia says. "Anyway, I better go before Mr. Johnson puts me in detention again for another act of heinous vandalism. See you in the auditorium at four? You didn't forget, right, Max?"

"Er . . . no," I say. "That's definitely something I remembered . . ."

"Good," she says, "because I have a surprise for you."

"A surprise?" I say, but Alicia just smiles innocently.

"See you at four!"

She winks, twisting on her heel and heading back down the corridor, leaving a criminal trail of glitter behind her as she goes.

◀▶

What do you think?

Straight Expectations

Dad's message pings through on my phone as I take a shortcut across the soccer field on my way to the auditorium. And by shortcut I mean a route that's twice as long but *feels* shorter because I get to see Oliver in his uniform.

I open the message to see a picture of Dad's new tie. It's covered in brightly colored tap-dancing penguins. It's absolutely *hideous*.

I lie. Super cute, I write, immediately forwarding the picture to the GroupChat™.

We've been secretly rating Dad's tie collection for the best part of a year now. Dean quickly replies with an edited picture of Regina George saying it's the "ugliest effing tie she's ever seen," and Alicia pings one through of Anne Hathaway now proudly wearing the tie along with the iconic Chanel boots. It's incredibly well edited—she's an artist in everything she does, and apparently that even applies to spur-of-the-moment memes. I heart both of their messages and then tap back to the chat with Dad.

> How was the seminar?

Dad runs his own fintech company—whatever that means—and recently signed up his whole team for one of those diversity-and-inclusion away days. I can't fault him for trying.

> Great! Did you know gay people have their own flag?

He can't be serious.

> What?

> There's a gay flag for gay people! It's a rainbow. I'd have thought you of all people would have known that!

> It's for LGBT+ people. Not just gay people. Why do you think I have one hanging on my bedroom door, Dad?

You do?

He sends a shocked face for added effect.

> Only for like five years.

I just thought you liked the colors?

> Yeah and the posters of topless boys are just because I *really* admire the photography 😊

> Anyway, Mum thinks we should do something this weekend. Me, you, her, and Chris. You down?

I'd love to! What did you have in mind?

> I'll think about it. Talk to you later, okay?

I push my phone back into my pocket just as I hear a cheer from across the soccer field. I think our team must have won the game because they're bouncing up and down in one of those homoerotic huddles. I try to spot Oliver, but the only part of the tangle of limbs that's recognizably his is a pair of rainbow laces. I wish the rest of the team would wear them too. I should probably suggest we make that happen at Queer Club, but I'm not going to get my hopes up. There's only so much you can expect from a team of straight boys.

Dean meets me outside the auditorium with a spring in his step and a tray of four venti cups of Starbucks in his hand, each with the name of one of the Scooby squad members written on the side.

"Here you go, Daphne," he says, handing me a cup. "And hold on to this one as well," he adds, pushing the one marked *Fred* into my free hand.

"Thanks," I say, taking a sip of the iced vanilla latte. It's the only thing we ever order because gays quite simply do not drink hot coffee.

We head inside to find that what was left of the *Little Shop* set has already been dismantled. The chairs have been tidied away in storage, and there's now just a big empty space where the dance floor will eventually be. Woodside has three official celebrations a year: the Snow Ball at Christmas, the Leavers' Ball in the summer to celebrate graduation, and the Monster Ball for Halloween—this Friday. The school has practically no budget but, just like with the show, Alicia takes the reins and always finds a way to make it special.

"Um, Alicia?" Dean calls into the echoing space. "Where is she?"

"I'm back here!" a muffled voice shouts from behind the stage.

We go through to the dressing area. It's unrecognizable from the chaos of Saturday night. Dark drapes now hang from the ceiling, coupled with some colorful plants and fairy lights repurposed from the *Little Shop* set. It feels like being inside a huge, cozy tent, the floor scattered with giant cushions and an oversized beanbag stolen from the common room.

"This is amazing, Alicia," I say. "You did it all in a couple of hours?"

"It's nothing," she says with a smile, taking the drink marked *Shaggy* from Dean.

"So what is it?" I ask, relaxing down into one of the giant cushions, careful not to spill the two coffees.

"Well, the Monster Ball can be pretty intense. I figured people would need a quiet place to relax and unwind. Away from the music and the dance floor."

"So a make-out room?" Dean says.

"Exactly!" Alicia grins. "It's all anyone's thinking about anyway. Except we don't tell the teachers that. I told Mrs. A that it's a 'haunted grotto.'"

"And she really fell for that?"

Alicia gives me some side-eye. "She's not stupid. She knows *exactly* what it'll really be used for, but she'll turn a blind eye if anyone asks about it."

"Haunted grotto it is," I say, laughing. "Who's the lucky guy, then?"

"Absolutely no one," she says. "I'm on a testosterone detox after last year. Zach Taylor has put me off boys for good."

"He was *hot*, though," Dean says with a sigh. "All those muscles! Surely he was worth the headache?"

Alicia groans. "He was more like a migraine. I'm glad he's graduated and gone now. I'm so much better off without the distraction."

"I wouldn't mind being distracted by *that*," Dean says.

"Since when are you interested, anyway?" I reply. Dean never talks about boys, and yet suddenly he has the hots for Zach Taylor?

He shrugs. "Since always. High-school boys aren't really my thing. I like my guys older. A little more rugged."

"Rugged?" Alicia laughs. "Zach Taylor?"

"Well, whatever! Boys just aren't the center of my universe, you know? We're not all totally obsessed, Max."

"He's right," Alicia says. "I've got art school to think about; boys can be put on hold for a while. It's not like they're going anywhere . . ."

"That's so easy for you to say!" I protest. "You've got boys lining up around the block! What us gays wouldn't give for that! Back me up on this, Dean."

"Well, Max is right," he says. "You do have guys lining up around the block, Alicia. And I can't deny that I'm not just a *little* bit jealous of that. But, Max, there's probably hundreds of guys in your future. You just might have to wait a little while to get them. So maybe shift your priorities elsewhere for a bit?"

"Like where?" I say. "You both have your whole careers mapped out. What am *I* supposed to focus on?"

Dean shrugs again. "You love . . . *shoes?*"

"Okay, wow," I say, laughing. "Way to make me sound shallow, Dean. *Max's interests include boys and shoes.* Like Barbie before they made her a yassified feminist."

"You *do* like boys and shoes, though," says Alicia.

"Boys *in* nice shoes," I correct her with a grin. "My kryptonite."

"Well, okay," Alicia finally says. "I'll be sure to check my straight privilege. But being harassed by horny teenage boys isn't exactly most girls' idea of fun."

"It isn't?!" I say. "That sounds like exactly my idea of fun."

She shakes her head. "Dean's right, though. You've got plenty of hot guys in your future so don't even worry about it."

"I guess," I say half-heartedly. But I don't want them to be in my future. I want them to be in my right now. "What is it you need us to help with, anyway?"

Alicia reaches over to what looks like a stack of paper plates. She takes one and twists it until it pops open into a lantern shape.

"They look a bit cheap now, but wait till you see them lit up. I've done a bunch already. Dean, you can help me hang those in the auditorium, and, Max"—she pauses as a mischievous smile spreads across her lips—"you can stay here and make the rest with Oliver."

"Wait, what?!"

Alicia beams. "Told you I had a surprise for you, didn't I?"

"Alicia, no! I can't!" I say, genuine panic setting in. I've managed to say a grand total of eight words to Oliver in the entire year he's been at Woodside. And now she expects me to join him for an evening of arts and crafts? "I'll help hang the lanterns. Dean can stay here with Oliver."

"And ruin your romantic evening? I wouldn't dream of it," he says, grinning.

"You *both* planned this, didn't you?"

Dean smirks. "I don't know what you're talking about." There's a clank as the auditorium doors open.

"We're back here!" Alicia yells, and I hear the sound of footsteps approaching.

Alicia opens her compact mirror and holds it up so I can quickly check my hair. I do look cute, admittedly, but not date-night-with-Oliver-Cheng cute. I need to run home and change, I think—it's just a *very short* forty-five-minute sprint—but it's too late because Alicia has already put away her mirror, and now Oliver's standing in the doorway.

"Hey, Alicia," he says.

He must have showered after soccer because his hair is all floppy and unstyled, and he's wearing a pair of skintight jeans and an oversized green T-shirt with some sports team logo across the front of it. The Greendale Jaguars, whoever the hell they are.

"Hey, Max. Hey, Dean," he adds, nodding at both of us with a smile.

I must be dreaming. There's absolutely no way Oliver Cheng knows my name.

"Thanks for coming, Ollie." Alicia smiles. She did *not* just call him Ollie. "I thought you could help Max make some paper lanterns?"

"Sure!" he says, surprisingly enthusiastically. Maybe a little *too* enthusiastically to be real.

"Oh, and Max got you a coffee," Dean adds.

I look down to see I am indeed holding two coffees. This is a complete and utter setup.

"Oh . . . yeah," I say, handing him the drink, turning around to mouth *I fucking hate you* to Dean as I do.

"Oh, you didn't have to," Oliver says with a smile, his hand brushing against mine as he takes the cup. "*Fred?*" he says, reading the side.

"Velma," Dean says, revealing the writing on his.

"Shaggy," Alicia says proudly.

"So that means you must be . . ." Oliver says, turning back to me.

"Daphne," I grumble.

"Well, that means I must have the hots for you, then?" he says, and I almost collapse dead on the spot. "Well, thanks, Max," he adds with a smile that nearly kills me a second time.

"No, thank *you*," I reply for some reason, and Dean chokes back a laugh.

"Right, get to work, boys," Alicia says, clapping her hands together before I can embarrass myself any further. I can't believe she's about to leave me with Oliver unsupervised. I haven't even planned out a conversation!

"How many of these do you need?" Oliver asks.

"I don't know? A hundred?"

A hundred?! She has to be joking.

"And you're sure you don't want me to help you instead?" I plead.

"No, I specifically need Dean for this," she says. "He has a really good eye for . . . lantern placement."

They're not even *pretending* to hide what they're doing, and yet Oliver is somehow just smiling along obliviously. The pair of them disappear before I can argue any further, but I bet they're not hanging up lanterns at all—I bet they're just sitting outside, listening.

"So how do we do these?" Oliver says, picking up one of the flat lanterns and turning it over in his hands.

"Here," I say, trying to steady my shaking fingers as I take the lantern from him and twist it the way Alicia showed me. It's trickier than I thought, but it eventually pops open.

"Cute," he says, taking a stack of them and going to sit down on one of the giant cushions. I sit down opposite him, my heart racing. He looks even prettier up close.

"I don't see you around school much," he says, taking a long sip of his coffee with those full, delicious lips. "I guess we don't share any classes?"

"I don't think so," I say, knowing perfectly well we don't. "You moved here from London, right? That must have sucked."

"You'd think so, but not really," he replies. "At first, I didn't wanna come to the countryside. I thought it'd be boring and that there'd be nothing going on. But I dunno, I won't admit this to my parents, but now I actually kinda like it here?"

"You're lucky," I say. "I've always wanted to live in a big city. Everything just seems so much more exciting. What's it really like? In London?"

"You've never been?"

"A few times when I was younger. My parents took me to some musicals before they separated. *The Lion King. Billy Elliot. Wicked.* The usual stuff. It was nice, I guess, but I didn't really see that much of the city."

"It's not as great as everyone makes it out to be." Oliver shrugs. "I don't know if I really miss it that much. My best friend still lives there so I guess I mostly just miss her? And good dim sum! You can't get that here in Woodside. But aside from that? The novelty of London wears off pretty quick. There's a lot going on, but it's not really that different from living anywhere else."

"But being gay there must be so much easier."

"How so?" he says. He seems puzzled by the statement.

"Well, just, like, it's London? The streets are painted with rainbows!"

He laughs. "The streets aren't painted with rainbows, Max."

"They are! I saw it on Instagram!"

"There's, like, *one* rainbow crossing," he says. "I've never even seen it. There is a gay bookshop, though. Gay's the Word. I do miss that."

"I didn't know you liked to read?" I've never seen him so much as turn a page before.

"Are you joking?" he says, abandoning the lantern he's working on to reach for his bag. He unzips it and tips out a whole rainbow of multi-colored books. "This one's my favorite," he says, pushing one of them into my hands. "It's about a gay kid who goes to a queer summer camp."

"Is that a thing?" I say, turning the book over and reading the back cover.

"Maybe in America? I dunno. Can you imagine if it was, though? There's something so romantic about the idea of summer camp. Playing games, staying up late around the campfire, swimming in the lake . . . I'd be there in a heartbeat."

"Same," I say, imagining Oliver and me diving into a big, beautiful lake, fireflies hovering just above the surface as the sunset reflects off the water. "Just like in the movies," I continue, imagining his wet hands finding my body, staring into his eyes, wanting nothing more than to kiss him . . .

"Do you want it?" he says then, looking me dead in the eyes.

"Huh?" I say, a little flustered. "Do I . . . want it?"

"The book," he says, pulling me back to reality. "Do you want to borrow it?"

"Oh," I say, trying to disguise my embarrassment, "I'm not much of a reader actually. I'll wait till they make it into a movie."

Oliver groans. "You're killing me, Max. But how about one of these, then?" He hands me a graphic novel called *There Are Things I Can't Tell You.* Two teenage boys grip each other on the cover. "They've got lots of pictures."

"You make me sound like I'm ten years old," I say, laughing shyly. "Are these hentai?" I say, noticing the distinctive art style.

Oliver's eyes widen a little. "What?"

"That's what they're called, right?"

"Do you mean manga?" he says, raising an eyebrow.

"Well, what's the difference?"

"Hentai is porn, Max."

"Oh my God," I say. I turn bright red.

"I think I should hold on to this actually." Oliver takes the book back from me. "Don't want you stickying up the pages."

"I wouldn't!" I say in protest, but honestly he's probably right.

"If you say so," he says with a wink, and returns to his stack of lanterns. I don't know what to say to that, so I go back to making lanterns too.

We work in companionable silence for a while. He's so cute when he concentrates, the way his tongue sticks out just slightly between those soft lips . . . I've never wanted to kiss somebody more.

Sitting there with him, it's hard not to notice the differences between us. He's so sporty, and I'm so . . . well, not. I wonder what he thinks about my painted nails and my fashion sense. I know they say that opposites attract, but sometimes I can't help but feeling like I might be putting guys off. "*Straight* acting"—that's what all the guys go for, right? Sometimes I think I'd be better off if I just tried to blend in . . .

But then something happens that puts all those thoughts out of my mind. Oliver glances up and catches me staring, and we lock eyes for just a moment. Then he tilts his head inquisitively.

Oh my God, is he going to kiss me?

He reaches his hand up toward my face. I'm not imagining it—this is it, this is real, and my whole body is quivering because this is actually, genuinely happening . . .

"Eyelash," he says, plucking a stray from my cheek and holding it out in front of him. "Make a wish," he says with a little smile.

"A wish?" I say hesitantly. "Oh, uhhh . . ."

It really shouldn't be that difficult, but with him staring at me with those beautiful eyes my mind goes completely blank. What did I tell Dean I'd wish for? *A Friday-night sleepover with Oliver Cheng.* That's stupid, but right now it's all I can think of, so I close my eyes for a second and gently blow the eyelash out of his fingers.

"What did you wish for?" he asks, his gaze following the eyelash as it's carried away on my breath.

"I can't tell you," I say, "or it won't come true. Everyone knows that."

"Okay," he says. "You don't have to tell me. As long as you promise you didn't wish for something stupid."

"I can't promise that," I say. "Why? What would you wish for?"

"A hundred more wishes, of course," he says with a grin. "And a really cute boyfriend."

I laugh. "That's cheating. You can't wish for more wishes. Everyone knows that."

"Okay, just the boyfriend, then."

He blushes slightly, and for the first time I wonder if he *might* actually be interested. I've always thought of him as out of my league, but maybe Dean's right. Maybe he would consider somebody like me after all.

"I really like your bracelet," he says suddenly, as if looking for a way to change the subject.

"Oh, this?" I say, clutching it. "It's a friendship bracelet. Dean gave it to me years ago. I know it's a bit childish, but I like to wear it on special occasions."

"What's the occasion?"

"Oh, I dunno," I say. "I put it on for the show and, well, after that amazing performance, I guess I didn't wanna take it off?" I pause. Am I talking too much? I'm definitely talking too much. "I don't know—it's stupid."

"No," he says. "Not at all. It's actually really sweet."

We continue working for a little while, not saying much at all, the lanterns piling up around us. Maybe I *should* do what Dean and Alicia have been pushing me to do all this time and actually ask him out. We're preparing decorations for the Monster Ball: it wouldn't be too much of a stretch to ask him if he'd like to go with me. Would it?

"You know, Oliver . . ." I say. *I'm going to do it. I'm actually going to do it.* "I was wondering if maybe . . ." I hesitate, and he looks at me expectantly. This is it, this is finally my moment. "I was thinking that it might be cool if—"

His phone rings. Buzzing noisily in his pocket, demanding attention. I will him to ignore it, but he doesn't.

"Sorry, I need to get this," he says, pulling it out. "Hold that thought?"

He stands up and answers it, walking away so I can't hear him. I'm sweating. I can't believe I almost did it. He's gone for no more than a minute.

"Sorry, Max," he says. "My parents want me to come home early. They're going away in a couple days—a second honeymoon—and they want to run through the 'house rules' again."

"House rules?" I say.

"Oh, you know—no drinking, no parties, no boys in my bed . . ."

"Oh yeah, sure." I swallow hard. "That's cool. It's just I was about to . . ."

"Yeah?"

"Nothing, don't worry."

"Tell Alicia I had to go? And I'll make it up to her?"

"Yeah, no worries," I say.

"You're the best, Max," he says, and rushes out the door.

Chapter Five

"*Make a wish, Max,*" Dean says, putting on a ridiculous deep, sexy voice as he plucks an imaginary eyelash from Alicia's face.

"*Oh, Oliver!*" she cries, falling back onto her bed. "*I wish you'd take me right here!*"

The two of them shriek with laughter.

"Very funny," I say, unamused, just as Darius knocks and opens the door.

"Are they still tormenting you, Max?" he says, opening the pizza box.

"Relentlessly," I say, my mouth watering at the smell of double sausage, extra onion, and a thick layer of barbecue sauce. The Williamses have always had excellent taste in food; between Darius's traditional barbecues and Shonda's Thanksgiving dinners, Alicia's parents utterly spoil us.

"Well, I'll leave you in charge of the pizza. How's that? They'll be groveling in no time." He winks and pushes the box into my hands. "They're just jealous that they're not as popular with the boys as you are."

"I've got better things to worry about than boys, Daddy," Alicia says.

"Damn straight!" he replies. "They're just a bunch of slobbering horndogs anyway. Best not to waste your time with them."

"You should hear the way Max obsesses about Oliver," Alicia says, flicking her hair back. "If anyone's a slobbering horndog, it's him."

Darius raises an eyebrow and shoots me a disapproving look. "You better not be disrespecting that boy, Maximillian. Or any boy for that matter."

"I'm not!" I protest. "I just wanna go on cute dates and do cute boyfriend things. Nothing you wouldn't see on the Disney Channel!"

Dean smirks. "Well, that's not what you said earlier . . ."

"Oh, whatever! Don't listen to him," I say to Darius. "He's just jealous that I'm your favorite."

"I don't have favorites," says Darius, holding his hands up. "Although, Dean, I am still waiting for you to make good on your promise . . ." He holds his hands out, presenting his unpainted nails. "That might just be enough to swing it in your favor."

"Name the time and place!" Dean grins. "We just need to figure out your color. I'm thinking a deep purple to match that beautiful complexion. Or maybe something fiery to turn some heads at the gym." He pirouettes as he says it, catching some air in his cropped pink hoodie.

"Oh, don't encourage him," Alicia says. "You're so embarrassing, Dad."

"Well, your embarrassing father will be downstairs. Behave yourselves."

"We'll try our best," Dean says, and Darius chuckles, closing the door.

"So, *Freaky Friday*?" I say, picking up the TV remote.

"*Again*? Do we have to?" Alicia says. "I just don't understand the obsession with Lindsay Lohan. She's not even that good an actress."

"I'm sorry?" Dean says in faux outrage. "Have you not seen *The Parent Trap*? How they made that movie with just one Lindsay Lohan is a feat of cinematic brilliance!"

"And *Mean Girls*!" I add. "Don't forget about *Mean Girls*!"

"Exactly. Don't be homophobic, Alicia!"

"Okay, fine," she says, laughing. "But you at least have to agree that the plot of this movie is all over the place. I mean, a magic fortune cookie? Really? Could they seriously not come up with anything better?"

"The absurdity is what makes it brilliant," I say. "Now shh—it's starting."

I love sleepovers at Alicia's house. Her room sits in the huge, converted attic space and looks like a Tumblr aesthetic come to life, all exposed brick and rope lights suspended from the ceiling beams. She has an inspiration pinboard above her desk filled with magazine cuttings and Polaroids she's snapped over the years with her fancy vintage camera. There's a blank canvas resting on an easel in one corner, and paintbrushes cluttering every surface. The whole room is a living, breathing work of art, but my favorite thing is the watercolor that hangs over her bed. A painting of the three of us re-created from a photo we took on our trip to the lake a few summers back.

"How do you get your Instagram to look so good?" I ask, barely paying attention to the movie. I have a slice of pizza in one hand and her account open in the other. It's gorgeously curated and full of so much color. A mix of her recent work and set designs with the occasional artistic selfie thrown in.

"With great difficulty," she says. "They won't admit it, but I've heard rumors that the top art schools search out applicants on social media now."

"That is absolutely not true," Dean says, aghast. "They're not looking up teenagers' Instagrams. That's so totally creepy."

"Well, it wouldn't surprise me," Alicia replies. "I know you're anti–social media and everything, but you should probably think about creating an account. Apparently casting directors look at how many followers you have now too."

"Yeah, that's called stunt casting," Dean says, rolling his eyes. "I'd prefer to get cast because of my *talent*, not how many followers I have."

"I'm just saying it wouldn't hurt," she says. "Besides, you're way too hot to not be on Instagram. The gay boys would eat you up."

"That's true." Dean grins, fluttering his eyelashes. "Honestly, I don't think Instagram is ready for *this*."

"Aw, that one's cute!" Alicia says, leaning over my shoulder and pointing at one of the photos on-screen. I'd switched over to Oliver's page while they were talking.

"Oh yeah?" I try to act casual, tapping into the photo as if I've not already looked at it a thousand times.

It's a picture of him on a beach somewhere. He's giving the camera a big cheesy grin as he poses with a giant sea turtle just at the edge of the surf. His hair is wet, he's not super muscly or anything, but his body is *really* nice to look at, and his long red swim shorts cling to him in a way that leaves very little to the imagination. I know that's not what I should be paying attention to—it's just supposed to be a cute turtle selfie—but judging by the comments I'm not the only person who's noticed. There's a whole load of London boys telling him just how hot he looks.

"Do you think he's slept with any of these guys?" I ask, reading a comment from a guy called Cole. He's written "run me over with a truck" coupled with five drooling emojis, three chili peppers, and an eggplant.

"Does it matter?" Dean says. "Who cares?"

"I do," I say. "I mean, what if he's *experienced*? What if he's already hooked up with one of them? I can't compete with that."

I open my own profile and tap into one of my most recent pictures—me and Dean with matching nails. It has just eight likes and one single comment.

Nice nails boys xoxo love mum

"Like, what if it came down to it, and I didn't know what to do?"

"Oh puh-*lease*," Dean says. "You're hardly sweet and innocent, Max. I've seen your search history. Besides, I know you practice with the contents of the vegetable drawer."

"Oh my God," I say, burying my head in my hands.

"What, like . . . a whole cucumber?" Alicia says. "Or do you, like, cut a hole in a pumpkin? Either way, remind me never to eat the salad at your house."

"I have *not* been practicing with the vegetable drawer!"

"I wasn't judging. What you and the turnips do is none of my business." Dean is laughing now. "Look," he says, "this whole conversation is pointless. You're never gonna get the chance to find out what it's like with Oliver if you don't message the boy. Stop making up excuses and just do it."

"Absolutely not," I say, and they both sigh in frustration. We've been going around in circles with this all evening.

Alicia groans. "Oh, come on, Max! You can't avoid this forever!"

"She's right," Dean adds. "Just say hey and ask if he wants to hang out. It doesn't have to be a big deal. Just be chill about it."

The two of them are staring at me as *I* stare down at my phone. Maybe they're right. Messaging him would certainly be a whole lot easier than doing it in person. That way I won't get distracted by how pretty he is like I did earlier.

"Okay, fine," I reluctantly say, and begin carefully crafting the message.

It takes many agonizing minutes, writing and editing, editing and deleting, throwing my phone across the room and saying, "*I can't do it!*"

but eventually, long after the movie credits have rolled, I think I have something okay.

"Here," I say. "Can you read it before I send?"

Dean takes the phone from me and clears his throat.

"Really cool chatting with you earlier, loads of fun. I was just wondering if you'd maybe like to maybe hang out or something sometime, maybe? No worries if not. Smiley face. Kiss kiss.'"

He pauses for a moment, and I can tell they're both trying not to laugh. "Is that it? That's what took you all night?"

"Loads of . . . fun?" Alicia repeats, and the pair of them crack up.

"So helpful. Thanks, guys," I say. "Really mature, honestly."

"You know you used the word *maybe* three times?" Dean asks.

"Did I? Wait, let me change it."

"Too late," he says, grinning. "Sent."

"What?!" I gasp, trying to snatch the phone back. "I wasn't ready!"

"You were never going to be ready," Alicia says. "And look, he's typing!" She points at the three dots as they appear at the bottom of the screen.

"Dean, give it back!" I demand, wrestling the phone from him.

I watch the little dots, waiting for the inevitable polite rejection. Oliver types for what seems like forever, and then, just when I think I can't bear it any longer, the typing suddenly stops. I wait a moment for the message to come through, but there's nothing. Alicia and Dean stop laughing.

"Give it a minute. He's probably just thinking of what to say," Alicia says, but I can tell by her tone that even she isn't convinced. A minute passes, and then another, my heart sinking a little deeper with each one.

Alicia tries to stifle the awkward feelings by putting on another movie. *To All the Boys I've Loved Before.* Usually my favorite, one of our go-to rom-coms, but right now it's a terrible, terrible choice.

"I expected better from him," Dean finally says after a full hour has passed. "He always seemed pretty decent, but leaving you on read? Literally who does that?"

"Just be patient," Alicia counters. "Do you think Oliver would sit around checking his phone, waiting for a boy to message him back?"

"No," I say grumpily, knowing she's probably right.

"There you go, then. You shouldn't either. Let's talk about something else."

Dean grins. "Like how we're gonna sneak alcohol into the Monster Ball?"

"Exactly!" she says. "But that's easy. We'll just stash it in the haunted grotto beforehand. Mrs. A will never check—we just need to make sure we get there earlier than anyone else. We don't want a repeat of last year."

"Whose idea was it to hide it in the boys' bathroom anyway?" Dean says.

"That would be Max!" She laughs, but I don't join in. I barely even look up from my phone. All I can think about is that *stupid* message, and how I've officially ruined my chances with Oliver. There's a reason I never asked him out before, and that reason is exactly *this*. Humiliation. Rejection. All hopes of my high-school romance disappear just like that.

"Come on, Max, he's just a boy," Alicia says, putting her arm around me.

"He's not just a boy," I say, annoyed, and push her off. "You wouldn't understand. How old were you when you had your first kiss? Like, eight? Well, I'm almost eighteen and still waiting. I'd kind of given up hope, to be honest, and then Oliver showed up, and I thought that maybe it could finally happen . . ."

"Oh . . ." Alicia says, and I can tell she doesn't know what else to say. "Well, there's more to life than kissing boys, Max. It's not all it's cracked up to be."

"Yeah, well, that's easy for you to say when you can have anyone you want. But that's not my story, is it? I'm going to finish high school without ever being invited to the dance, without ever finding secret love notes in my locker. I'll never get in trouble for making out somewhere I shouldn't, and there'll never be rumors about who I may or may not be dating."

I gesture to the TV where Noah Centineo and Lana Condor are making out in a hot tub.

"Dating, romance, maybe even sex—that's what high school is *meant* to be about . . . but I don't get to experience any of it." I'm staring down at my hands now. "It's not fair," I say. "I hate being different."

"Come on, Max," Dean says. "You don't mean that."

"But I do," I say. "I want what the straight kids have. Endless options for love and romance. Even just for a couple of days. I know you don't care about that stuff, Dean, but I do."

"Of course I care," he says. "But you said it yourself, Max—gays don't peak in high school. We've got the rest of our lives for all that."

"Yeah, and that's easy for you to say when you have your whole life planned out. You both do. Drama school. Art school. What have I got?"

"You're literally going on a gap year paid for by your parents," Dean says, laughing. "That's pretty good if you ask me. Besides, what if I don't get a scholarship? What do you think happens then?"

"Not this again." I roll my eyes. "Of course you're going to get one."

Dean clicks his tongue in frustration. "But you don't *know* that, Max! There are *hundreds* of kids chasing those scholarships. You keep acting like it's a done deal, but I don't think you're listening to me . . ."

"No, I don't think *you're* listening to *me!*" I shoot back. "I'm trying to tell you how I feel, and you're making it all about you and your stupid auditions."

"Okay, wow," Dean says, leaning back. *"My stupid auditions?"* Well, I'm sorry if I think my whole future is more important than talking about boys! We all have to deal with rejection eventually. You'll be fine in the morning. You're a big girl, Maxine."

"I'm not a girl," I reply bitterly, looking down at my painted nails. "No wonder Oliver isn't into me when I dress like this. He's literally on the soccer team. I'm taking it off," I say, going over to the vanity table and reaching for the nail-polish remover.

"Don't you dare," Dean says. "Don't you dare do that, Maxine!"

"My name is MAX!" I snap, taking off the lid.

"Max, don't," Alicia says, but it's already too late. The smell of chemicals is thick in my nostrils as I scrub the color from my nails.

"I can't believe you just did that," Dean says after a pause. "You're the definition of white gay privilege. You realize not all of us can take off our identity whenever it suits us?"

"Dean's right," Alicia says. "Think of all the queer people who fought for what you have, Max. You're really gonna literally wash your hands of them? Just like that? Turn your back on who you really are?"

"But maybe this *isn't* who I am!" I say. "Has it ever occurred to either of you that sometimes I might just wanna blend in?"

"Blend in?" Dean snorts. "Max, you're literally a walking Pride flag!"

"That's rich coming from you!" I sneer. "I mean, just look at yourself. This is real life, Dean. How's anyone supposed to take you seriously? If you're so worried about your precious auditions, why don't you start dressing the part?"

"Max!" Alicia gasps.

Dean's face is stony.

"You know what?" he says, pulling his hood up defensively. "Mum was right. You white men *are* all the same. Be like everyone else! See if

I care! I believed you were different, but I guess that was just wishful thinking."

"And that's exactly it! All you've ever done is try to force me to be like you! But I'm not you, Dean, and I never will be. So just let me live my own life."

"Well, go on, then," he says. "You know where the door is."

"Fine!" I say, heading for it.

"Max, come on . . ." Alicia tries to stop me. "You don't mean any of this. I know you're upset about Oliver, but he really is just a stupid boy . . ."

"He's not just a stupid boy!" I yell, and my eyes start to well up now. "But of course *you* don't understand. You're just like the rest of them . . ."

"Max . . ." She looks genuinely hurt, but I'm too angry to care.

"You know what? I wish I could have what you have, Alicia. I wish I could be one of the *normal* kids."

"Oh, grow up, Max," Dean says. He actually looks at me with disgust.

"You know what?" I say, grabbing the friendship bracelet on my wrist and pulling with all my strength. "I wish we were never even friends."

I look Dean dead in the eye as I say it, and as the bracelet snaps, I feel something snap inside me too.

Chapter Six

"Max!"

There's a thud at the door as I jerk bolt upright. The curtains are pulled tight, just a sliver of light breaking through the darkness. I look at my alarm clock and see it's flashing 11:11. Shit. I'm already two hours late.

"Yeah?" I call groggily, rubbing my face.

There's nothing worse than being woken up unexpectedly. My body feels like it's been hit by a truck, and my eyes are so heavy it's as if they've been set with industrial cement.

"I thought you left hours ago!" Mum yells back. She sounds angrier than she has in a long time. "I just got a call from school saying you weren't in class this morning. You can't keep doing this, Max!"

"I overslept," I say, grabbing the white T-shirt lazily thrown over the back of my chair and scooping a pair of blue jeans off the floor.

"Well, get a move on," she says, and I can hear her heading back downstairs.

I fumble around for my phone. It's usually charging by my bedside, and the cable's there, but the phone is missing. Sometimes it falls down and ends up under the bed, but it's not there either. And you know what?

Fuck it. After last night, I'm not sure I want to talk to anyone right now anyway. Part of me wonders if Oliver ever replied, but even if I had my phone, I'm not sure I could bring myself to look. I'd rather live in ignorance than face that rejection.

I grab the first shoes I can find, a pair of worn-out black-and-white Adidas that had been pushed underneath the bed. I swear I've never seen them before, but they're kinda cute so I slip them on anyway. I catch a glimpse of myself in the mirror as I do. It's dark, but I can just about make out my reflection, and it's funny because in this outfit it almost looks like I'm one of the straight boys. But a little bit more stylish. Obviously.

I make it to school in record time, and I'm kinda glad I missed the morning because it makes it easier to avoid everyone. The last thing I want right now is to have to face Dean and Alicia, and I certainly don't want to see Oliver after I completely humiliated myself. As if to add salt to that wound, though, Rachel Kwan and Simon Pike collar me on the front steps, holding hands and looking obnoxiously happy.

"Hey, Max," Rachel says, waving. She's wearing a plaid skirt, chunky platforms, and a sleek button-down top in black. It looks really good on her. I never really noticed that she had such a great figure before, but that outfit is doing *wonders*. "Where were you this morning? Alicia was looking for you everywhere."

"I overslept," I say with an exaggerated groan. "My mum's pissed with me—apparently the school called to ask where I was."

Simon laughs. "Yikes!" He's wearing one of those awful band shirts with skulls and flames and completely illegible writing scrawled across the front.

"*The . . . Distorted Reality?*"

"You know them?" He looks down at his shirt proudly.

I shrug. "Can't say that I do."

I used to have a crush on Simon a couple years back but looking at him now makes me wonder what I was thinking. It's not that he's unattractive; he just couldn't be any less my type. Right now, I genuinely think I'm more attracted to Rachel. At least she knows how to turn a look.

"All right, well, we'll see you at lunch?" Rachel says. "We're gonna go check out the new sushi place if you and Alicia want to come with?"

"Oh, I dunno . . . We kinda had a fight," I say, looking down at my feet.

"Trouble in paradise?" Simon says, wiggling his eyebrows.

"Uh . . . yeah. Something like that . . ."

"Well, romance isn't always easy, Max," Rachel says.

Oh God, she already knows about Oliver. My stomach turns over. I know gossip travels fast around Woodside, but it's barely even midday.

"It's always worth it, though, right, Simon?"

"Right," he replies, and they share a sickeningly sweet kiss.

"Well, it's not that simple. Who told you anyway?" I ask, imagining the cringeworthy details of my message to Oliver captured in a screenshot and sent to every single person in school. Oliver wouldn't do that, surely, but if Oliver shared it with Thomas? He absolutely would.

"Huh?" Rachel says. "Who told us what?"

"About Oliver," I say, but she just looks at me weirdly. Of course she's going to play the innocent. "Oh, forget it. I've gotta go."

"Okay . . . see you later?" they call, but I'm already hopping up the steps two at a time, heading for the double doors that lead into the main corridor.

I brace for impact as I walk through, expecting everyone to stare, but people barely notice me at all. The hallway is alive with the usual buzz of students grabbing their books and rushing between classes, but something doesn't feel right. The sensation is a bit like stepping into school on your first day and not knowing anyone. I can see all the familiar faces, but they seem strangely different, as if there's some intangible change about them that I can't quite put my finger on.

At Woodside, the soccer boys have always taken center stage, with their loosely hanging shorts and mud-spattered calf muscles, but now it's almost like they've faded into the background, as if the popularity paradigm has spun on its axis, and now it's the girls from drama class who are taking the spotlight. I watch as they idly chat by their lockers, pushing back their hair and filling the air with the scent of their perfume. I don't know if it's new outfits or haircuts, but there's definitely something different about them, and I can't bring myself to look away.

"Hey, Max," Double P says, giggling, as if she's noticed me staring.

"Oh, uh, hey," I say, scratching the back of my neck. Why am I blushing?

"Are you going to the party on Wednesday?"

"Party? No, I don't think so. I wasn't invited . . ."

"Not invited to your best friend's party?" She laughs. "*Ouch!*"

"He's throwing a party?" I say, confused.

Dean *never* hosts parties. I know I'm prone to forgetting things, but I would definitely remember *that*.

"Yeah, everyone's going," she replies, twirling her hair. "I'm sure you'll get the invite. I'll see you there?"

"I mean . . . sure?" I say, continuing down the hall. Why is everyone acting so weird today?

I turn the corner and head toward the common room, and that's when I hear Alicia call out from behind me.

"There you are!" she says, grabbing one of my arms as she catches up to me. She's the last person I wanted to bump into, but I suppose I have to face her eventually. I can't hide from her and Dean forever.

"Alicia, hey, about last night . . ." I begin, turning to face her, but then it's like the air is knocked out of me, and all I can manage to say is "*Wow.*"

She's straightened her hair and is wearing a cute green top that matches her eyeshadow, with a pair of tight black jeans. There's a spark in her deep brown eyes, and her glossed lips are full and alluring. I know she's always been one of the prettiest girls in school—you'd have to be blind not to notice that—but today she doesn't just look pretty, she looks kinda . . . hot? Like, we're talking five drooling emojis, three chili peppers, and an eggplant. Three eggplants, in fact. And, oh my God, I think I'm turning full eggplant just looking at her. I know it's really gross and weird, like admitting I like my cousin or something, but I mean . . . I think I might have a crush on Alicia?!

"Last night?" she says, those soft lips twitching upward into a smile.

And that's when I notice she has boobs. Two of them, in fact, and they're looking right at me. I know I shouldn't stare, but it feels a bit like being nine years old in the men's underwear section all over again. Bulges absolutely everywhere, but you mustn't look or everyone will realize you're a massive pervert.

"Max?" Alicia says, and I realize I'm just slack-jawed and staring.

"Alicia, g-g-gosh," I stammer. "I mean . . . hi, good morning, hello."

"Hello, Max," she says with a laugh and gives me a cute little look.

Is it possible I've liked girls this whole time, and I'm only now having my big bisexual awakening? That's a thing, right? Loads of people don't realize their sexuality until much later in life. Maybe I've been the B in LGBT this whole time.

"I'm late for class," Alicia says, checking her watch. "But I'm glad I found you. I didn't get my good-morning kiss."

"Huh?" I say, but before I can even process what's happening, she puts her hands on my hips and leans into me. This is a dream—it has to be. It's the only explanation. Alarms sound in my head, but it's like I'm frozen to the spot as she sighs softly and goes to push her lips against mine.

"Wait, stop!" I say, pulling away just before she can kiss me. "We can't do this!"

She laughs. "Afraid you'll get another detention? You're such a Goody Two-shoes, Max. There aren't even any teachers around."

She leans in again, but I jerk away.

"Detention? What are you talking about? I—"

"You look different," Alicia says thoughtfully, stepping back to take me in. "New hair or something?"

She reaches out and musses up my fringe as I stand there, speechless. Her features soften, and she looks at me in a way she's never looked at me before.

"What did I do to deserve such a cute and dorky boyfriend? You're a weirdo, Max, but you're my weirdo. Right, I've gotta go," she says, kissing me on the cheek. "I'll see you later?"

I nod, unable to form words as she blows me another kiss and turns on her heel.

Boyfriend? Did she just call me her *boyfriend*? That confirms it: this *must* be a dream. I pinch the back of my hand as hard as I can, then slap myself on each cheek.

"*Come on, Max*," I say out loud, slapping myself harder between each word. "*You. Need. To. Wake. Up.*"

"Well, that's certainly one way to wake yourself up," a familiar voice says mid-slap. "I prefer coffee myself, but to each their own."

I turn to see the boy of my unrelenting adoration standing behind me.

Except it's like his usual glow has been snuffed right out of him. He's not the same perfect boy I've fantasized about for months. He's just ordinary, friendly, plain old Oliver Cheng. His hair is messy and sticking up at all angles. He should probably run a brush through that or something. Like, seriously, dude—you look like a bichon frise that got trapped in a car wash. His cheeks dimple in that way that usually brings the world to a standstill. Normally my heart would be beating out of my chest, but right now I don't feel anything at all.

"You still good to come over Wednesday night?" he says.

"Come over? What? Like a sleepover?" I imagine the matching pajamas.

"We're not ten years old," Oliver says, laughing. "But yeah, you can stay. My parents leave tonight, so you can have their bed as long as you promise not to jizz all over the sheets. Unless you wanna share my bed and cuddle?" He wiggles his eyebrows suggestively.

"Oh no," I say. This is totally overwhelming. "I don't think we should. I—"

"I'm joking! Jeez, Max, what is with you today? You do realize not every gay guy wants to sleep with you, right? You straight boys are so ridiculous."

Straight boys? He did *not* just call me a straight boy. I rub my temples as I try to process everything.

"What day is it?"

"Monday," he says, deadpan.

"But we literally just had Monday."

Oliver laughs. "Yeah, they come around once a week, Max."

"Oh . . . yeah . . . I'm just feeling a little out of it today," I say. "What year is it? No, wait—who's the president of the United States?"

I don't know why that was my go-to question, but isn't it what they always ask in the movies whenever anyone hits their head?

"Donald Trump of course," Oliver says. "A landslide victory too!"

"What?!" Oh God, maybe I am concussed.

"I'm fucking with you," he says, grinning. "Of course it's Biden. Jeez, who are you and what have you done with my best friend?"

"Best friend?" I splutter. "I barely even know you . . ."

"Okay, ouch," he says, holding his heart in mock pain. "That hurts, Max."

"I didn't mean it like that," I say. "I'm just a bit confused. I think I might be dreaming." I slap myself a couple more times.

"Okay, stop doing that," Oliver says, grabbing my hand. "You're starting to freak me out a bit. Do you need to lie down?"

"Maybe. I didn't sleep so well," I say, trying to recall the events of last night.

I remember the argument and storming out of Alicia's house, but then . . . nothing. It's like everything just goes black. The next thing I remember is waking up and everyone acting weird. Maybe I got hit by a car on my way home or fell and hit my head. Maybe this is all in my imagination, and I'm actually lying in the road with Dean and Alicia crouching over my body and the ambulance on its way. *"Don't go into the light, Max!"* they're pleading, but what if it's too late because I'm already DEAD? Or maybe I'm in limbo? Or heaven? Or hell? Like, I know the whole gay thing supposedly upsets the man in the clouds, but I never actually kissed a boy, so that shouldn't even count, right? I *did* watch a bucketload of gay porn, though, and I lied about the vegetable drawer. Should I have maybe confessed that to a priest or something?

"Max?" Oliver says, and I must have zoned out again because now he's staring at me like I've actually lost it. "Do you need to see the nurse or something?"

Ah yes, the school nurse. A cold compress and a Band-Aid are bound to sort this right out. They can't give me a Tylenol without a signed letter from my parents, but yes, I'm sure they'll have no problem straightening out the space-time continuum!

"No," I say. "I'm okay. I think I just need to head home."

"Do you want me to walk you? Or call your mum?"

"I'm fine, honestly," I lie.

"All right," he says, sounding unconvinced. "I'll see you tomorrow, then, okay?"

"Yeah, okay," I say as calmly as I can, but I can't get out of there fast enough.

I practically run out of school. Everyone's staring at me, but with the very fabric of reality crumbling around me the last thing I care about right now is the opinion of some bratty freshmen. I just need to get home and work things out. There has to be a rational explanation for all this.

Chapter Seven

There's no rational explanation for any of this.

My mind is in overdrive as I shut my bedroom door and throw myself down on the bed. Mum was busy on the phone as I came in, which is probably for the best because I'm not sure I could handle her asking questions that I don't know how to answer right now. I take a deep breath and try to reorient myself. I guess I left my room in such a hurry this morning that I didn't notice that this isn't really *my* room at all. It's similar, but ever so slightly *off*.

Most noticeably, all my pin-up heartthrobs are gone. The only familiar poster that remains is a double fold-out feature of Ariana Grande. She's a gay icon, so a poster of Ariana makes total sense for a gay kid's room, right? But looking at her now, I realize *that* isn't why it's hung in this bedroom at all.

Worst of all, there's now a totally tasteless poster of the girls from the terrible remake of *Baywatch* above my bed. I can feel them staring at me. I try to avert my eyes, but I keep being drawn back to their sleek red swimsuits.

Shirtless Zac Efron is there too, but now it's like I barely even notice him. Can you imagine? Looking at Zac Efron and *not* being turned on?!

Oliver called me one of the straight boys, and I can't get those words out of my head. I don't know why this is happening, but it absolutely can't be true. I can't be straight. I refuse. It goes against every single fiber of my campy, fluorescent being. I look back up at Zac and will myself to be attracted to him, just like I once tried to will myself to be attracted to girls, but it's hopeless. So much for "*being gay is a choice.*"

I go over to the wardrobe to see what horrors Straight Max keeps inside.

I don't wanna see any fucking H&M, I hear Mama Ru say in my mind as I pull open the doors, but actually the clothes aren't half bad. Obviously they're not as exciting an array as I have in the real word—no glitter, no mesh, not a crop top in sight—but there are definitely some things we can work with. My favorite piece is a stunning blue varsity jacket with yellow sleeves and a big '06 (the year I was born) embossed with intricate stitching on the back. It's suede and has that vintage smell and feels amazing to the touch. I slip it on and look in the mirror and that's when I notice my hair is cropped slightly shorter than usual. It doesn't look terrible, though, and coupled with the jacket, it actually kinda works. I sort of hate to admit it, but it's true—Straight Max actually has some taste!

And that's when my computer calls to me. Just like it's called to every curious teenager who's ever been left alone with the internet. There's only one surefire way to confirm my new heterosexual credentials. I go over and lock the door.

My hands are clammy, and my heart is racing as I click into my search history. Ordinarily, I'd routinely wipe it clean, but I guess straight guys don't have years of repressed sexuality to shame them into hiding their secrets because—lo and behold!—the entire thing is pristine and intact. I can see every single thing this hetero version of myself has ever searched for.

> Am I addicted to porn?
> Can too much jerking off really make you blind?
> Do penis-enlargement pills actually work?

So I guess straight guys are just as insecure as the rest of us. But this doesn't confirm anything. A gay kid could easily have searched for any of those things. If I'm honest, they seem a little bit *too* familiar, come to think of it . . .

I open a new tab and click into my browsing history, the holy grail of a teenage boy's interests, and a guaranteed way to confirm my sexuality one way or the other. And right there is a list of Pornhub videos with increasingly unimaginative names. It seems I have quite a varied taste, but the one thing they all have in common? They all revolve around *women*.

As I remember it, last night I was out with Dean and Alicia, but according to my search history I was just sitting at home, mindlessly hammering away. I must have been watching from 10:57 to 11:11 because that's when the videos suddenly stop. Fourteen minutes. Congratulations, Max, you may have just broken a record.

I click into the Pornhub home page. The little pop-up asks me if I like guys or girls or both, and I have to stop myself from instinctively pressing the button that'd take me to the world of daddies and twinks and bears (*oh my*). Instead, I click the button that says I like women and am immediately presented with dozens of categories, their compelling thumbnails all begging me to click on them. I can navigate a gay porn site in my sleep, but this is brand-new territory. I hesitate for a moment before something catches my eye.

TWO GIRLS HOT TUB DATE NIGHT

I let my newfound straightness guide me and tentatively click. The page takes far too many frustrating seconds to load, and just as I'm about to click away onto something else, there's suddenly two girls splashing around and moaning, and my speakers are on FULL BLAST.

"Fuck!" I say as the girls on-screen scream something similar. In my panic, I dive for the mute button but accidentally send the speakers crashing to the floor, the wires sweeping everything off my desk along with them. The two girls are now very vocally celebrating each other's efforts, and the sound *still* isn't off.

"Max?" Mum calls as I try frantically to close the video. "Max, is that you?"

Well, it's either me or two very noisy lesbians have broken in to have sex on my bedroom floor. I can't believe I'd be so stupid—everyone knows the first rule of watching porn is to make sure everything is on mute. In all my years of being gay, I never once got caught watching porn, but somehow I've managed it in just a few hours of being straight.

"What are you doing back so early?" Mum demands, rattling the door handle. "And why is this locked?"

Honestly, Mum, don't ask questions you don't want to hear the answers to. Why do you *think* your teenage son's bedroom door is locked?

"I wasn't feeling so good . . ." I say, cracking it open. "I was just a bit overwhelmed and needed to get away from it all."

Not *exactly* a lie.

Her expression is angry at first, but as she looks me up and down it's like she's seeing something for the first time. "Max, you're pale as a ghost."

"I am?"

I glance into the mirror, and I guess I am a little washed-out. I really must have caught a bad case of heterosexualitis. A pandemic that has plagued humanity since the very dawn of time and yet for which, shockingly, there's still no known cure.

"Is that why you overslept?" she says, her blue eyes swimming in worry now. "You should have stayed home if you weren't feeling well."

"I didn't really notice until I got to school. I would have texted to tell you, but I can't find my phone. You haven't seen it, have you?"

She laughs at that. "Nice try, Max. The bug hasn't stolen your sense of humor, then. You can have your phone back at the end of the week, like we agreed."

"You took it?" I wonder what heinous crime Straight Max could have committed to deserve such a cruel and unusual punishment. "Can I just have it for a few minutes, maybe? It's important. Like really important. For . . . school stuff."

"School stuff?" She raises an eyebrow. "Well, as convincing as that explanation is, I'm sure the 'school stuff' can wait until Sunday."

She pauses and reaches out to touch the sleeve of my jacket. "God, you've not worn this in years, Max. It still looks good on you. Do you remember when we bought it?"

"Remind me . . . ?" I say, turning to look at myself in the mirror again.

"It was from that vintage market, for your birthday. Your father nearly had a heart attack when he saw the price."

She laughs and comes to stand behind me, smoothing down the fabric and resting her chin on my shoulder. And that's when she says something I don't think I could have ever been prepared for.

"He'll be home in a couple of hours."

It knocks the air right out of me.

"Dad's coming home?" I say, hoping I haven't misunderstood. "Here?"

"I know." Mum laughs. "Not working late for once! I'll get him to bring some Chinese food, maybe? Your favorite?"

"I'd love that," I say, and I think I genuinely mean it, despite the spinning sensation that's threatening to overwhelm me.

Because, whatever has happened, it's bigger than I could have imagined. It seems it isn't just my sexuality that's changed: the whole world has changed along with it.

But if Dad's coming home, that means in this reality my parents managed to work out their differences and stayed together. My being straight can't have had anything to do with that, though. If anything, I was fortunate enough to have parents who saw my being gay as a good thing. So if not that, then what? What else is different here, what could have possibly caused this? I spent so many years praying that this would happen, but I never actually believed it would.

I'm sure this isn't permanent because how can it be? Maybe it's just a temporary glimpse into a world I always wondered about, and I'll wake up tomorrow, and everything will be back to normal. But what if it's not? And what if I don't?

"All right," Mum says. "Well, rest up, okay?"

She smiles and goes over to the door. "And, Max?" she adds, nodding toward the computer. "No, they don't work, and I'm sure you don't need them anyway."

"Huh?" I say, and then, to my absolute horror, turn to see that the search results for penis-enlargement pills are still open on the screen.

"Hey, champ," a voice calls softly, and I sleepily open my eyes to see Dad standing in my bedroom doorway. He's still got his coat on, a long beige button-down that matches his hazel eyes, the cuffs of his white shirt peeking out. I must have dozed off because it's dark outside now.

"How are you feeling?" he asks, coming to sit at the foot of my bed, the smell of Chinese food wafting up from downstairs.

"A lot better," I say, and I actually mean it. Just having him here in my room fills me with a feeling of warmth and security. This may not be real, this may not truly belong to me, but it certainly makes me feel like I'm home.

"Do you want me to bring some food up? Or are you all right to come down?"

"I'll come down," I say, sitting up and stretching into a yawn.

This whole scenario reminds me of the time I had tonsilitis as a kid and had to stay home for two weeks. Dad would come in to check on me the second he got back from work, still in his coat, all worried eyes and five-o'clock shadow. Sure, I couldn't swallow anything and was in constant pain, but looking back now those feel like two of the best weeks of my life. Mum and Dad were happy then, their arguments few and far between, and something like me being unwell really made them rally together.

"Did you forget the chow mein?!" I hear Mum yell from the kitchen.

"Looks like I'm in trouble," Dad says with a wink. "See you downstairs?"

"Yeah, I'll be down in a few. Thanks for getting the food."

"Anytime, champ," he says, disappearing just as Mum starts shouting about prawn crackers. He yells back as he descends the stairs. Like an old married couple because, well, I suppose that's what they are.

I get up to fix my bed head in the mirror and then lazily follow Dad downstairs. This will be the first family dinner we've had together in years, and it surprises me how normal it feels, how easy it is to slip back into old habits. Mum is taking warmed plates out of the oven; Dad is fussing over the box of food as he unwraps different bags and containers.

Aromatic duck with plum sauce and pancakes, chili fried crispy beef, garlic chicken and sweet-and-sour pork, a huge tray of special fried rice, and a noticeable lack of chow mein and prawn crackers.

Seeing the feast laid out before us reminds me of one of the last times we ate together as a family. The night I came out to them. That evening might have brought us all closer, but it wasn't enough to keep the two of them together. I guess they'd grown apart over the years. I never wanted to admit it, but even I could see how different they were. Opposites attract, I guess, until they don't.

"So do you think you need to see the doctor?" Mum says, lighting a candle in the center of the table as we sit down to eat. I waste no time loading up my plate with a little bit of everything and smothering it all in sweet-and-sour sauce.

"No," I say, maybe a little too quickly. "I don't think so."

I mean, what would a doctor even prescribe? Season six of *Drag Race*? An emergency glitter transfusion? Historically, nobody has ever tried to "cure" heterosexuality. It's only the queers who "need to be fixed."

"Well, let's just keep an eye on it," Dad says, getting plum sauce everywhere as he attempts to roll a pancake. He looks tired, the bags under his eyes weighing him down. He's always been a bit of a silver fox in the making, but tonight he's a little more salt than pepper.

"How are things at the office?" I ask.

"Same old." He shrugs. "Too much work, not enough people. One of these days, I swear I'm just going to quit and start my own business."

"Didn't you already do that?"

He laughs. "No. You don't pay much attention, do you, Max?"

I give myself a mental slap. Not everything in this reality is the same as the old one.

"Well, I think you should," I say. "Just walk in tomorrow and quit! I mean, why not? What's stopping you?"

"The bills? The mortgage? That garlic chicken you're eating?"

"Well, you've got savings—we're not exactly poor . . ."

"And that's because your father has a job," Mum interjects. "Responsibilities."

I frown. Mum's normally the rebellious one. Clearly not this version.

"Well, whatever." I shrug. "I still think you should do it." Dad doesn't say anything to that but does give me a small appreciative smile. "How's that girlfriend of yours, anyway?" he asks, changing the subject.

"You mean Alicia?"

I've not quite come to terms with the fact that the two of us are supposedly now a couple. Hearing it from Dad just feels wrong.

"Unless you have another girlfriend you haven't told us about?" he says jokingly.

"No, just Alicia. My girlfriend. Right," I say. "Things are okay, I guess? We're just busy with the school show, the dance, Queer Club—"

"Queer Club?" Mum says, clearly confused.

"Oh yeah . . . I mean, we just go to help out . . ." I improvise. "Support the queer kids."

"'Support the queer kids'?" Mum puts down her fork. "Come on, Max. I thought we raised you better than that."

Oh God, please tell me my alt-parents aren't homophobes . . .

"You shouldn't use that word," she continues. "It's offensive."

"Oh!" I say, relieved. "You mean *queer*? That's fine—we've reclaimed it. It's empowering now!"

"Who's 'we'?" she asks. "I don't think that's up to you to decide, Max. It's a horrible word. Just say LGQB2."

"El-gee-queue-bee-two . . . ?"

"That's better," she says, and Dad nods in agreement. I guess Straight-World Dad never made it to his diversity-and-inclusion away day . . .

"You should invite Alicia over for dinner sometime," Dad says.

"But no sleepovers," Mum adds promptly. "And no sneaking her in through the window again."

Wow, did I really do that? As iconic as it sounds, it just seems like something from a teen rom-com rather than my actual life.

"And how are your other friends doing?" Mum says. "It feels like ages since we've seen them. Ollie and . . . what's the other one called?"

"Dean," I say. As if anyone would ever forget his name.

"Oh, I can't keep track," she says with a shrug.

It frustrates me that my parents seem so clueless about my social life now. They were always so invested—a little *too* invested, in fact. Mum used to be able to tell me Dean's shoe size, and now she can't even remember his name? It makes me miss him more. I know it's only been a single day, but it feels like so much has happened. I'd do just about anything to talk to him right now. I don't know how I'd even begin to explain any of this, but if there's one person in the world who I know will understand, it's him.

"I was thinking," I say, pushing my plate away, "maybe I could use my phone after dinner? Just for an hour?"

Mum smiles sympathetically. "Max, we agreed it'd be good for us all to have a little digital detox. Cut back on our screen time. It's only been two days and look how much you're struggling! Maybe that's a sign you *do* need a break?"

"A digital detox?" I say. "So this isn't a punishment?"

Mum laughs. "Of course not. Why would we be punishing you?"

"Ah, come on," Dad chips in. "Just let him have it for a little bit?"

"We already talked about this," Mum says, shooting Dad a look.

It's a warning sign, one I know all too well. The last thing I want is to be the cause of a big fight. I know what that's like. To feel like something I said or did sent them off down that path, shouting for hours, long after I've gone to bed.

"It's fine," I say, attempting to nip their argument in the bud. "You're right. I can manage just fine without."

"Of course you can," Mum says. "You've just got to break the habit, that's all. You know, when we were younger, if we wanted to see our friends, we had to call them up on the landline, or go to their houses and knock."

"Primitive times," I say. "I don't know how you got anything done." Dad chuckles. "With great difficulty!"

"Like, what did you do before Google?"

"We read books, Max," Mum says. "Ever heard of an encyclopedia?"

"Ew, gross," I say, and they both laugh.

Crisis averted. It's been a while, but I still know how to play the puppet master.

"Here, Max," Dad says, tossing me a fortune cookie.

I catch it without thinking (sports!), but then, as I stare down at the shiny red packet, I wonder if this could be it. My Lindsay Lohan moment—the moment when everything suddenly makes sense, the moment that explains why my whole world has been knocked out of orbit. The idea's ludicrous, of course, but right now it makes about as much sense as anything else.

I tentatively tear open the packet and crack the cookie, the little message falling facedown on the table. Mum and Dad both look at me expectantly, but I can't bring myself to read it. I'm too afraid of what it might say.

"Well, go on, then," Dad prompts me finally.

"Here, you read it," I say, and slide the paper across to him.

"All right." He picks up the fortune and looks at it. "Oh, this is a good one," he says. "'*The solution to all your problems*'"—he pauses, holding eye contact, the rising anticipation slowly killing me—"'*is to order more Chinese food.*'"

Six Years Ago

"Get off, Max—you're too heavy!"

Dean laughs as he tries to pedal us up the hill. The warmth of the sun beats down on us while the summer breeze blows gently between the leaves of the overhanging trees. We don't know it yet, but it's the kind of evening that will one day inspire nostalgia. An evening meant for *change*.

We both hop off the bike, and Dean starts wheeling it up the hill. The view from here is the best in town. You can see Dean's house on Brimsby Road on one side, and all the way down to Woodside Academy on the other. We'll both be starting there next month. Dean was offered a scholarship to go to the private school over at Grove Hill, but he turned it down because he "doesn't want to be surrounded by rich kids." And I get that. I wouldn't want to go there either.

"Your mum got to this one too," I say, pointing at the poster stuck to the streetlight. BATTLE FOR BRIMSBY is written in bold lettering with a couple of paragraphs of information beneath it.

"'*Gen-tri-fi-cation*,'" I say, reading one of the words aloud. "She likes that word. She's used it about fifty-eight times."

"It means ruining something by making it nice," Dean says. "Yeah, I don't really get it either," he adds in response to my baffled expression.

"Have you *seen* the pictures of the new apartments the developers wanna build? They low-key look sick. I wouldn't mind living in one of those."

"You're such a goober," I say. "As if your mum could afford it."

"Hey!" He laughs, taking a swipe at me. "Just wait until I'm a superstar—you'll be begging to come live in my mansion."

"Nuh-uh," I say. "You'll be begging to live in *mine*."

"Whatever," Dean says with a twirl and drops onto a bench that overlooks the town. "I'm the fabulous one here."

"I guess," I say, sitting down next to him.

The sun is starting to disappear behind the rows of old townhouses now. If you look closely enough, though, you can still just about make out which one is Dean's. Small and unremarkable, but still special in its own way. Special because it's his.

"It is pretty, though. Maybe your mum's right, and they shouldn't spoil it."

He sighs. "I just don't wanna have to move away. I'd hate that."

"Because you'd miss me?" I say with a grin.

"Well, who else am I gonna share all my secrets with?"

"Yeah," I say, and then pause because I've been keeping a secret this whole time. I've wanted to tell him; it just never seemed like the right moment.

"Would you be mad at me for hiding something from you?" I ask.

"Furious," he says jokingly, pulling his legs up onto the bench and turning his whole body around to face me.

"Well, go on, then. Tell me. Did you finally have your first wet dream?"

"Ew!" I laugh. "It's nothing like that. It's about . . . *someone*."

"*Someone*?" He raises an eyebrow.

"Someone I like," I say. "Like, *like* like."

"A crush, you mean?"

"Kinda."

"Someone I know?"

"Someone in our class . . ."

"Poppy?" he asks. "It's Poppy, isn't it? No, it's Rachel!"

I shake my head.

"Hmm," he says, tapping his fingers on his chin as he thinks. "Well, if it's not Poppy and it's not Rachel . . . Oh my God, it must be me!"

I laugh at that, which cuts the tension a little, and then I finally spit it out.

"It's Simon."

I look down at my feet, bracing for the inevitable impact.

"Oh," says Dean. It takes him no more than a second to process it. "Well, he's cute!" he continues enthusiastically. "He's not my type, but I totally see it!"

"Yeah?" I say, looking up at him hopefully.

"Total hottie!" he agrees, and I smile.

"So it's not a big deal?"

"Of course not," he says, and then he pauses for a moment as he unties the rainbow bracelet from his wrist. "Here. I made this for you anyway. Hang on to it until you're ready to wear it. Welcome to the club, Max."

Chapter Eight

A big part of me expects to wake up back in my old reality, so I'm surprised when I'm actually woken by the sound of Dad making breakfast. He's clattering around the way he always does whenever he makes his famous blueberry pancakes, a specialty reserved for sick days and special occasions.

"Morning, Max!" He beams at me as I appear in the kitchen and slides a plate across. Mum seems to have already gone out, so it's just me, Dad, and a big bottle of imported Canadian maple syrup. "Feeling any better today?"

"I guess?" I say, wasting no time in emptying half the bottle. A fifty-fifty syrup-to-pancake ratio is a must. "I think I'll head into school today actually."

"Oh yeah?" he says. "You bounced back quick. You had us worried for a minute." He sits down at the table opposite me. "If you're feeling up to it, I thought maybe we could do something this weekend? Just the two of us?"

"Like what?" I say. In the real world, Dad has learned not to try to force me into typical hetero activities, but here? Oh God, is he gonna take me to the soccer game?

"We could go for a drive, do a little shopping, maybe?" he says. Both acceptable choices. "Grab lunch? Whatever you wanna do, Max."

"Yeah, sure," I say, though honestly I fully intend to be back in my own world by the weekend. I just haven't figured out how yet. "Maybe we could go see a movie? Raid the pick 'n' mix stand?"

"Sounds good," Dad says. "Just nothing with guns and explosions, right?"

"Right," I say. "How'd you guess?"

I'm impressed he still seems to know me. Not the heterosexual version of me, but the *real* me. Maybe Straight Max and Gay Max aren't that different at all.

He laughs. "I know my own son, Max," he says. "Right, I've got to get to work, but I'll see you later, okay?" He grabs one of the pancakes and takes a bite. "Not my best," he says with a frown. "Can't be perfect every time, I suppose."

"They're great, Dad, but here," I say, offering him the syrup. "Drown them in this, and you won't be able to tell the difference."

"Thanks, Max." He squeezes a little onto the pancake, careful not to get it all over his hands. "Right, see you later."

"Yeah, see you, Dad," I say. "And remember to quit your job, okay?"

He chuckles as he goes, leaving me alone with the pancakes. It feels strangely natural to have him here. In the space of a single day, we've slipped right back into old habits, and it makes me wonder if this world actually has the potential to be better. Maybe this change is a blessing and not a curse. I might be straight here—that's definitely the big catastrophic downside—but I'm still me, still the same person. At least that doesn't seem to have changed.

What I can't figure out, though, is whether this new reality is my old world that's been altered somehow, or a parallel world that's always been here, running alongside it. Is it possible that there's always been a

Straight Expectations

Straight Max in this parallel world? And is it possible that we've in fact switched places, and right now he's in Gay World just as confused as me, and trying to work out why his bathroom is full of nail polish and Oliver Cheng is suddenly supernova hot? I don't know what the answer is, but I'm going to have to be careful what I do here. If Straight Max *does* exist, I can't mess up his reality—and I just have to hope he's not out there somewhere messing up mine . . .

With Mum and Dad both out of the house, it gives me some time to really think and begin to come up with a plan for dealing with this *situation*. To everyone at school yesterday, it must have seemed like I was acting really *off*, so today I need to act *normal*, play the role of the straight boy, at least until I can figure out how to fix this. But I'm going to need help. And, if there's one person I can convince that I've slipped into some sort of Lindsay Lohan–type situation, that person is Dean. All I need to do is find him, get him alone, and explain everything from start to finish. He'll know what to do—he always does.

I head to the seniors' common room first, wearing my straight-boy kicks, skinny jeans, and my surprisingly stylish varsity jacket. I'm hoping Dean might be there—it's usually where we meet before first period—but the place is empty except for Oliver and Thomas in the kitchen. Thomas is boiling the kettle while Oliver bounces a soccer ball that is definitely going to smash something. Apparently they're friends in this world too. Joy.

"Max!" Thomas beams as he spots me. And then Oliver yells, "*THINK FAST!*" and kicks the ball at my head. I half expect Straight Max's instinctive hetero sports powers to take over, but instead I'm paralyzed by gay fear. I don't "think fast" at all, and the ball hits me squarely in the face, knocking me flat on my back.

"Ow!" I say as Oliver rushes over to help me up. Please tell me that Straight Max isn't known as an all-star soccer player because, if that's the case, I may as well quit this charade now. The jig is up. Max is gay and can't catch a ball to save his life.

"I'm so sorry," Oliver says, laughing and offering his hand. "Are you okay? It's really amazing how you're *so* bad at sports. It's like you're broken or something."

Phew. That's good to know. I guess I can't blame my lack of sporting ability on my desire to kiss boys after all. It's almost as if those two things have absolutely nothing to do with each other. Who'd have thought?

"We missed you yesterday," Thomas says. "You feeling any better?"

"Yeah," I say. "I was just a bit out of it, is all."

"Well, whatever you had, don't give it to me, please."

Oliver grins at me, but I don't think he needs to worry about that. It's not like heterosexuality is catching. "We tried texting you, but I guess your mum still has your phone on lockdown?"

"Yeah, what's that about?" Thomas says. "It's not like you even did anything wrong, right? Like, who takes a teenager's phone for no good reason?"

"Something about him spending too much time staring at screens." Oliver elbows me playfully. "Been watching a bit too much porn, Maxxie?"

"Oh my God," I say.

The entire world has been flipped, and yet I still manage to have a reputation for being a pornoholic. Of all the personality traits I could have carried over to Straight World, that's the one that sticks.

"Coffee?" Thomas says to me, grabbing another cup.

"Sure."

Hot instant coffee. Gay Max would never, but right now I need to blend in. I look over to the door, hoping Dean will burst through with iced vanilla lattes for both of us.

"So anyway," Oliver continues, "how long have you been questioning your sexuality, Max?"

"What?" I squeak, my voice jumping about three octaves. "What do you . . . I mean . . . huh?"

Oliver is laughing again now. "Your Spotify playlists are public," he says, taking out his phone and opening up my profile. "A lot of musical theater. Troye Sivan. Lady Gaga. Kylie Minogue . . ." He carries on scrolling through the gayest playlist you've ever seen. "And 'It's Raining Men' is your most listened to song of all time? Something you're not telling us, Maxxie?"

"It's a good song!" I blurt out, because it is. That's an objective fact and any straight man who disagrees with you is lying. "Thomas, back me up on this," I say. Sometimes you have to find allies in the most unlikely places.

"You're on your own with that one!" he says. Fucking typical.

"Ah, I'm just teasing, Maxxie," Oliver says. "We've all seen the way you look at Alicia. There's no faking that. There's a lot of things I doubt about this world, but your heterosexual credentials aren't one of them."

Can you imagine? Me? Having heterosexual credentials? I imagine how Dean would react if he heard that. He'd probably choke to death with laughter.

"Speaking of which," Thomas says, turning to Oliver, "please tell me you've invited some girls tomorrow? I don't want it to be a massive sausage fest like last time."

"It wasn't a massive sausage fest!" Oliver protests.

"I've literally seen more girls in the guys' changing room," Thomas says. "I reckon I can swipe a few bottles when my parents aren't looking, but *only* if you promise that there's gonna be girls there . . ."

Oliver laughs. "I promise, but I wanna keep it chill, okay?" He grimaces as he sips on his terrible cup of coffee. "It can't turn into a massive party."

"Yeah, like, no more than fifty people?" Thomas grins.

"I was thinking more like fifteen," Oliver replies. "Do you think you can bring a few drinks too, Max? I don't want you to get grounded like last time, though . . ."

"Drinks? Uh, maybe?"

"My hero!" He beams at me.

I've played out so many fantasies where Oliver would say those words to me, but right now it's like they mean nothing.

"All right, I've gotta get to drama," Thomas says, checking the time.

"Ready for English?" Oliver says, turning to me.

"Yeah. Sure."

I don't usually take English, but I guess I chose different subjects in this world. Maybe Straight Max has a clearer sense of what he wants to do with the rest of his life. Maybe I can actually learn from him.

I wish I could follow Thomas to drama, though. Dean will definitely be there, but I guess waiting another hour or two to see him won't hurt, so I go with Oliver to Mr. Grayson's English class instead. He's one of those old professorial types, overdressed for a Woodside classroom in his Atticus Finch glasses and half a corduroy suit. He was my English teacher for every year before senior year, but something about the slow way he speaks never managed to capture my imagination. We're studying *The Handmaid's Tale* apparently, and I'm just grateful that Dean and I watched the TV series so I can at least pretend to know what the book's about.

"I finished it last night," Oliver says, slumping down into his chair as we pair up at the back of the room. Mr. Grayson has instructed us to make a list of the themes we think the author is trying to explore. "I know we're not supposed to read ahead, but I can't help myself. Everyone else is so slow . . ."

"Always a rebel," I joke. "I hardly think you're gonna get detention for doing too much reading, Oliver . . ."

"Oliver?" he says. "Nobody's called me that in years."

"They haven't?" I hesitate. "So . . . Ollie, then?"

"Nah. I quite like it when you say it." He smiles dorkily. I smile too. "So how far have you gotten?" he adds, tapping the book.

"Not very," I say, flicking through the pages. I hope the TV adaptation didn't deviate too much from the book. "I kinda struggled with it, to be honest. Like, what's the message?"

Oliver frowns. "Isn't it obvious? The events of this book are portrayed as fiction, right? But they're not. At all. It's written as this dystopia, but actually there's nothing in the story that isn't happening somewhere in the world right now." He speaks in the same passionate tone he'd used when we were talking about books while making paper lanterns. "It's scary, really. I mean, this was published back in the 1980s, but it's describing things that are happening today."

"And I guess it's good representation for LGBT+ people?" I say, trying to recall the events of the TV show and not sound like an idiot who quite clearly hasn't read the book. "Like the inclusion of queer characters?"

"Well, it's hardly great representation to see us being murdered, Max . . . But I know what you're getting at. You mean the way Gilead puts so much emphasis on people's ability to have kids? As if that's the only thing that makes you valuable as a human being? And the way the Aunts talk about anyone who goes against the cis-hetero norm being 'gender traitors'? It's bringing queer issues to the forefront."

"Uh . . . yeah," I say. "That's exactly what I meant."

Oliver smiles at that. It's obvious I'm not keeping up with him, but he isn't judging. If anything, I think he's enjoying playing the role of teacher.

"On the surface, the book is about women's rights, yeah?" he continues. "But it's super intersectional. It's like society falls apart, and it's the rights of the minorities that are the first things to go. All women are oppressed, but it's queer women, disabled women, and women of color who feel that oppression the most. It's a pretty accurate view of what a dystopia would actually look like, don't you think? If we were facing an end-of-the-world-type scenario tomorrow, I reckon we'd see a lot of the things that happen in this book play out for real. The author knew that then, and I think it's still true now."

"But what would cause such a dramatic shift?" I ask. He's actually caught my interest now. "Like, things have been getting better for decades, haven't they? What would turn that progress back in the opposite direction?"

"I don't know," Oliver says. "Could be a nuclear event, like in the book? But I think our biggest worry is climate change. Do you think people would still care about queer rights if we reached the point of fighting over resources? I'm a mixed-race gay boy. I think they'd string me up for a mouthful of bread and a splash of water."

"I don't know if I believe that," I say. "I mean, you make people sound so primitive. Humans are inherently good, aren't they?"

"Are they?" he says. "The civilized world is so fragile, Max. You have the privilege of going through life as a straight white guy. Not all of us are so lucky."

I know why he thinks that, but just hearing him refer to me that way makes me itch.

"I guess," I say. "You've really thought about this, though, haven't you?"

He laughs. "That's literally the assignment, Max, but yeah, of course I have. You have to think about these things when you're queer."

"Do you?" I say, because that doesn't ring true to me at all. Oliver reminds me of Dean actually—the way he's always talking about "the fight," but I guess I don't feel it. Maybe that's what Dean meant when he said I have white gay privilege. But what is there left to fight for? Sure, we have to put up with bigots like Mr. Johnson, but beyond that? Is there really still a *fight*?

Oliver is quiet for a moment, chewing his lip as he weighs me up. "Finish it," he finally says, tapping the book. "Try to put yourself in the shoes of these women. Try to understand that, if we're not careful, this could be our future. Then maybe you'll get it."

"Okay," I say, looking down at the pages.

I'm not totally convinced, but I want him to know that I understand allyship. This isn't my world, but it still *feels* real. And I still care what he thinks about me.

"So, what should we write?"

"Everything you just said," I say. "All of it. That's bound to get us an A."

Alicia practically jumps on me when we get back to the common room, swinging her arms around my neck and pulling me in to kiss my cheek.

"This whole no-phone thing is driving me crazy," she says. "How did people ever manage without them?" She slides her hand down to meet mine. "Ollie said you weren't feeling great yesterday?"

"I was just spaced out," I say. "I'm better now, though."

"Good," she says, leaning in to kiss me again.

"Sorry—morning breath," I say, dodging her advances. It's not that I don't *want* to kiss her—she looks amazing, and my feelings from yesterday haven't diminished, if the tightness in my underwear is any-thing to go by—but it doesn't feel right. It feels like taking advantage.

Alicia laughs. "It's midday! Please tell me you didn't forget to brush again this morning."

"That's gross, Max," Oliver teases. "Honestly, you two need to get a room anyway," he says, sliding his body between us and pushing us apart. "If I have to watch you make out one more time . . ."

"Don't be jealous, Ollie," Alicia says with a smirk, going to mess up his hair. "Just because I bagged the hottest guy in school and you didn't."

"Ha!" Oliver says. "Hate to break it to you, but Max isn't exactly my type."

"Okay, ouch," I say.

I may no longer have feelings for him, but that one still hurt. I guess at least it finally clears something up, though—I didn't blow my chances with him in the real world because he was never into me in the first place.

"So what *is* your type, then?" Alicia asks. "Someone big and burly? Someone to throw you around? A bear, maybe? A big masc daddy?"

"Oh my God, stop," Oliver says. "Hearing you try to use gay slang is so cringe. Besides, I'm not interested in what a guy looks like. As long as they've got a big one." I almost choke as he says that. "A brain, I mean, obviously," he adds mischievously. "A massive, juicy, big, beautiful brain."

"I'm sure that's *exactly* what you meant," she says, raising an eye-brow. "That's what they all say anyway: 'I don't care about looks—it's all about the personality.' But everyone has a type, Ollie. That's just the basic law of attraction."

"I don't know what to tell you." Oliver shrugs. "We don't all want to settle for the first above-average guy that shows an interest."

"You both realize I'm standing right here, yeah?"

"Sorry," Alicia says with a smirk, taking my hand.

"So, *Fortnite* tonight?" Oliver says. "I call Goku."

"Sounds good," I say instinctively. "As long as I can be Spider-Man."

A world where Oliver Cheng and I casually play *Fortnite* together? I think I could actually get used to this . . .

"Aren't you forgetting something?" Alicia says, looking cross.

"Oh, um—um . . ." I stammer, trying to read her for clues.

"We already have plans tonight," she says, looking even more annoyed. "You're not telling me you forgot again?"

"Sorry, that's my bad!" Oliver jumps in to save me. "We can play another time. Max has already told me about your big date."

"Yeah?" she says, smiling at me now. "Why, what are you planning?"

"Oh well . . . That would ruin the surprise, wouldn't it?"

"Just no strawberries this time," Alicia says, and she and Oliver laugh like it's the most hilarious thing anyone's ever said. "If I never see another strawberry as long as I live . . ."

"Honestly, ever since you told me that story, I haven't been able to look at soft fruit in the same way," says Oliver, giggling. "Especially not cherries."

"Don't get me started on the cherries!" Alicia howls. "Cherries, Max?! What on earth were you thinking?"

"Ha ha, well, you know me!" I say. "Strawberries . . . cherries . . . blackberries . . . you should see what I can do with a pineapple!"

"*A pineapple?*" she says, horrified. "Okay, I don't wanna know, Max . . ."

"Yeah, there's a line, and you've definitely just crossed it," Oliver adds.

Oh God, what did I just admit to?

"You'd think that would have totally put me off my lunch," Alicia says, "but somehow I'm still hungry. Are you guys ready?"

"Sure," I say. "Shouldn't we wait for Dean, though?" I do a quick scan of the common room. Some of the drama kids are already here.

"Huh?" Alicia says. "Dean? Who's that?"

"Dean," I reply. "Dean Jackson." But she just stares at me blankly. I look to Oliver to back me up, but he simply shrugs.

"I don't know who that is," she says. "Is he on the soccer team?"

I try not to laugh. "Of course he's not on the soccer team. Dean Jackson! The gayest kid in school!"

"I'm pretty sure that's me," Oliver says, grinning, and all I can think is, *Oh please*. All-star, straight-acting Oliver Cheng thinks he's the gayest kid in school? I'm still gayer than he is, and I have a girlfriend now. I understand things are different here, but how can they not know who Dean is when he makes a grand entrance every time he comes into the room?

"You seriously don't know who I'm talking about? This isn't just some elaborate windup?"

"I really don't know who that is, Max," Oliver says. "You're being weird again. Are you sure everything's okay?"

"No," I say. "It's really not. You mean to tell me that neither of you know who Dean is? My best friend since I was, like, eight? That Dean?"

"Sorry, Max," Alicia says. She looks genuinely concerned now.

"I . . . I need to go."

"Go where?" Oliver says, reaching out to put a hand on my shoulder, but I move out of the way. Alicia tries to grab my hand, but I pull away from her too.

"To find Dean," I say, backing away from both of them.

I don't care what they say, Dean has to be here somewhere—and you better believe I'm gonna find him.

Chapter Nine

The drama department is near empty when I burst through the doors, colliding with one of the mannequins usually used to model the outfits for the show. Mrs. A is sitting at her desk, peering at a dog-eared script as she eats a sandwich. She watches me wrestling with the dummy for a moment and then sighs, lowering her script and peering at me over her half-moon glasses.

"Can I help you?"

"Dean Jackson!" I blurt as the mannequin falls to the floor with a clatter, leaving one of its arms in my hand. "I'm looking for Dean Jackson!"

She sighs. "Who?" Her usual upbeat flair seems beaten out of her. She seems tired and frustrated, as if she can't bear to deal with another student right now. Usually I'd know to come back later, but this is an *emergency*.

"Dean Jackson—you must know him!" I gesticulate with the lifeless limb for added emphasis. "He's the star of Woodside Academy!"

She snorts. "Is that so? And who might you be?"

"Max," I say. "Max Baker."

"All right, Max." She nods to the chair in front of her desk. "Take a seat."

"Thanks," I say, a little calmer now. I sit down opposite and place the arm on the desk in front of her.

It's not so surprising Mrs. A doesn't know me here, but it does make me a little sad. I was never *really* one of the drama kids, but I always felt like I was an honorary part of this family.

"Well, Max," she says, "I know all my students, and I don't have a Dean Jackson in my class. Are you sure he's a drama student?"

"I'm sure," I say.

If there's one thing I'm certain of, it's that there's no world in which Dean isn't a theater star.

"I'm sorry." Mrs. A shrugs. "I don't know what to tell you."

I look around the room, feeling my desperation start to trickle back. It all looks pretty unchanged: the same peeling green wallpaper, the same uncomfortable plastic chairs, the same graffitied tables decorated with declarations of love and cartoon dicks. But then my eyes drift over to the cabinet where the pictures of the school productions are on display.

"The photos!" I exclaim. I know if I'm going to find Dean anywhere, it's there.

"You're the first person to get excited about those in years!" Mrs. A laughs as I go over to examine the display. "Most kids don't even stop to look at them."

The show photos have always been a testament to the drama department's past glories; "proof of what can be achieved with a little budget and a lot of talent" is how Mrs. A would always put it. I scan the collection for Dean. He usually stands out, pulling focus in his over-the-top costumes, but this is just a dreary display of unappealing performances. And Dean isn't in any of them.

It seems in place of last year's production of *Legally Blonde* they put on *West Side Story*. And the year before that, to my absolute horror, I see they did *Grease*. If there was ever a musical made for straight people, it's that. Summer Lovin' 2022 is written across the bottom of the photo in Comic Sans.

Dear God, Mrs. A, what have the heteros done to you?

Part of me is glad Dean isn't here to see this. No wonder he isn't in any of the photos: he wouldn't be caught dead in a production of *Grease*. The boy is talented, but he at least needs *something* to work with. Alicia's set designs are gone too, replaced with some lackluster painted backdrops that have been given zero love and attention.

"Is everything okay, Max?" Mrs. A says. "Do you need to sit down? I feel like there's something you're not telling me."

"Why on earth did you do *Grease*?" I say, slumping back down into the chair. "*Grease*? With the awful biker jackets? Whose idea was that?"

Mrs. A laughs. "Well, it wouldn't have been my first choice, but I run my class like a democracy. I let the students decide."

"But what about *Legally Blonde*?" I say. "Or *Little Shop of Horrors*?"

"A little too kitsch for my liking," she replies. "I'm more of a *Hadestown* gal myself. I prefer something a bit dark and gritty."

"I had no idea," I say.

I remember how enthusiastic she'd been when Dean suggested *Little Shop*. She'd reacted like it was one of her all-time favorites.

"Well, Max." Mrs. A gives me the same reassuring smile she's given a thousand times before. She doesn't even know who I am, and yet she still seems to have time for me. "I'd love nothing more than to sit and talk musical theater, but back to this Dean kid you're looking for?"

And suddenly I want to tell her everything. She has that effect on you, a way of making you feel as if everything will be okay. But how do I even begin?

"I don't know how to explain this," I say, "but I woke up yesterday morning, and everything was different. I know it sounds ridiculous, but it's like I'm suddenly living somebody else's life."

Mrs. A leans back in her chair and considers me for a moment, as if reading me like an old script.

"That doesn't sound ridiculous at all."

"It doesn't?" This is a little *too* understanding, even for Mrs. A.

"Of course not," she says. "Senior year is tough. Everything's changing. Old things are ending; new things are beginning. It's enough to make anyone feel unsettled."

"Well, yeah," I say. "But that's not what I meant. I mean I feel like I've slipped into a parallel universe. Like this world isn't the one I belong to."

Mrs. A chuckles. "I think we all feel that way sometimes, Max," she says. "I couldn't tell you the number of times I've wished for someone to get me off this planet."

"But what if that wish came true, and suddenly the world you knew was gone, and everything was all backward and messed up and . . . different. Then what?"

"Well . . ." Mrs. A says, thinking on that, "I suppose I'd find a way to put things right. But this isn't about me, is it? This is about your friend." She pauses as if something has just clicked into place. "Did the two of you have a falling-out? You'd be amazed by the chaos that can be caused by a rift between friends."

And that's when the answer finally hits me. It's been staring me in the face the whole time. I look down at my bare wrist, where Dean's friendship bracelet used to be, and think back to the argument and all the horrible things I said.

"I wish we were never even friends."

I did this. Somehow I wished all this into existence. *That* was my fortune-cookie moment.

For a second, all I can do is sit in stunned silence, taking it all in.

"So what do I do?" I finally say.

"Find your friend." Mrs. A smiles. "I'm sure, if you patch things up there, then everything will start to feel right again."

"You really think so?" I say hopefully. "I've no idea where to start, though. I've asked around, and nobody knows where he is . . ."

"Well, have you tried his house?" she says. "He's probably just out sick or licking his wounds or something. It's not rocket science, Max."

"Of course!" I say. "Oh, Mrs. A, I could kiss you!"

She laughs. "Please don't! I'm happy to talk anytime, Max. Even during my lunch break," she adds with a twinkle.

"Thanks, Mrs. A. You're a real one."

I think back to the day Dean gave me the friendship bracelet as I climb the hill that overlooks Brimsby Road. It may have been years ago, but that moment is crystal clear in my memory. Dean had been so understanding then, and, although I hope things will be as simple now, I still have no idea how I'm going to put all this into words. How am I supposed to get him to believe something that I barely even believe myself?

Hi, you don't know me, but we're gay best friends in another universe. Do you mind if I come in?

I'm so caught up in my thoughts that I don't notice the noise to begin with, but, as I climb farther up the hill, it becomes impossible to ignore. It's something mechanical. Something loud. The sound becomes more and more unsettling until it forces me to break into a run. I sprint all the way to the top of the hill until the street where Dean lives comes into view.

Except he doesn't live there. In fact, nobody does because Brimsby Road and the whole neighborhood around it is nothing more than rubble. A huge fence now surrounds the perimeter, and the metal jaws of noisy construction vehicles are busy tearing everything apart. Destroying the place I thought of as my second home and all hope of finding my friend along with it.

I look at the lamppost where the BATTLE FOR BRIMSBY poster had once hung. In its place, there's now a bright pink developer's notice proudly boasting about the new apartments that are *"coming soon."*

Dean's mum was a fighter like no other, but in this world, it seems that this fight was lost—or, worse, that it never even happened at all.

No, I think. Dean wouldn't have let them take Brimsby without a fight, and I'm not going to let them either. Without even thinking, I start running down the hill, the machinery grinding louder and louder as I approach the perimeter fence.

"Stop!" I hear myself calling, my voice breaking as my fingers catch in the chain-link. "Stop!" I yell again, but nobody hears me. "Please stop . . ."

A couple of the construction workers look over in my direction, laughing among themselves, because obviously my misery is *hilarious.* One of them isn't laughing, though. He's the smallest of the bunch and looks concerned.

"You all right, mate?" he says as he starts to walk over toward me. He takes off his hard hat and goggles, and instantly I recognize him.

"Chris?!" I say. "What . . . ? What are you doing here?"

"Sorry, do I know you?" he replies, scratching at his stubble. But then he looks down at the name badge on his hi-vis jacket and laughs. "Oh right."

"It's me—it's Max," I say. Helplessly, because I already know he doesn't have a clue who I am in this world. But I'm too upset to be logical right now.

"Sorry, mate, I think you're confusing me with someone else."

He looks back at the others, shrugging as if he thinks I'm a lunatic, and they all laugh again, like I'm not standing right here.

"How did all this get approved?" I say, looking around. One of the Brimsby Road street signs lies bent and crumpled in a pile of torn-up asphalt. "Didn't anyone try to stop it? What about the Battle for Brimsby?"

"The battle for what?" he says, looking even more confused now. "Listen, mate, I don't know about any of all that. I just work here, you know?"

"But this is where Dean lives! Dean!" I scream.

I *know* he doesn't know who Dean is, and I *know* that none of this is his fault, but it still makes me angry, even if that's irrational, because how fucking dare he?

"Look," Chris says, surprisingly gently, "I don't know what's going on here, but you seem pretty torn up about something, so maybe you should head home."

"Whatever," I say, pushing myself off the fence. "I never liked you anyway."

"Never liked you either, mate," he says, laughing, as if it's nothing. If Mum heard him say that, she'd have dropped him in a heartbeat. "Get home safe, though, okay?"

"Don't tell me what to do!" I yell back, turning and walking away.

It's obvious Chris isn't going to be able to help me, and I'm not sure I want his help anyway. The only person I want right now is Dean. But, if he doesn't live here, then where is he? Nobody at Woodside seems to remember him—not Oliver, not Alicia, not even Mrs. A.

I hate to admit it, because there's nothing more frightening, but I'm starting to think that maybe in this world there isn't a Dean Jackson at all.

Chapter Ten

Right now my bedroom is the only place I feel safe. I've spent the past few hours using my computer to search for Dean, but it's no good. He wasn't on social media in the real world, but I was hoping he might be in this one. There are a thousand Dean Jacksons on Snapchat. Another thousand on Insta. None of them are him. It's like looking for a needle in a haystack.

I've gotten so desperate I'm even thinking about telling Mum and Dad what's happened, but what are the chances of them actually believing me? I'm not sure even *I* would believe me right now. In fact, I'm pretty sure that I wouldn't. But what other choice do I have?

But, as I open my bedroom door and head for the stairs, up from the kitchen comes an all-too-familiar sound.

"Please, can you give it a rest for just five minutes. I'm exhausted!" Dad barks. "You don't work—you don't get how tiring it is."

"I don't work?" Mum snaps back. "So what do you think I do in this house all day? Sit around with my feet up? Who cooks dinner? Washes your clothes? Who do you think keeps this place from falling apart?"

"I didn't mean it like that," Dad says. "I just . . . can't cope." They must hear me on the stairs because their argument suddenly stops.

"Max?" Mum calls. "Is that you?"

"Yeah, it's me," I say reluctantly. I want to head straight back up the stairs and lock myself in my bedroom, but if I want their help, I'm going to have to face them eventually. So I walk through into the kitchen.

They're standing on opposite sides of the room, the breakfast bar dividing them. Mum looks pale, as if the life force has been sucked right out of her. Dad doesn't seem much better.

"What's going on?" I say, glancing back and forth between them.

"Nothing," Mum says. "We were just having a little discussion. That's all."

She tries to mask her mood with an unconvincing smile, and my heart sinks. This is exactly how I remember it, exactly how it'd been before they got divorced. But if they're having the exact same arguments, then why are they still together in this world? It just doesn't make any sense. Mum and I have always had such an honest relationship, and it hurts that she's now point-blank lying to my face. It makes it feel like she's not my mum at all, just a stranger who looks like her.

"Well, you were clearly fighting," I say, leaning against the door-frame. "So let's talk it out, okay? Instead of bottling it up and doing whatever *this* is."

Dad sighs. "You're right, Max. We're both dealing with a lot of stress at the minute. It's fine, though. There's really nothing for you to worry about."

"If you say so," I reply, trying my hardest not to roll my eyes. As much as I'd *love* to play marriage counselor right now, that's not why I'm here. "In that case, there's something I want to talk to you about. You might not understand, but I just need you to hear me out, okay?"

"Is it about your grades?" Mum says. "Because we've talked about this, and we can always get you a tutor . . ."

"My grades? No, it's not that. It's—"

"You got suspended again, didn't you?" Dad says wearily.

"Again? What do you mean *again*? No, it's—"

"Alicia?" Mum says. "Well, we've been meaning to have *the talk* with you anyway. Haven't we, Henry?"

"Oh yeah," Dad says. He couldn't be any less enthusiastic. "*The talk.*"

"The talk?" I say. "Please tell me you don't mean the sex-education talk because we should have probably done that four years ago . . ."

"Well, we think you might need to hear it again," Mum says, raising an eyebrow. "What with you sneaking off to Alicia's house and everything."

"*Sneaking off to Alicia's house?*" I splutter. "We're not having sex, if that's what you mean. Alicia's not that type of girl."

"Well, just in case you do," Mum says. "We don't know what you know, and we just want to make sure you're prepared . . ."

"Condoms. Babies. Morning-after pill," I say. "Anything I'm missing?"

"Periods?" Dad says, and Mum looks at him like he's insane.

"We don't need to talk about periods, Henry."

"What about consent, then?"

"Yes!" she says. "We *definitely* need to talk about consent."

"I understand consent!" I growl. "And periods for that matter! And, by the sounds of it, I should be the one educating you two! Sex is more than just penises and vaginas. You know that, right? LGBT people need sex ed too!"

"What is it with you and LGBT at the minute?" Mum says.

"Oh, I don't know. Because maybe we shouldn't always just assume heterosexuality as the default? Jesus Christ, can we really not do this right now? I'm trying to tell you something!"

"See, I told you this was a bad idea," Dad says.

"Oh well, thanks for the support!" Mum snaps back. "So much for us working together as a team!"

"Stop it!" I say. "Can you just stop fighting?"

"He's right," Dad says. "Stop trying to cause an argument."

"Cause an argument?" Mum throws her hands up. "You're the one who started it!"

"Here we go . . ." Dad rolls his eyes. "Everything's my fault. What a surprise!"

"You know what? Forget it," I say, turning back out of the room.

"No, come on, Max. Tell us what's the matter," Mum calls after me.

"Nothing!" I shout back, heading for the front door now. "Everything's just peachy."

"Where are you going, Max?" Dad shouts, but I ignore him. "Max?"

"Call me if you need me!" I say. "Oh wait, you can't because you won't let me have my phone!" I slam the door behind me. That last part felt good.

"I told you we shouldn't have taken it!" I hear Dad yell as I storm off down the drive. "How's he supposed to reach us in an emergency?"

"I offered him the Nokia 3310!" Mum yells back. "But he said he wasn't interested in some dusty old relic!"

I hear the front door open and them both calling after me, but it's too late because I'm already halfway down the street.

If they won't help me, maybe somebody else can.

Dean's house would usually be my first port of call in a crisis, but with that no longer an option, I head for Alicia's instead. I still don't know how to deal with the new feelings I have around her, but right now she feels like the only thing I have left that still resembles normality. She's still my best friend, even if things are a little *complicated*.

Darius opens the door, sweaty from a workout, and eyes me suspiciously.

"Maxwell?" He sounds surprised. "Well, better late than never, I suppose."

Maxwell is technically my name, but the only time I ever hear it is when Mum is particularly angry with me. *"Maxwell Timothy Baker, what is OnlyFans and why is there a charge for it on my credit card?"*

That's right, I'm Max T. Baker. Which, if you say it fast enough, sounds like one of every teenager's favorite pastimes. Imagine the glee of the entire seventh grade when they figured that one out halfway through biology class.

"I ought to slam this door in your face," Darius continues. "I respect my daughter enough to let her make her own decisions, but I don't like you, Max. And I don't know why she keeps defending you. You clearly don't deserve it."

"Huh?" I say. Who is this man and what has he done with Darius Williams? "Did I do something wrong?" I ask, but he just clenches his jaw. I've never found his physique intimidating before, but right now he looks like he might crush me.

"Your date?" he finally says. "You're only two and a half hours late."

"Shit!" I reply. "I completely forgot."

"Why am I not surprised? Alicia!" he calls, his voice powerful enough to cause a small earth tremor. "That 'boyfriend' of yours has finally decided to show his face. Shall I tell him where to stick it?"

"Coming!" Alicia calls, and then a moment later appears at the top of the stairs. "Max!" she says, rushing down to throw her arms around me. She looks genuinely relieved. "Is your phone still on lockdown? I've been trying to get ahold of you all evening."

"Yeah," I say. "Sorry." Darius keeps staring at me disapprovingly.

"Well, don't just stand there like an idiot," she says, grabbing me by the hand and pulling me inside. "You had me worried. Ollie as well."

"I know, I'm sorry," I repeat as she starts dragging me up the stairs.

"Keep that bedroom door open!" Darius calls after us.

"Will do!" Alicia calls back, but then immediately shuts it. "What's going on, Max? You're just gonna disappear? Run out of school? And then miss our date? As if Dad needs another reason to dislike you! I've had to do *so much* damage control. Do you know how humiliating it is to be stood up by your *own* boyfriend?"

"I'm really sorry. It's just that everything got really intense at school all of a sudden. Like, totally overwhelming, and I didn't know what to do."

"You have been acting a little strange, Max," she says, more sympathetically now. "Ollie said the same. Even Thomas said you haven't been yourself lately, and he's about as perceptive as a guinea pig . . ."

"Things have just been . . . weird," I say. "Like *really* weird."

"Weird how?" Alicia replies. "You keep speaking in riddles . . . Why are you shutting me out, Max? Why can't you just tell me what's going on? Is it your parents? Are they fighting again?"

"I mean, yeah . . ." I say. "How'd you know?"

She shrugs. "Just a guess. I'm sorry, I thought things were getting better between them. I just hope they figure it out soon."

"Thanks," I say. At least this is something I can share with her.

She leans over and kisses me on the cheek. Her lips feel nice, comforting even.

"And that Dean kid? What was that about?"

I look at the empty wall over her bed where the painting of the three of us used to be. His absence is crippling; the room feels hollow without him. I want to tell Alicia what's happened—that's why I came here—but now that I'm standing in front of her, I just can't find the words.

"Oh . . . it's nothing."

It hurts to say that about Dean. I want to scream at Alicia to wake up, to comprehend that our best friend is *gone*, but it's not her fault she can't remember him. This reality is all she's known—and Dean isn't part of it. I have to stick to the plan. *Act normal.* At least until I can figure this out.

"Okay," she says. "But I'm here, Max. You don't need to shut me out."

She places her hand on my shoulder and runs it all the way down my arm to catch at my hand at the bottom. Static grows between us. *Uh-oh . . .*

"Thanks," I say, squeezing her hand for a moment before releasing it.

She cocks her head to one side then, as if suggesting a kiss, and I'd be lying if I said I didn't want to. I almost lean in, but no. I can't do that. If I cross that line, I'll never be able to go back.

I pull her into a hug instead, her arms lacing around my lower back, and for just a moment it feels like the outside world doesn't exist, as if she's lifted all the troubles off my shoulders. Is this what it's like to be in a relationship? It's nice, even if, deep down, I know it isn't right.

I glance over to her vanity table, remembering the last time I was here. Shouting and scrubbing off my nail polish. It all feels so childish now, it's hard to even understand what I was so mad about.

I look around the room a bit more, belatedly noticing how different it is. The easel from the corner is missing, the paintbrushes that once cluttered every surface are gone, even the inspiration bulletin board above her desk is now noticeably absent.

"What happened to your art stuff?"

"What do you mean?" she asks, looking puzzled as she releases me. "It's right here."

She goes over to her desk and holds up a sketchpad, the only remaining proof of her artistic talent. I take the pad and open it, my heart sinking as I see that the collection of radical art has been replaced.

"There's a lot of pictures of . . . us," I say, leafing through the pages, the guilt setting in deeper now. "What else are you working on?" Her set designs were missing from the drama department, but she must be using her talent for *something*.

"What do you mean?" she says. "I'm not working on anything."

"Nothing at all?"

She rolls her eyes. "You sound like Dad. I don't have to be working *all the time*, you know? What are *you* working on?"

"Well . . . nothing . . ."

"Exactly. And that's absolutely fine. We're allowed to have some fun, Max."

"But I thought you said creating things *was* fun?" I say. "You're never as happy as when you're working on your next big project . . . What about the Monster Ball?"

"What about it?"

"You could do the decorations, maybe?"

"What?" she says. "Why don't *you* do them?"

"Because you're the artist! You've got the talent here."

"You really think hanging a few paper ghosts counts as art? You really think that's my passion, Max? What I wanna do with my life?"

"But you could do something special. Transform the auditorium, make a little haunted grotto!"

"A haunted *what*?"

"Like a make-out room, but you could call it a grotto!"

"Have you been huffing glue?" Alicia says. "Where's this coming from, Max? As if I've got the time for any of that!"

"But you've always made the time!" I say. "You love the Monster Ball!"

"And yet you haven't asked me if I want to go with you . . ."

"Well, I'm your boyfriend, aren't I?"

"Simon is Rachel's boyfriend, and he did a huge promposal."

"But it's not prom . . ." I protest. "It's the Monster Ball."

"Yeah, and he organized a massive flash mob! He did the 'Monster Mash'!"

"Was it a *graveyard smash*?"

"You're not funny."

I frown. "I just don't get how that's supposed to be romantic. I mean, talk about typical straight people . . ."

"What do you mean, 'straight people'? *We're* straight people, Max!"

"Ugh, don't remind me," I groan.

"What's that supposed to mean?"

"Just forget it," I say. We sound like Mum and Dad. Always arguing about *something*, and yet always arguing about *nothing*. "I'm sorry, okay? I'm sorry for not promposing to you, even though it's not prom."

"That's not the point . . ." She sighs, and I don't know what to say to that. As insignificant as this all is, she looks genuinely upset. This may not be *my* world, but she's still Alicia, and I can't bear to see her hurting.

"I'm sorry," I finally say, a lot more sincere now. "I'm not a very good boyfriend, am I?" She doesn't answer. Just turns her head and looks away. "Because I should be. You deserve me to be."

She looks back at me then, and, for the first time since I got here, her face softens, and she gives me a little appreciative smile. I pass back the sketchpad.

I wish I could have what you have, Alicia. I wish I could be one of the normal *kids.*

This is exactly what I said I wanted, but, now that I have it, I realize how wrong I was. I close my eyes and silently wish for things to go back to how they were before. I don't know what I expect to happen, but nothing does.

"So that's it, then?" I say under my breath. "This is my life now?"

I look down at my bare nails. My hands look as if they don't belong to me.

"Life gets shitty sometimes, Max," Alicia says. "People say it gets better, but I don't subscribe to that. Sometimes things don't get better. Sometimes they get worse. Sometimes we get stuck . . ."

"Is this supposed to be a pep talk?" I ask. "Because it's not very peppy."

"It's just that I don't think we should sit around and wait for life to improve. We don't need permission to be happy, Max. There's always joy to be found somewhere, even in the little things. Even just a little bit."

"I guess," I say, but I really don't mean it. Where's the joy in a world without Dean, where my parents are unhappy, where I can't be my true self?

My eyes are inexplicably drawn back to Alicia's vanity, where they catch sight of a bottle of glittering nail polish. It's a sparkling blue color, not dissimilar to the one Dean was wearing the last time I saw him. It's absolutely gorgeous, and, as I pick it up and turn it around, I watch the shimmer of the liquid as it rises and falls in the bottle. It would look so good with the blue-and-yellow varsity jacket I found in my wardrobe. I know it doesn't fit with my new straight-boy persona, but honestly I don't care anymore. If I'm going to be trapped here, I don't think this is too much to ask for. Maybe Alicia is right. Maybe I can still find some joy.

"Do you think I could try this?" I ask, holding up the bottle.

"You wanna wear my nail polish?" Alicia says, looking at me weirdly.

"Never mind," I say quickly, realizing what an insane suggestion it is. *Straight guys don't wear nail polish, Max. Don't be so ridiculous.*

Alicia gives a light laugh. "Of course you can," she says, gently taking the polish from my hands. "Find something that brings you a little joy, right? Here."

She pulls out her desk chair and wheels it over to me.

"Thanks." I smile, a real one this time. This is the Alicia I know and love. "I could get used to this," I say, sitting down and spinning around to face her.

"You know, Rachel says I'm really lucky?" she says as she unscrews the top. "To have a boyfriend so comfortable with his identity. Do you know how many girls would love to paint their boyfriend's nails?"

I laugh. "Not many? I'm pretty sure that's not a thing."

"Well, it is for me," Alicia says simply, beginning to apply a base coat. "You need a really steady hand for this. Guys really don't give us enough credit for how difficult it is. Even Ollie can't manage it."

"He's never seemed like much of the nail-polish type," I say.

"That's what he said at first too. He changed his mind as soon as he saw how good it was on him. He looked really cute." She pauses for a moment to gaze up at me. "Maybe not as cute as you, though," she adds as I watch the color returning to my nails.

It feels nice, comforting even, like reclaiming something that's mine. It makes me feel closer to Dean too, and that gives me hope. I'll find a way to get back to him. I have no idea how, but I will. I owe him that much.

"Do you remember when we first met?" Alicia says. She doesn't look up from what she's doing, but I can tell she's smiling, reminiscing.

"Of course," I say. "We were twelve."

That much I'm pretty sure of. We met at Woodside, having come from two different elementary schools.

"And do you remember the first thing you said to me?"

"No idea," I admit. Who knows what Straight Max might have said?

"Nice shoes," she says, and it takes me by surprise because that's exactly what I'd said to her in the real world. "What kind of a lame pickup line is that?"

"You're joking, right? They were incredible!"

She'd had on a new pair of crisp white Vans that she'd doodled on with colored marker. Only this is Alicia we're talking about so, when I say "doodled," what I mean is "decorated like the roof of some fantasy palace." I knew we'd be friends from the moment I saw them.

"You remember!" She beams at me.

"Of course," I say, and I don't know why it surprises me that Alicia and I had the exact same introduction in this reality as in mine. The more time I spend in Straight Max's world, the more I realize that we're really not that different. I think of the well-organized wardrobe—I still seem to have an eye for fashion, that's something. And there *are* hetero stylists and designers after all. I remember Mrs. A putting me down as "Fashion Consultant" in the *Little Shop* program. Maybe she was onto something. Maybe she saw something I couldn't.

"There," Alicia says, inspecting my nails to double-check her work. "Finished."

I hold my hands up, the shimmer dazzling under the light.

"Fabulous," I say, perhaps a little too effeminately, and Alicia laughs.

"They suit you," she says, just as we hear thumping footsteps on the stairs.

"I told you to keep this open!" Darius growls. "You better not be—" He stops mid-sentence as he pushes open the door to see me inspecting my freshly painted nails. "What in the . . . ?"

"Yes, Daddy?" Alicia blinks her eyelashes innocently.

"This is . . . not what I was expecting. You're painting each other's nails?"

"Well, she's painting mine," I say, holding them up so he can get a closer look. "I don't think she trusts me to paint hers yet."

"Maybe with a little practice," Alicia replies mischievously. She's enjoying this a bit too much.

It feels mean to tease Darius like this—he and I have always been friendly up till now—but, at the same time, I'd be lying if I said I wasn't enjoying it too.

"Right, well, okay," he grunts, clearly unsure of what else to say. "Carry on, then. I'll be downstairs. Keep this open, though. I won't tell you a third time. I'm not above throwing you out of this house, Maxwell."

"Sure thing, Darius," I say.

"That's Mr. Williams to you. Don't get cocky now."

"Yes, sir," I say, and try to stop myself from smirking.

"I'll be listening," he says, leaving the door wide open as he disappears back down the stairs. Alicia laughs just a little too soon; he definitely heard her.

"He puts on this tough-guy act," she says, "but he's a big softie, really. You just haven't seen that side of him yet."

"I've seen the signs," I say, thinking of him asking Dean to paint his nails. "He's just protective, that's all."

"You're right about that," she says. "Ollie is just about the only teenage boy he trusts. You should see the two of them. I have to pry Dad away from him every time he comes over. He says he wishes all guys were a bit more like Ollie."

"Maybe he just needs to see a different side of me, then?"

She shrugs. "Maybe. Just don't count your chickens."

"Already counted them," I say with a grin, and she smiles at that.

"I really am the luckiest girl in the world, huh?"

She hugs me again, and I gently hug her back, careful not to mess up the polish. There's a silence between us then as I look up at the empty space where the painting of the three of us used to be. Even in the moments where things start to feel right, I have to remind myself that I can't get too comfortable. I can't let myself slip into this life. I have to get back to the real world. Back to Dean.

Maybe just for tonight, though. Maybe I can enjoy this just for one night.

"Do you think I could stay over?" I ask. "Like on the floor, sleepover-style? Not in the bed with you obviously," I add a little awkwardly, and Alicia straight-out belly laughs.

"I don't know what made you think Dad would *ever* allow that," she says. "But absolutely no way in hell. Nice try, though."

"Oh," I say. "Yeah, of course. I just don't really wanna go back home tonight."

"I know," Alicia says, her tone softening. "I wish you could stay, I really do."

"I get it." I smile back. "Maybe we could watch a movie or something before I head home, though? One of those trashy rom-coms you love so much?"

"Sure," she says. "I'll go make us some popcorn."

"Sweet?" I say hopefully.

"Salty. You're already sweet enough."

Eight Years Ago

I don't know what it is about new shoes, but I feel a spring in my step as the lunch bell rings and I make my way out of class. They're the brand-new Air Max I'd been asking for, pristine and gleaming white, with so much intricate detail. Mum and Dad bought them for me as an extra-special treat. They were supposed to be for picture day next week, but they let me have them early.

"Hey, Max," Thomas says, flicking me on the back of the head as he finds me sitting on the grassy slope by the side of the soccer field. I don't enjoy his company, but I put up with him because we share a lot of the same friends. "You playing today?" he continues, passing a soccer ball back and forth between his hands. "Or you gonna wuss out again like last time?"

"Not today," I say, getting up to move away just as some of the other boys come over to join us. "I'm gonna go and eat inside actually."

"Oh, come on, don't be so gay," he says, rolling his eyes.

"I'm not," I say firmly. "I just don't wanna wreck my new sneakers."

"Sounds pretty gay to me." Thomas laughs and some of the others laugh too.

"Whatever," I say, turning away, but he yanks my hood and pulls me backward. "Get off me," I say, pushing him away. "Just leave me alone."

"*Just leave me alone*," he parrots in an exaggerated high-pitched voice and goes for my hood a second time. "Come on, Max, stop being such a loser."

I try to wrestle myself free, but he just yanks harder until I trip backward down the slope. I try to keep my balance, but my feet slip in the mud, and I end up toppling.

I roll over twice, trying to scramble away from him, but everyone around us just laughs. I don't dare to look down at my shoes. I already know they're ruined. I want to cry but know better than to do that in front of him.

"Why are you being such a dick?"

I look up to see that it's Dean talking. We share a few classes, but we've never really spoken.

"What's it to you?" Thomas says, rounding on him.

"You really have nothing going for you, do you?" Dean says. "And that's why you push people around. To try to hide the fact that you're a *nobody*."

Some of Thomas's friends laugh at that, and it leaves Thomas fumbling for words. "At least I'm not gay," he mutters, at which Dean immediately lights up.

"That's right, Thomas, I'm gay. And I know you probably think that means I *really* like you. But, if it was a choice between you and every other boy in school, you'd be the last person I'd pick. At least your little friends here have personalities. And talent. Lyle's an incredible athlete, Jack's actually hilarious, and Santiago? Everyone wants to date Santiago. But you, Thomas? What exactly have you got?"

Thomas goes quiet as his friends stare at Dean in amazement.

"Cat got your tongue?" Dean says, arching one perfect eyebrow, and Thomas just mumbles a meek, "Whatever," and skulks off down the field.

I wonder if his friends will turn on Dean now, but instead they just call him "a bit of a legend." Dean takes a graceful bow.

"He's gonna come after you later," I say once it's just the two of us. Dean shrugs. "Let him. I'm sorry about your shoes."

"It's fine," I say, looking down at them. "But my parents are gonna kill me. They were supposed to be for picture day."

"I think we can get them clean again." Dean smiles. "In fact, I know we can. Come on—I'll teach you how."

Chapter Eleven

"Oh, for God's sake!"

Mum's voice from somewhere downstairs wakes me in a cold sweat. Dad starts yelling back, and I feel a familiar sinking feeling as I realize that nothing has changed overnight. It's my third day in Straight World, and three days is quite enough, thank you very much. I don't know if it's what Alicia said about finding joy or the fact that I have a brand-new set of sparkling sapphire nails, but I've decided that today's the day I'm going to fix this.

The first item on the agenda is to get my phone back. Mum may think she's keeping it till the end of the week, as if a digital detox will somehow fix the mess that is this family, but I know *exactly* where she's hiding it. I've been pre-checking my Christmas presents since I was fourteen. There's only one place she could be keeping it prisoner, and it's time for a little jailbreak.

"I don't care if it's full of calories!" Dad yells. "I work hard enough without having to worry about a bit of extra butter on my toast!"

"You're the one who keeps complaining about the beer belly!" Mum yells back. "But fine, go ahead and gorge yourself on fat. See if I care!"

My parents, everyone—champions of body positivity. If you have "Max's parents arguing about butter" on your Family Feud bingo card, you can go ahead and cross that one right off. Congratulations!

I pull on a pair of sweatpants and creep onto the landing. As hard as it is to listen to them like this, it does provide the perfect cover for a stealth operation.

Their bedroom looks different. Weird even. I'm so used to this being just Mum's space that it feels strange to be in a room that splits their personalities down the middle. The vanity table I used to steal makeup from is pushed over into the corner on Mum's side. Dad's bedside table is cluttered with unread Dan Brown novels and about a hundred different variants of the same gray tie. I never thought I'd say this, but I miss the dancing penguins.

I guess that's the thing that continues not to make any sense in all this—why are Mum and Dad still together in this world? And why did Dad never leave his dead-end job? The best thing he ever did was start his own company. I'll never forget the day he swapped his black trousers for a pair of jeans. He pulled off the smart-casual vibe so effortlessly, and it was amazing to see how much his confidence grew.

"Lemon jam?" Mum yells. "There's no such thing as lemon jam, Henry!"

"Well then, what do you call *this*?!" Dad shouts back. I imagine him triumphantly—but incorrectly—holding up a jar of marmalade.

"That's lemon *curd*!" she sneers, and that's when I tune them out. I don't have the bandwidth to listen to an argument about breakfast preserves.

I quickly go over to the wardrobe, Mum's colorful clothes a carnival of chaos on one side, and Dad's monochrome suits a shrine to conformity on the other. I lean down to find the false panel at the bottom, and, as I slide it open, sure enough, there's my phone. Predictable as ever, Mum, and that's why I love you.

I've still got half an hour before I need to leave for school, so I sneak back to my room and lie down on the bed. I play LANY from my computer to drown out Mum and Dad's argument and turn on my phone. I wait a moment for the 26,000 notifications to ping through. There's countless messages from Oliver and Alicia, a couple from Thomas apparently too, but, I suppose unsurprisingly, nothing from Dean. He isn't in my contacts either. I guess part of me was still holding on to the hope that the two of us were somehow still in touch—secret pen pals or something—but my phone suggests otherwise.

I do another quick Google search and then continue scrolling through the endless Dean Jacksons on Instagram. Still nothing. The internet is telling me that he simply doesn't exist.

I tap through into Alicia's profile in case there are any clues there, and I'm immediately horrified by what I find. Just like in her sketchpad, all her art is *gone*. Her illustrations, her paintings, the selfies with her "magnificent sets." She's still clearly incredibly popular—there are loads of photos of her at parties, hanging out with big groups of friends, that's still the Alicia I know—but every piece of art seems to have been replaced with pictures of the two of us. It's like a big part of her is now missing. I have to scroll back more than two years to find any of her artwork, but then suddenly it appears in abundance.

What changed? I wonder, but I already know the answer to that.

The thing that changed was *us*.

I check my own profile, and the contrast is striking. I have to scroll back pretty far to find any pictures of Alicia and me at all, and when I do, it's just one of us kissing outside a fish-and-chip shop. Hardly the stunningly choreographed #LoveWins photos I always fantasized about posting with my future boyfriend. I tap into the comments.

Cuties!
You look so good together!
Pineapple emoji for no reason!

ThomasMulbridge69 has written "#CoupleGoals," but I'm honestly not sure we're hashtag couple goals at all.

The rest of my profile is a little less vivid and colorful than my profile in the real world, but it's still well put together, and weirdly I have more followers. I'm mostly just glad to see that I'm still doing my outfits of the day. They need work, of course—they're missing that undefinable *something*, that flair, that understated pizazz—but it's ten out of ten for effort.

There is one picture that particularly stands out, though. It's from just last week, and I'm wearing tight fitted khaki joggers, rolled up to show a flash of ankle. I've coupled them with a pair of plain white Nikes and an off-white hoodie that I've cut off at the sleeves. It seems like I've run a pair of scissors along the cut to give it a distressed appearance, and it actually looks pretty sick. It's very *straight boy*, admittedly, not something I'd usually go for, but I'm quite impressed with my handiwork. I've even put overnight salt-spray curls in my fringe for added effect. Straight Max really thought this one through. There may be hope for the heteros yet.

I do a quick scroll of my timeline and am completely unsurprised to see I'm following both Kim Kardashian and Kylie Jenner. Straight Max evidently thinks with his penis. In the real world, I only follow the accounts of people who inspire me. People like Tom Holland and Wi Ha-joon and that guy from the toothpaste ad with the washboard abs . . .

I close my phone and open up my wardrobe to see what we've got to work with. "On Wednesdays, We Wear Pink" is a cardinal rule, obviously, and I'm pleasantly surprised to see that Straight Max does have two pink T-shirts, one salmon and one peach. I go for the salmon and pull a cerulean sweater over the top to match my nails—very *Andy Sachs on her first day at* Runway.

I complete the look with a blue watch I find at the back of my drawer, and a pair of white jeans. The look is screaming for a pair of baby blue Converse, but I don't have anything like that in my current arsenal, so I settle for blue socks paired with white shoes instead. It's not quite the look I'd usually go for, but I remind myself that I am hetero now and so can't be expected to turn heads *every* time I walk the corridors. The look has to say *I'm here, I'm* not *queer, get used to it.* I still style my hair to perfection, though. I'm not an animal. Today is a day for changing the world, and I absolutely need to look the part.

The look is finished, and I'm ready to go. I slip in my AirPods to drown out my parents' argument and rush out the door, sidestepping breakfast. There'll be no butter for Max today, and certainly no lemon jam.

I play some retro Pet Shop Boys and George Michael as I break into a power walk, the playlist culminating with Ariana Grande and Troye Sivan as I make my grand entrance into the main corridor of Woodside Academy—mine and Dean's catwalk.

I spot Shanna rummaging through her locker and, knowing that she'll definitely appreciate the outfit, beeline in her direction.

"Hey, Max," she says, peering out from behind her locker door. "New look?"

She's checking me out, but *she's* the one who has the new look. Her rainbow hair is back to its natural brunette and all the Pride pins are missing from her backpack. She's dressed in black, like her colors have been drained.

"Just experimenting," I say, leaning back against the lockers, making sure she has a good view of my fabulous nails.

"You look good," she says with a smile, and I see a little of her color return.

"Thanks," I say, giving her a little twirl. "How are you anyway? What's new? And where's Gabi?"

"Huh?" she says, confused. "Gabi? Who's that?"

"Gabi Jimenez," I say, but she just looks at me blankly.

I blink fast. "So you're not dating anyone?"

"No," she replies, glancing anxiously around as if she's worried someone might hear us. "What made you think I was?"

"Nothing," I say, but my brain is now once again in a tailspin. "I'll catch you later."

I turn away from her and head on down the corridor. First Dean is missing, now Gabi? It's like I'm a homophobic Thanos or something. One little snap and I've erased half the queers in existence.

I pull out my phone and do a quick Insta search for Lil Nas X, and—thank God!—he's still there because what would we do without him? It's taking everything in me not to descend into panic, but I have to stay focused. All this is temporary. I can fix it. I have to be able to fix it . . .

"Cute outfit," Oliver says as I walk into the common room. I forget myself for a moment and have to look down to double-check what I'm wearing. "And nice nails," he adds, pouring himself a cup of coffee. "Alicia got you too, huh?"

"Oh," I say, trying to get my bearings, "it was my idea actually." I hold my nails up so that the blue reflects in the light. "They look good, right?"

"They look amazing," he says. "I have to say I'm a bit surprised, though. Like, your fashion sense has never been pure straight boy . . . but this!"

I laugh. "I'm gonna take that as a compliment!"

"It was definitely intended as one," Oliver replies with the hint of a blush. "Who knows? Maybe it'll rub off on some of the other guys."

"We can only hope."

Either way, it feels nice not to have to pretend anymore. Like I can finally just be myself. For the most part anyway.

"Look, I'm sorry about yesterday," I say, remembering how I'd stormed off, looking for a person he's never even heard of. "My head was all over the place."

"Don't worry about it. We all have days like that, right? Do you wanna talk about it? Go get a Starbucks, maybe?" He grimaces as he takes a sip of his instant coffee. "I don't know why I bother with this stuff."

"Do we have time?" I look at my watch, completely unsubtly lifting it just high enough to show off that it does, in fact, perfectly match my outfit.

"Yeah, we've got another half hour till English. Come on, my treat," he says, tapping me on the arm in the affectionate way that straight guys sometimes do.

"All right," I say, readjusting my backpack and following him out of the common room.

A morning coffee date with Oliver Cheng. Gay Max would be losing his mind right about now, but actually it just feels pretty chill.

"So what's up?" Oliver asks as we walk side by side across the soccer field. The grass is still dewy, the smell of autumn lingering.

"It's one of those things you can't really explain," I say. "Like, nobody can possibly relate to what I'm going through, so why even bother, you know?"

"Try me," he says, and there's something quite comforting about walking alongside him like this, not having to look him directly in the eye. "Feeling like you're alone and nobody really understands you? I get that. I don't know any other queer kids at Woodside. There must *be* more, but sometimes I feel like I'm the only one."

I think of Shanna then and wonder if she's not out in this world at all. And then I think of Dean and Gabi, both of them missing. I wish I could tell Oliver about all of them. It stands to reason that the more kids come out, the more will have the confidence to follow, but it's hard to shake the feeling that, in Woodside at least, Dean was the first domino that set all this in motion.

"Have you thought about starting a Queer Club?" I say. "Maybe that'd encourage some kids to come out?"

"Maybe. We had one in London. A whole bunch of us. Not just gay kids either. There were out-and-proud kids from all over the rainbow. Here, I'm all on my own."

"You're not alone, Oliver," I say, and I wish he understood how much I really meant that. "Like, obviously I don't understand what it's like to be gay." I don't want to sound as if I'm coming out to him. I can't do that to Straight Max. "But I'm here for you. As your totally straight-not-gay-at-all hetero friend."

Oliver laughs. "It's cool, Max. I don't think you're gay—don't worry. I'm not gonna try to hit on you, if that's what you're worried about."

"I'm not," I say. "Worried, that is. I mean, you said it yourself—I'm not your type, right?"

"Right," he replies quickly. "You *are* quite adorable when you get panicked, though." His dimples twitch as he grins at me.

"Is that so?" I say, wiggling my eyebrows, the two of us laughing.

It surprises me how easily we get along. The more time I spend with Oliver, the more I realize I've been missing out on such a great friendship back in my own reality. If only I could've seen past my crippling obsession to the person he really is.

"So what are you gonna do after school?" I say. "When we graduate?"

"I'd really like to write for a magazine. In Manchester? Birmingham? Or Brighton to be with the gays!"

"So you're not sticking around, then?"

"Well, are you? Woodside's nice and all, but there's a great big world out there. Besides, you've gotta go where the jobs are."

"You sound like Alicia," I say, laughing. "She never shuts up about her career."

"I've literally never heard her talk about it," Oliver says. "She mostly just complains about you."

"Are we talking about the same Alicia?" I say, and it's only as I say it that I remember we aren't. *Christ, Max, get it together!* But, for some reason, I can't just drop it.

"What about art school? That's still her dream, right?"

Oliver shrugs. "I dunno, Max. She's never mentioned it to me."

I feel the same sense of hollow anxiety that I did looking at her Insta this morning. I've got to somehow get her back on track.

We reach the door to Starbucks then, and I follow him inside. Despite my worry about Alicia, I'm delighted when Oliver orders a pair of iced vanilla lattes without even asking me. Straight Max likes iced coffee! I'll take the small victories where I can get them.

"Name?" the girl behind the counter asks.

"Thelma," Oliver says.

"Louise," I add, and she nods, writing it down with a little smile.

It warms my heart a little to see that I'm still playing this game, even when Dean isn't here. But that warmth is coupled with a pang of guilt. I can't just replace him with Oliver. I still have to find a way back to him. I'm not giving up on that. Not now, not ever.

We sit on the curb outside Starbucks for a little while, as people come and go with their extra-hot macchiatos and venti cups of chai.

"I love this," Oliver says. "Just watching people—it's nice, huh?" His eyes are following an attractive guy with curly blond hair and exceptionally tight trousers.

I laugh. "I bet you do. You're such a skeez, Oliver."

"What?" He blushes, looking back at me. "I didn't mean it like that. I mean, hot guys, obviously that too, but also I just love people watching. Everyone living their own lives and their own stories. It's all inspiration, right?"

"I guess," I say, sipping on the cool vanilla. "But inspiration for what?"

"Well, anything," Oliver replies. "I've been thinking about trying to write a book, and any one of these people could inspire a new character. And you're into fashion, right? You must get ideas from other people's style? Like that guy with the glasses?"

"Or maybe her?" I say, gesturing to a young woman in a patchwork duffel coat. I love the way you can hear her heels clacking from across the street.

He elbows me in the ribs. "Of course you'd suggest the hot girl," he says. But actually I didn't even notice that. I guess she's not really my type?

"It's a nice way of seeing things, but right now style is not the inspiration I'm looking for," I say, thinking of my fruitless search for Dean. "What do you wanna write anyway? The next *Hunger Games*, maybe? Dare I say the next *Harry*—"

"Don't!" he interrupts with mock horror. "How dare you compare me to *her*."

"Sorry! So what, then? Horror? Mystery? Sci-fi?"

"Maybe romance?" he says, and then looks away as if he's embarrassed. "Or I dunno, whatever. Definitely something queer."

"Yeah? You really wanna box yourself in like that?"

"Box myself in?" He frowns. "You've gotta write what you know, Max. You're telling me you wouldn't read a book just because it has gays in it?"

Straight Expectations

"Well, of course *I* would," I say. "But straight people"—*Fuck!*— "*other* straight people, I mean . . . you know what they're like. If it doesn't have some Olivia Rodrigo type swooning over some Joshua Bassett lookalike, they're just not interested."

Oliver laughs. "That's really quite *specific*, Max."

"And so is the taste of straight people! They made *three* movies about time travel that all star Rachel McAdams. And she never even gets to time travel! She just has to sit around and wait for the man to finish!"

"Waiting around for the man to finish?" Oliver says. "I think that's something that a *lot* of women can relate to actually . . ."

I almost choke on my coffee. Who knew Oliver Cheng could be so sassy?

"Maybe you could write a book about time-traveling gays, then?" I suggest. "They could go back in time and fix all the mistakes made by straight people."

"Like not giving *Mean Girls* an Oscar?"

"Exactly! Rachel McAdams was robbed!"

"You have surprisingly strong opinions about Rachel McAdams," Oliver says, chuckling. "So you'd really read a book with a big gay romance that culminates in a pair of guys making out?"

"Of course," I say. "I mean, why wouldn't I?"

He beams. "I'll be sure to send you a list of recommendations, then."

"I'm a slow reader, though, so don't get your hopes up. It'll probably take me six months just to get through one."

"You remind me of Laci—my best friend back in London. I think she's still working through a book I gave her, like, a year ago . . ."

"I'm easily distracted!" I say. "I get halfway down the page and then start thinking about the shower scenes from *Elite*."

"I haven't seen it," he replies. "A lot of naked girls, then?"

"Oh . . . yeah," I say. Thank *God* he hasn't seen it. *Stop referencing your past gay viewing habits, Max!*

"So, Laci?" I quickly change the subject. "Tell me more."

"I only talk about her, like, ninety percent of the time."

"I know," I say. "But I like the way you light up when you do."

"Is that so?" He smiles. "Well, I told you how she gave me the courage to come out, right?"

I need to be careful here. "Remind me?"

"Well, she came out long before I did—told me one day and the whole school the next. Just like that. She had it hard too. Teachers using the wrong pronouns, deadnaming her, the works. But she did it. And seeing her do all that made my struggles feel insignificant."

"But they're not insignificant," I say. "They matter."

"That's what she said too."

He opens up Instagram and flicks through to a picture of him and a beautiful girl with wavy blond hair and pink streaks. She reminds me a bit of Emma Stone when she played Gwen Stacy—the same heart-stopping, innocent blue eyes. The two of them are ugly laughing into the camera, the way you only do when you're with that someone you really know and love. I've seen the picture before while stalking his Instagram, but I never really looked at it then. Now it's like I'm seeing it with new eyes.

"I still speak to her, like, every day," Oliver says proudly. "I'm thinking about inviting her down soon, so you can finally meet her. I reckon you'd get on like a house on fire. She's feisty, though, eats straight boys like you for breakfast."

"I used to have a friend like that once too," I say, thinking of Dean.

"Once? What happened?"

"It's . . . complicated." I sigh. "But he's gone now, and I miss him."

"Well," Oliver says, thinking on that for a moment, "is there anything you can do to fix it? Like, did you have an argument or something?"

"I said some things I didn't mean," I admit. "And now I can't take them back."

"We all say things we don't mean sometimes, Max."

"I know. But this time it's like my words are stuck. And now *I'm* stuck."

"Well, it's never too late." Oliver puts his arm around me. "I'm sure you'll figure it out. And if there's ever anything I can do . . . ?"

"Thanks, Oliver," I say. "I feel a little bit better actually."

"Yeah?" He smiles, and our eyes catch.

"Yeah," I say, and, for just a moment, it almost feels like there's a spark between us. Like a flash of lightning that's gone as fast as it was here. I instinctively look away, but then look back, searching for something I so badly want to believe is there. But there's nothing. Maybe I just wanted it to be true.

"We'd better head back." Oliver clears his throat, taking his hand off my shoulder. "We don't wanna be late for English."

"Oh," I say. "Yeah, okay." I throw my backpack on. "I'm really glad we're friends, you know?"

Oliver grins. "Me too," he says, and then we head back to school as if nothing had happened at all.

Chapter Twelve

Alicia and I sit on the grassy bank at the side of the soccer field, the floodlights illuminating it as the players' shadows chase them around the grass. It's already dark, even though it's barely 6 p.m. There's never more than a handful of spectators, not like in those American movies where the whole town shows up to watch some high schoolers throw a ball around. We don't have cheerleaders either, but Alicia whoops and claps her hands and makes the noise of a whole squad every time literally anything happens. I'm on my second coffee of the day. It's getting cold now, so I've committed the cardinal sin of abandoning iced coffee for a hot one. It's pumpkin spice, though, so forgivable.

Woodside is up two to one against Grove Hill, the private school on the other side of town, and it's nice to see that for once Oliver isn't the only player with rainbow laces. One of the rival team members is wearing them too. Built like a truck, with a hi-top fade and expertly twisted curls, he's ruggedly handsome, the kind of guy that looks too old to be on a high-school soccer team.

I guess it never occurred to me that here, on the soccer field of all places, would be somewhere to meet other LGBT+ people. Dean and I always steered clear of anything sports-related. We never even came to watch Oliver play.

"What's his name?" I say to Alicia, nodding to the mysterious player. He grins as he tackles Oliver and steals the ball. Oliver is smiling too, his tongue poking out with determination as he sprints after him.

"Kedar," she replies. "He's the captain. Ollie talks about him sometimes."

"It's cool that he's wearing rainbow laces. Do you think he's . . . ?"

"Gay? I dunno, probably. Or just trying to show his support?"

She takes my free hand and wraps it around her shoulder, nestling into me. It's nice to be close to her like this and doesn't feel like I'm crossing any line. Alicia and I have always been very tactile with each other.

"That's nice," I say. "It can be a bit isolating sometimes, feeling like you're one of the only queer kids in town."

Alicia looks at me strangely.

I hurriedly correct myself. "For Oliver, I mean. I'm talking about Oliver."

"Oh yeah." She nods. "I still think he misses his London friends. He knew a lot of LGBT+ kids back there. It must have been hard leaving them . . ."

"Well, he has me," I say. "I'm always here for him."

"And me too, obviously, but we don't know what it's like to be gay, Max. Sometimes I think he just needs someone who understands him."

"What about Mrs. A?"

Alicia snorts. "She's like a hundred years old but, sure, she and Ollie should start having sleepovers. You should *definitely* suggest that."

I shrug. "I bet she'd be good at *Fortnite*. Something tells me there's dexterity in those fingers."

Alicia turns to look at me. "Was that a lesbian joke?"

"No, what do you—? Oh my God, ew!"

There's a shout from the field as Kedar kicks the ball into the back of the net. He pulls his shirt over his head to celebrate, revealing a six-pack that makes it look like he's been chiseled out of stone.

"*Jeeeeez*," Alicia says, eyeing him up like she can't look away. "His body is insane. How does a person even get that ripped?"

I laugh. "Your dad is literally a personal trainer."

"I know that, but Kedar is, what, eighteen? How's that even possible?"

"That's gotta be a hundred thousand sit-ups right there," I say. "What I wouldn't give for washboard abs like those . . . The guy looks like an Adonis."

"All right, calm down, Max," says Alicia, laughing.

"I'm just saying that with a body like that everyone's probably dying to get his number . . ."

"You're starting to sound like *you* want his number," she says teasingly, just as the referee blows the whistle to end the game.

The match is a draw, two to two. Oliver shakes hands with the members of the rival team as they take turns patting each other on the back and saying "good game" over and over again. It fascinates me how Oliver slips into ritualistic heterosexuality so easily. He spots us sitting on the bank and grins as he runs over. Now that he's closer, I can see that mud is spattered all the way up his legs, his pristine white uniform shorts ruined.

"You did great," I say. "Really fantastic ball kicking."

He laughs. "Thanks, Max. I've invited the teams to come over for the gathering tonight. I can't wait for you guys to meet them."

"You mean the party?" Alicia beams, jumping to her feet.

"It's a *small* gathering," Oliver reiterates.

"Whatever you say, Ollie," she says with a grin. "You realize Thomas has invited half the girls in school, right? Literally anyone with a pulse."

He groans. "Oh God, I'm gonna kill him. You're still coming, right, Max?"

"Oh yeah, of course," I say.

Honestly, I'd completely forgotten about Oliver's "gathering" tonight. I was planning on using the evening to think of new ways to find Dean, but I suppose one night off couldn't hurt. If Dean is out there, it's not like he's going anywhere. Besides, right now I'll take any excuse to get out of my parents' way. If I have to listen to them argue about condiments again, I think I'll actually lose it.

Mum's ears must be burning because my phone starts to ring.

"Urgh, I better take this," I say, getting up and walking just out of earshot.

"I knew it!" Mum says as soon as I answer. "You can't just go rummaging through my things, Max. I thought we'd been robbed!"

"Well, it's a bit ironic, don't you think?" I reply. "That you're now calling me on the phone you didn't want me to have?"

"Well, never mind that," she says. "We've barely seen you all week, and we're worried about you. When are you coming home?"

"I dunno," I say. "Tomorrow probably?"

"Tomorrow? Why, where are you tonight?"

"I'm gonna stay at Oliver's place."

"Oh," she says, and there's a long pause while she considers that. "Well, I suppose that's okay. As long as the two of you aren't . . . ?"

"Jesus, Mum." I roll my eyes so hard that she can probably hear it on the other end of the line. "I'm with Alicia, aren't I? And just because Oliver's gay that doesn't mean he's sleeping with every single guy he has over to his house."

"I didn't mean that!" she protests, but that's *exactly* what she meant.

"It's just a few of us staying over—don't worry," I say. "And, if I do suddenly decide I need to get railed by the gay kid, I promise I'll use a condom."

"Oh my God, Max," she splutters, but honestly she was asking for that.

"It's just a small gathering, okay? I promise nothing bad will happen."

Bad things are happening. And on a school night.

Oliver's "small gathering" has gotten a bit out of hand, and I'm *more* than a little worried about the soft furnishings. Alicia wasn't joking: word really has gone around and pretty much every kid from the senior class has turned up. Kedar and his teammates are here too and, considering that most of us aren't eighteen yet, an obscene amount of alcohol has managed to materialize into existence.

I used to fantasize about coming to Oliver's house and what it would be like, but I never pictured somewhere quite as extravagant as this. His parents are clearly loaded—the house is huge, with a massive garden and perfectly manicured hedges running around the perimeter. It looks like one of those Hollywood homes that you see on TV. There's a giant fridge with an icemaker, one of those sexy modern fireplaces that wraps all the way around the living room's shiny hardwood floors, and a sick speaker setup that runs through the entire house—including *all four* bathrooms. You can tell they've only been here for a year, though. The whole house has that "new" feeling about it. I can't quite put my finger on what it is, but I can just tell people haven't lived here very long.

Unsurprisingly, Oliver has already run out of glasses, and without the standard red party cups on hand (small-gathering planning) he's resorted to handing out mugs and whatever else can serve as a container for alcohol. I'm pretty sure I saw Kedar in the kitchen drinking wine out of a Pyrex jug. He may as well have abandoned all pretense and cut out the middleman by drinking it straight from the bottle.

"Here, try this," Oliver says, sipping from a mug shaped like the pig from *Toy Story*.

We're sitting at the bottom of the stairs, and he winces as he swallows the concoction and passes it over to me. It tastes like Red Bull mixed with paint thinner. I'd wanted to whip up some margaritas (I'd found a how-to video on YouTube and everything), but the tequila I spotted earlier has already been commandeered by the soccer boys who are now shooting it out of eggcups.

"You're right—it's rank. I'm gonna make something else," Oliver says. "Do you want anything?"

"Like a vodka cranberry maybe?" I say. "Anything that doesn't taste like battery acid."

"I'm making no promises," he says with a grin, leaving me at the bottom of the stairs.

"Hey, Max!"

Poppy Palmer instantly slips into Oliver's spot.

She's curled her hair and it falls in ringlets around her shoulders. She looks really hot. I never thought she'd be my type—a little bit *too obvious* perhaps—but right now she's undeniably pushing all the right buttons.

"Double P," I say with a smile. "How are things?"

She's wearing a cute white top with A LITTLE BIT DRAMATIC printed in bold pink type across the front. It's familiar, but I can't place it.

"Things are great, Max," she says. "But my eyes are up here."

"Oh sorry, I was just . . . the top . . . I recognize it from somewhere."

"I'm sure you do." She winks, and I feel her leg push up against mine. "Regina George?" she says, and finally it clicks. "It's the one I wore at my birthday last year. You know, before the incident with *Big Steven*."

"Oh yeah," I say. *"Big Steven . . ."* I've literally no idea who that is.

"I was sore for, like, a week afterward."

"You were?" I say. This feels a bit TMI, even for Double P.

"My dad had to help me up the stairs when I got home. I literally couldn't walk."

Dear God, her poor father.

"So I guess Big Steven really lives up to his . . . reputation?"

"You can say that again," she says, laughing. "And poor Ollie! He'd been at Woodside for what . . . two weeks? And he goes bareback in front of *everyone.*"

She giggles, and I practically choke on my own saliva.

"Big Steven is a horse!" I blurt. "Please tell me he's a horse?"

"What?" she says. "Big Steven isn't a horse, Max."

"He's not?" I swallow.

"No," Poppy says. "He's a mechanical bull—you know that. You were there."

"Well, yeah, course I was," I say. I'm actually sweating. "I was just messing with you."

"You're a bit weird sometimes, you know that, Max?" Poppy laughs a bit too loud, and her hand very unsubtly moves toward my knee. "I do wish we hung out more, though. I think that every single time I see you. We really ought to see *more* of each other . . ."

"I guess," I say. "I'm just busy, I suppose?"

"With Alicia?" she asks. "You know if you ever need some time apart . . ."

I feel my heart begin to beat faster. My whole body is getting hot and flustered. I could never do this to Alicia, but I'd be lying if I said a part of me didn't want to. Poppy's fingers are on my thigh now, and, although I'm not morally on board with any of this, there's nothing I can do to stop it—I'm on a one-way trip to boner town.

"Maybe it's time to try something new?" she says, and I guess she makes a good point. I've gone through life attracted to guys; maybe I should try it with a girl. I mean, life is about experiences, right? Maybe I could just . . .

"No," I say, getting up and moving away from her. "I mean, no thanks," I add, remembering my manners. "I'm flattered, but I'm happy with Alicia," I say, lying through my teeth.

"Oh . . ." She laughs innocently. "Max, I wasn't suggesting we do anything behind her back. I mean, Alicia's my friend . . ."

"Yeah, sure," I say, but she isn't fooling anyone.

"Just text me sometime, okay?" she says, standing up and touching my arm. I see Rachel Kwan shoot me a look from across the room, so I quickly pull away. Thankfully, Alicia has her back to us.

"All right, Max, I get it," Poppy says, withdrawing her hand. "I'm just trying to be friendly."

"I know," I say, "and I appreciate it. Maybe if things were different?"

"Maybe," she says, twisting one of her curls. "Back to your girl-friend, then." She nods in Alicia's direction. "But I'm not finished with you yet, Maxwell . . ."

Poppy winks, flicking my hair as she moves on to talk to somebody else.

My hands are actually shaking. Who knew being a hormonal straight boy could be so difficult? Being gay always left me with so few romantic options, I never actually considered what it would be like to have not one but TWO people into me? I mean, I'm flattered, but how do the straights handle this?

I've always despised those awful guys who cheat on their girl-friends, but I think I was just one more thigh graze away from being one of them. I slip my hand into my pocket to adjust myself and awkwardly wait for a moment for the swelling to go down. The sensation brings back memories of being fourteen and getting called to the front of the class. Always at the worst possible moment.

"Never Have I Ever?" Thomas says as I join Alicia and the others. Usually my go-to drinking game, it's the last one I want to be playing right now. My past in this reality is unknown territory. I don't *know* whether I have ever . . .

"I'll start," Simon Pike says. He and Rachel are sitting together on the couch, their limbs entangled because God forbid they spend even one moment out of touching distance. Rachel is wearing a sleek black turtleneck, coupled with a pleated green skirt that matches the colors in Simon's hideous band shirt. I appreciate the effort, even if Simon hasn't noticed. In fact, I'm probably the only person here who has.

"Never have I ever . . . been caught watching porn," Simon says.

Well, at least I know the answer to that one because it literally happened two days ago. *Off to a fantastic start, Max.* I coyly take a drink.

"Aw, Max!" Alicia laughs as I take a sip. "It can happen to anyone," she says, but evidently not because I'm literally the only one who drinks.

"Never have I ever . . ." Rachel begins, looking around the group, scanning our faces for clues to our deepest, darkest secrets. "Never have I ever . . ." she repeats, "masturbated at school."

I don't know why, but everyone turns to look at me. It's as if the minute anything remotely embarrassing happens, everyone just assumes it must be Max.

"I haven't!" I say defensively. "I mean . . . at least I don't think I have."

And then, to everyone's surprise, Oliver coyly sips his drink. Thankfully, it takes the heat off me.

"Oliver Cheng!" Alicia squeals. "Where was it, Ollie? The back of English class? Mr. Grayson do it for you, does he?"

"Oh my God," he says, blushing. "I'm not giving you details!"

"Spoilsport," she says, and I agree. I'm curious to know where it was. The common room at the end of the day when everyone else had left? The changing-room showers after practice? My gay feelings may be dormant, but that image still lingers in my head for longer than it probably should.

"All right, my turn," Alicia says. "Never have I ever . . . kissed a boy."

Rachel and Alicia sip their drinks. Oliver practically downs his. One gulp for every thirsty Instagram boy no doubt. *"Run me over with a truck . . ."*

"Drink up, then, Max," Thomas says, clinking his mug against mine.

"Huh? I'm straight," I squeak, perhaps a little too defensively. Never have I ever imagined *those* words coming out of my mouth, and yet here we are.

Thomas leers at me. "Weren't so straight when you were sucking my face off in Alicia's back garden," he says.

"What?!"

There's no way Thomas and I have kissed—what the fuck?!

"I forgot about that," Alicia says, laughing. "At my thirteenth birth-day party! Truth or Dare! You frenched him—you must remember!"

"Oh yeah, right," I say, grumpily taking a sip. I can't believe Straight Max made out with a boy before I did. And that boy was Thomas of all people.

"My turn?" Oliver says then. "Never have I ever . . ." He takes a look around the circle, from Rachel, to Simon, to Alicia, and then me.

". . . fallen in love with my best friend."

Everyone except for Oliver drinks. I guess I should probably drink too, so I do.

"That was cute," Alicia says, smiling. Oliver's dimples twitch, and he shrugs. "Aw, don't worry, Ollie. We'll find someone for you yet. Which reminds me: That's the Kedar you're always talking about, right?" She nods to the kitchen where Kedar is now loudly playing Ring of Fire with his teammates.

"Six! Dicks!" I hear them yell, raising their glasses to toast each other.

"I'm not *always* talking about him!" Oliver protests. "I've mentioned him, like, twice. He's a good guy, though. Great athlete too."

"And even greater abs," Alicia adds. "Even Max took a liking to those."

"Oh my God, no I didn't!" I say, embarrassed.

"I'm just teasing! But really, Ollie, you never mentioned how hot he was. Keeping secrets from us now, are we?"

"I guess I never noticed," Oliver replies. "Yeah, he's all right, I suppose."

"Oh, whatever, Ollie! He's gorgeous. Of *course* you noticed."

"I'm starting to think maybe *you* want to date him, Alicia," I say.

"Yeah, maybe you've got some competition there, Maxxie," she says teasingly. "And the rainbow laces, Ollie? What's that about?"

"I suggested it!" he says proudly. "I've been trying to get the captains of the local teams to wear them, to show their support. He's the only one who actually did, though. It's a bit like pulling teeth from a baby."

"Like pulling teeth . . . from a . . . baby?" Alicia squints at him.

"Yeah," he says, a little too confidently.

"Pulling teeth. From a baby?" she repeats, thinking he'll hear the mixed metaphor, but he just nods at her, confused.

"Okay, let's loop back to that one." She takes a very large sip of her drink. "So Kedar isn't gay, then?"

"Oh, I don't know," Oliver says. "I didn't ask."

"You didn't ask! Oh for God's sake, Ollie, you're useless at this. Completely and utterly useless. Here, hold my drink." She pushes a jam jar of murky liquid into his hands. "I'm gonna have to do it for you."

"Oh God, I'll stop her—don't worry," I say, going after her. The truth is, I don't want her to set Oliver up with Kedar. I can't explain why. I just don't. "Alicia, wait!" I call, but she doesn't stop.

"So," she says, walking right into the middle of their game.

"Just in time!" Kedar says with a wicked smile. "You have to take a drink."

"And why's that?" she asks. Kedar holds up the card he just drew.

"Four," he says. "It's just the rules of the game. Six is dicks, and four is . . ."

"A derogatory term for a sex worker?" Alicia says, raising an eyebrow.

"I was gonna say 'girls,' but . . . yeah. I mean, I didn't make up the rules . . ."

"And I should hope not," she teases. "All right, pour me one, then."

She gestures to the near-empty bottle of tequila on the table. Kedar pours her a shot and hands it over. She downs it without flinching.

"Anyway," she continues, all eyes on her now, "are you single . . . or?"

"Oh my God," I say, spluttering on my drink. "Alicia!"

"What?" She laughs. "We're friends of Ollie's. I'm Alicia, and this is my boyfriend, Max."

"Hey." He laughs a little nervously. "I'm Kedar."

"Oh, I know. Ollie's told us *all* about you," she says, grinning. "Obviously I wasn't asking for me—Max is just being jealous—but are you? Single, I mean?"

"No," he says. "I have a boyfriend, sorry."

"Shame," she says. "Sorry, I mean 'shame.' That's great for you obviously. I just thought you'd be a good match for one of my friends, is all."

"Sorry to disappoint," he says. "It's newish, but we're really happy actually. That's sweet of you, though. Who's your friend?"

"He's not out," she says. "Still keeping things discreet."

"I get that," he says. "I was that way too until recently. It's not easy coming out to a town full of straight people."

"Yeah, poor Ollie is like the only gay guy in our class. I guess there aren't many other gay kids at Grove Hill either?"

"Well, I'm bi actually," Kedar says. "But yeah. Just a handful."

"Oh yeah, of course. Sorry. We love all the letters of the LGBT," she says, attempting to pry the foot out of her mouth. *The LGBT.* Oh my God, Alicia.

"I think Oliver wants us to help with something," I say.

A blatant lie, but if I have to stay in this conversation for even a second longer I think I may actually just pass away. *Here lies Max Baker, loving son and totally hetero boyfriend. Died of a cringe overdose. There was nothing that could have been done.*

"Yeah, coming, Oliver!" I say to absolutely no one, grabbing Alicia's arm.

"Nice talking to you!" Alicia says as I practically drag her out of there.

"Oh my God. What are you playing at? That was so awkward!"

"I thought it went quite well actually." She grins at me as we go back to join Oliver. He's talking to Thomas, who is in the middle of a long and convoluted story about a pair of girls he supposedly slept with. Oliver is making a good show of feigning interest, nodding along, but clearly not believing a word of it.

"That's . . . *literally* incredible, mate," Oliver finally says as Thomas finishes telling his story. Thomas has already stopped listening, though, now distracted by the theater girls who've just walked through the front door.

"Hold that thought," he says, dropping out of the conversation.

"That boy is hopeless," Oliver says, squeezing the bridge of his nose.

"Now I know why he wanted to play the lead," I murmur, forgetting myself.

"Huh?" Oliver says. "The lead what?"

"Oh, never mind," I say as Alicia's phone rings and saves me.

"It's just Dad," she says. "Probably checking in to see how the 'small gathering' is going. I told him it was just gonna be five or six friends from school."

There's a huge crash in the kitchen, followed by a very masculine "*Wahaay!*" that echoes through the house.

"I better take this outside," she says, plucking her drink from Oliver and heading for the door. "Tell him about Kedar, Max!"

"What about Kedar?" Oliver looks panicked. "Oh God, what did she say?"

"She came *this close* to making a fool of you," I say, pinching my fingers together. "We found out he's bi, but he has a boyfriend." I pause. "Sorry," I add a little half-heartedly.

"What're you sorry for? You know I'm not actually into him?"

"You're not?" I say, a wave of relief washing over me.

"Nah, he seems nice, but he's just not my type, you know?"

"Alicia seemed to think you were a match made in heaven."

"Alicia thinks I'm a match made in heaven with literally any guy who isn't straight." Oliver shrugs. "She means well—it's not like we queers are spoiled for choice here in Woodside—she just wants me to be happy. I mean, I *am* happy but . . . a bit lonely sometimes, you know? I dunno, it's stupid."

"It's not stupid," I say. "I'm listening. Go on."

"Well, monogamy is what we have forced down our throats, isn't it? From the age of, like, four, we're taught that our whole lives revolve around finding a partner, but when you're gay that doesn't always seem like an option . . ."

"I had no idea you felt that way," I say. Who knew we had this in common?

"I guess I don't like to talk about it," he says, his eyes flicking away from mine. "So anyway, Mr. Fashion—who wins best dressed?"

"I'm not sure," I say, taking a long look around the room. "I hate to say it, but I think it might be Double P. The Regina George look? Sure, it's a little obvious, but she's absolutely nailed it. She's Rachel McAdams reborn."

"Rachel McAdams? Again, Max?" Oliver laughs. Poppy catches my eye then and smiles.

"You don't like her, do you?"

"Rachel McAdams?"

"Poppy," he says, raising an eyebrow. I stop staring.

"What? No," I say. "I mean, she's hot but . . ."

"Max."

"No. I'm not into her," I clarify, just as Alicia starts making her way back over to us with a fresh drink in her hand.

"Dad's already suspicious," she says, and then, before I have time to respond, she trips over her own feet and splashes her drink on both of us.

"Careful!" Oliver says, catching her. "How many of those have you had?"

"Maybe one too many," she says, looking at us with that dewy smile, and for just a moment I understand what Straight Max must have been feeling all along. Even when intoxicated, she's cute.

"Hope you enjoyed your trip," Oliver says with a cheesy smile, wiping some of the alcohol off his shirt. "Send us a postcard next time?" *He is such a dork.*

"Making dad jokes now, are we?" Alicia says, curling her arm around me. "That does remind me, though, Max. I've been researching a few places for us next year. I was thinking maybe the Amalfi Coast?"

"What do you mean?" I ask, and she frowns.

"For our gap year? We've only talked about it, like, a thousand times . . ."

"Oh . . . yeah . . ." I say, but this is all wrong.

The only reason I planned a gap year in the first place was because I didn't know what else to do with my life. It was supposed to be my chance to break away from Woodside, see a little more of the world, maybe even find a guy I could fall head over heels in love with. Gay bars were top of my agenda for that reason. Do they even have those on the Amalfi Coast? Where exactly is that, anyway? Greece? There's a reason I didn't take geography.

Alicia smiles at Oliver. "Have you ever been abroad, Ollie? Any recommendations?"

"I love Hong Kong. We've been a few times to see Dad's family. And Paris. We went to Disneyland for my tenth birthday. I got to meet Mickey Mouse," he says, beaming. "We've been to Scotland too, if that counts?"

"I'm not spending my gap year in Scotland, but Paris! The City of Lights! We should go there, Max. Maybe not Disneyland, but we have to see the Eiffel Tower!"

"What do you mean, 'maybe not Disneyland'?!" Oliver gasps.

"But what about art school?" I say. "That's always been your dream."

"Not this again, Max," she says, rolling her eyes. "I just want to go traveling, see the world with you. See Zimbabwe. America. Trace my heritage. That's way more valuable than some pretentious art school. Besides, if we go to Paris, we can see the Louvre!"

"Are you sure that's what you want?" I say, a little helplessly.

"Of course it's what I want," Alicia replies, her tone turning harsher now. "What's going on, Max? If you don't want us to travel together, why don't you just say so?"

"I don't think he meant that." Oliver tries to interject, but she ignores him.

"It's not that," I say. "I just don't want you to make any stupid decisions on my account."

"So now I'm stupid?" she snaps. "For wanting to travel with my boyfriend? Wow, Max. Why don't you tell me what you really think?"

"I don't think you're stupid! It's just . . . I know you, Alicia. And this isn't what you really want."

"Don't tell me what I want," she growls. "I'm getting another drink."

"Alicia, wait," I say, but she's already pushed away from me and is heading back through the crowd toward the kitchen.

"I don't know what's wrong with her," I say, but Oliver just frowns.

"What's wrong with *her*, Max? You handled that terribly. Am I going to need to give you another gay-best-friend talking-to? Because I'm not sure I have another one in me."

"I should probably go after her . . ."

"You think?" he says, nodding toward the kitchen where I can see she's now joining the soccer boys for another round of shots.

"All right. Thanks, Oliver," I say.

I start for the kitchen, but Thomas intercepts me. He must have already been rejected by the girls he went to hit on.

"Ugh, Max, I hate this," he says, blocking my path. "Like, what am I doing wrong? I'm so tired of being single."

"Thomas," I say, trying to get by him, "now's really not a good time."

"It just sucks," he says. "You and Alicia have it so good. You've no idea what it feels like. You know I've never even been on a date? Like, ever?"

"Is that so?" I say, not even trying to disguise the disinterest in my voice. Forgive me if I don't feel any sympathy for the straight guy who is oh so oppressed. "Look, Thomas, can we talk about this later?"

Thomas just sighs at that. "Yeah, fine. Later. Like always. You never have time to talk anymore."

"Huh?" I say. "What do you mean?"

"We used to be good friends, Max. But then you start dating Alicia, and then Ollie shows up, and now you're spending all your time with him. Like, when was the last time we hung out? Just the two of us? It's as if you don't wanna be friends anymore . . ."

Maybe because you're not a very nice person? I think but manage not to say out loud.

"I'm busy, okay?" I say, just as I see Alicia taking another shot. "And right now I need to talk to Alicia. She's had too much to drink and—"

"Oh, come on, Max—lighten up!" Thomas says, turning around to look into the kitchen. "She's having fun. It's a party—you don't have to be so *gay* about it."

My vision flickers red. "What did you just say?"

"Oh, don't get pissy with me," he says, rolling his eyes. "It's just an expression."

"It's not *just an expression*," I say through gritted teeth. "Oliver is literally standing *right there*. Why don't you go and say that to his face?"

Thomas scowls. "See! You're making it all about *him* again."

"Oh, whatever, Thomas," I say, pushing past him as I try to swallow down my rage. "Just leave me alone, okay?"

He calls after me, but I ignore him. I've tried to give this new Thomas the benefit of the doubt. In this reality, he may not have been the same kid that bullied me, but it's clear he's still a homophobe, and I don't want anything to do with him.

"You're a *machine*," Kedar says in awe to Alicia as I walk into the kitchen, and she downs another shot. "Save some for the rest of us!"

"Don't worry about that," she slurs. "If we run out, I know where Ollie's dad keeps the good stuff. Is your boyfriend coming tonight? I'd really love to meet him."

"Nah," Kedar says. "I wish he could, but he's really busy with school stuff, and he's gotta get ready for Friday. There's this big show and—"

"Alicia?" I interrupt. "Can we talk?"

She looks at me for a moment, anger buried deep in her eyes, but she lets it go and sighs.

"Okay, sure," she says. "He sounds lovely anyway," she adds, turning back to Kedar. "Maybe we could all hang out sometime?"

"I'd like that," he says. "I'll show you some pictures later, yeah?"

"Sounds good," she says with a smile, following me out of the room where it almost instantly disappears from her lips. "God, I wish we could be more like them."

"Like who?" I say as we elbow our way through the overcrowded party.

"Kedar and his boyfriend. The way he lights up when he talks about him. Like, when was the last time you spoke about me like that?" She sighs. "Why is it gay guys always have better relationships?"

"I don't even know how to answer that," I say. It's hard not to be annoyed by such a statement. Is she really implying that we have it easier? "Come on, let's find somewhere quiet."

I lead her up the stairs. Oliver spots us and throws me the hand sign for "*all okay?*" I give him a smile and a nod, but I don't think he's convinced. Honestly, I don't think I'm convincing anyone anymore. Being straight is one thing; holding down a relationship is another.

"This house is gonna get trashed," I say as we climb past a couple of people I don't recognize who are making out at the top of the stairs.

"You can say that again," Alicia mumbles woozily, tripping over her own feet once more. I catch her before she can topple back down the stairs.

"Are you sure you're all right?" I say, trying to steady her.

"I'm fine, Max. Chill," she says, taking my hand and leading me into the bedroom at the end of the landing.

She pushes the door closed behind us, and I instantly recognize the room as Oliver's. I've never set foot in here, but it's so obvious. He has a huge bookcase organized in a rainbow, red books at the top sliding down through the gradient to purple at the bottom. On his desk, there's a picture of him and Laci at a theme park, and two little flags sitting next to it—the *More Color, More Pride* flag with its black and brown stripes on one side, and the trans Pride flag on the other. He has his own ensuite bathroom, which I recognize from some of his pictures on Instagram, and a stack of graphic novels on the bedside table. It's like stepping into his secret little world.

"Okay, so I might have overreacted," Alicia says, before I can speak. "It just seems like you haven't been yourself lately, and sometimes it feels like I'm not enough. Sometimes I think I'll never be enough for you, Max."

"No, Alicia, you're right," I say. "I haven't been myself lately. I'm just going through a lot right now, but it has nothing to do with you, I swear."

"You keep saying that, but you can't keep shutting me out."

"I know," I say. "I don't mean to. I just . . . can't really explain it right now."

"You can tell me anything, Max. You know that, right? Anything."

"I know," I say. "I just need a little more time . . ."

"Okay," she says, and puts her arms around me.

She buries her head in my neck, and I inhale deeply, sighing and releasing everything as I let my body melt into hers. Her hands slide down my lower back, and she pulls me a little closer, squeezes me a little tighter.

"Max?" she says, her voice soft and delicate. "We haven't been close lately. I've missed you. I've missed this."

Her hands grip me even tighter then, and that's when the alarms start to go off in my head. My stylish designer underwear is starting to feel tighter now, and, as much as I try to stop it by thinking about the time I saw my great-aunt Ruth in the bathtub, it's completely hopeless. My body responds to Alicia. These Thunderbirds are go.

"Max," Alicia says again, her breath heavy as she slides her hand past the waistband of my jeans and gives me what I can only describe as sex eyes. She leans in to kiss me, and, for just the briefest moment, I almost let her.

"Wait, stop!" I say, pulling away.

This is totally taking advantage of her. She's drunk, and she thinks I'm straight. We absolutely cannot do this.

"Huh? Why?" she says. "I'm sure Ollie won't mind."

"No, that's not what I meant," I say. "I mean, you're probably right, but . . . I just don't think I'm ready . . . I don't think we're ready for . . . *this*."

Her brow furrows. "I don't understand."

"I just don't think tonight is the night. And in Oliver's room of all places. Like, don't you think this should be special? Don't you think we should wait?"

"For what? It's not like we haven't done it a hundred times, Max."

Suddenly my throat is dry.

"Done it?" I croak. "Like *it*, you mean? You're telling me we've had sex?"

Alicia throws up her hands in frustration. "Yes, Max, we've had sex," she says. "Why are you being weird again? Is this a joke? Because I honestly don't get it."

"So I'm not a virgin . . . We're not . . . virgins?"

"No, we're not virgins, Max! Seriously, *what* are you talking about?"

"I need some air," I say, going for the window. I can feel my whole body growing hot now, and my chest is getting tighter and tighter.

"Are you okay?" she says as I accidentally knock a bunch of Oliver's Dragon Ball figurines off the windowsill. "What's going on, Max?"

"I just need some space," I say, opening the window and taking in deep swallows of the cool outside air. "Just give me some space, okay?"

"Okay?" she says, backing off. She sounds really worried now.

"We shouldn't have done that," I say. "This isn't right, Alicia."

"Done what?" she says, her eyes wide. "You're freaking me out, Max."

"Sex," I say. "We never should have done that."

"Why not? That's what people who love each other do . . ."

"But I don't!" I say without thinking, turning back to face her. "I don't love you, Alicia. Not like that, anyway."

The blood drains from her face; her expression turns cold.

"Oh," she says. She opens her mouth to speak again, but there's nothing.

"I'm sorry," I say, but she goes to the door and slams it shut behind her.

Shit. What have I done . . . ?

"Max?"

Oliver pushes the door open.

I'm sitting on his bed, clutching a pillow, head between my knees, inhaling deeply. I don't know how much time has passed; the world feels like it's spinning out of control.

"Are you okay, Max? Do you wanna tell me what's going on?"

"You wouldn't believe me . . ."

"All right," Oliver says, sitting down on the bed next to me. "I'm not gonna push it, but I'm here if you need me, okay?"

He puts his arm around my shoulders, and for a moment we sit there with nothing but the sound of our breath.

Finally he asks, "Did Goku do something to upset you?"

"Huh?"

He nods to the figurine in pieces on the floor.

"Oh God, I'm sorry," I say.

"Don't worry about it. As long as you're okay?"

"I dunno. How's Alicia? She really doesn't deserve any of this."

"I'm not sure. She stormed down the stairs and into the kitchen."

"Oh God," I say, getting up.

"Why, Max? What's happening?"

"I said some things I shouldn't have," I say, going over to the door. "And she's already had way too much to drink."

"Oh shit, right," Oliver says, following me back down into the party.

The couple at the top of the stairs is still making out, and *I* almost trip over them this time. Things have definitely gotten rowdier, and I can hear the lyrics of a familiar drinking song breaking through the noise.

"We like to drink with Alicia, 'cause Alicia is our mate . . ."

I make my way to the kitchen door and see Thomas and a group of guys banging their hands loudly on every available surface.

"And when we drink with Alicia, she downs her drink in eight . . . seven . . ."

"Stop it!" I say, pushing my way into the room and trying to pull Alicia's drink from her lips. She splutters and almost chokes.

"Whoa, chill, dude!" Thomas says, stepping in.

"Yeah, I'm not your property, Max," Alicia says, batting me away.

"You've had enough." I grab her arm as she tries to finish her drink.

"Back off, dude," Thomas says, stepping in front of me. "Don't grab at her like that. What's gotten into you?"

"Fuck off with the macho bullshit," I say, pushing him, and he stumbles backward. "I told you she'd had enough, and now you're here encouraging her?"

"All right, calm down, Max," Oliver says. "Are you okay, Alicia?"

"I'm fine," she replies, turning to the back door.

"Alicia, wait," I say, but Thomas blocks me again.

"She can make her own decisions, Max. So she's had a few drinks? So what? Stop being such a loser."

"What did you call me?" It's been a long time since I heard him speak those words. "Go on, say it again. I dare you."

"Just chill," he says, but I'm seeing red again, and this time it's more than a flicker. I think back to all the times he tormented me, and something snaps.

"You're such a fucking bully, Thomas," I snarl. "That's all you've ever been."

"What?" he says, confused. "What are you talking about?"

"You know exactly what I'm talking about," I spit. "What is it you used to say? Loser? Reject? Gay boy?"

I shove him again, harder this time.

"What?" he says again. "Max? I would never . . ."

"Back in elementary school!" I shout. "Don't act like you don't remember!"

"Oh . . ." he says, like it's just dawning on him. "That was years ago, Max. I was just messing around. I never meant anything by it—you know that. We're supposed to be friends . . ."

"Friends? With you?" I laugh at that. "Get fucked, Thomas."

I shove him a final time, and he falls back against the fridge.

"Stop it, Max!" Oliver says, stepping in between us just as Thomas takes a swing at me. He takes the full force of Thomas's fist to his face.

"Oh shit, dude, I'm sorry!" Thomas cries.

"It's fine," Oliver says, bent over in pain, clutching at his eye. I go to help him, but he just pushes me back.

"Max, stop. Just go check on Alicia," he says. "I'm okay, really."

"I'm sorry," I say. "I didn't mean for this to happen."

"It's fine. Just go."

Alicia hasn't gotten very far. She's taken her shoes off and barely made it halfway around the block by the time I catch up with her.

"Leave me alone, Max!" she says as I approach. "I don't want to talk to you."

"Then don't," I say. "But at least let me walk you home." She reluctantly lets me put my arm around her as I guide her down the street. She stumbles with every third step. I do my best, but I'm barely strong enough to keep her upright.

"Are you sure you can make it?" I say. "Maybe we should call your dad."

She snorts. "Are you joking? He'll murder you, Max."

"Yeah, well, right now I don't think we have any other options."

Sure, he'll be mad if he finds me with Alicia in this state, but he'd be even madder if he found out she was like this and I did nothing. I take out my phone and find his number. It used to be saved as "Darius" with the sunglasses emoji, but now it's just "Mr. Williams." I sit Alicia down on a wall while the phone rings twice, then three times, and finally he picks up.

"Darius Williams speaking . . ."

"Mr. Williams," I begin, "it's Max."

"What is it?" His voice sounds instantly worried. "Is Alicia okay?"

"She's fine. Everything's okay. She's just had a bit too much to drink . . ."

"Where are you?" he says matter-of-factly, and I give him the address. "I'll be there in five. Just stay put."

Darius looks surprisingly calm as he pulls up next to us. I'm sitting on the wall with Alicia leaning on me, almost asleep.

"Alicia," he calls, stepping quickly out of the car. "Wake up, baby girl." He gently kneels down by the wall she's sitting on. "How much has she had?"

I wince. "A lot. She was doing shots with the soccer team."

"I'm fine, Daddy," Alicia slurs through her drunken haze. "Max is overreacting."

"It's all right," he says, and gently lifts her into his arms like she weighs nothing, placing her in the back seat and pulling the seat belt around her with a click. "Don't worry, sweet girl. We'll get you home," he murmurs in a gentle, reassuring tone, closing the car door.

He turns to me then, and I'm ready for him to rip my head off, but he doesn't.

"How much have *you* had?" he asks. Maybe he's just being a responsible adult, but he sounds genuinely concerned.

"Not much," I say. "Just a couple of drinks. Honestly."

"Well, I'm calling your parents to pick you up."

"No!" I say. "Please don't do that."

"Why not?"

"They're fighting enough as it is," I say. "The last thing they need right now is for me to throw more fuel on the fire. I already told them I'm staying at Oliver's tonight anyway."

Darius considers me for a moment and sighs. "Okay," he says. "But you promise you're all right to get back on your own? You don't need a ride?"

"It's just a couple blocks away."

"Okay, well, I have to take Alicia home." He gets into the car and starts the engine. "And, Max?" he adds. "You did the right thing calling me. At least you were man enough for that."

I don't say anything, just nod, and he drives away, leaving me with nothing but regret.

I sit back down on the wall and try to figure out where everything went so wrong. I should never have come to this party. I should have stuck with the plan, stayed home, stayed *focused*, and tried to find Dean.

"Um . . . Max, right?"

Kedar is standing at the end of the street, his hoodie pulled up over his head, his hands stuffed into his pockets. "I don't know what happened back there. I went to the bathroom for, like, two minutes and came back to find all hell had broken loose."

"Oh yeah," I say. "That's my fault, sorry. Is Oliver okay?"

"He's fine," he says. "He sent me to find you. Said you're crashing at his place tonight?"

"I honestly didn't think I'd still be welcome."

"That bad, huh? I guess he must really like you, then." He gives me a big, reassuring smile. "Come on—he's worried. Let me walk you back."

One Year Ago

"You know, I've been thinking," Alicia says. "Now that Zach's out of the picture, I have all this free time and nothing to do with it."

"Free time?" Dean laughs. "Alicia, you're literally always busy."

"Regardless," she says, "you've got *Legally Blonde* coming up, right?"

"*Legally Black*, you mean."

I laugh. "Mrs. A is never gonna let you call it that, Dean."

"Well, I was thinking maybe I could help out with the set design? Put a little Williams spin on it?"

"You'd do that?" Dean sits up, all eager. "Like, for real? But what about the Monster Ball?"

"I can do both," Alicia says. "Besides, it'll look great on my art-school applications next year, and it'll stop me from thinking about *him*."

"That's a great idea," he says.

"And what about you, Max? Have you decided what you wanna do yet?"

"Not really," I say. "Dad wants me to take a gap year. Says he'll pay for it and everything."

"What?" Alicia says, her eyes bugging out. "You're joking?"

"You're so lucky, Max," Dean says with a sigh. "I'm *beyond* jealous!"

"Same! My parents would never let me take a year off."

"Yeah . . . Well, I dunno. I'm not sure it's actually what I wanna do . . ."

"Oh, shut up!" Dean laughs. "You *don't* want to take an all-expenses-paid year off to explore the world?"

"Yeah, I know, but—"

"Well, you do you, Max," Alicia says. "But I'd think twice about passing that up."

"Yeah?"

"Absolutely!" She wiggles her eyebrows suggestively.

"Think about all the foreign boys you could kiss!"

"I don't think I can wait that long," I groan. "If I don't kiss somebody by the time I leave school, I think I'll actually combust."

"And there's nobody you like? Nobody at all? What about one of the soccer players?"

"Ew, don't be gross. Can you imagine *me* dating one of those brain-dead meatheads?" I say, glancing over toward the field. "But wait . . . who is *that*, please?"

"Huh . . . who?" Alicia says, tracking my gaze to one of the boys in the huddle. I've never seen him before. He's pretty, like *really* pretty. "That must be the new kid. He's in English with Simon and Rachel. Oliver something . . ."

"See you later, Cheng!" the pack of boys choruses as Oliver breaks away from them and starts coming right toward us.

Oliver Cheng. I think my heart actually stops. I'm in love.

"He's perfect," I say. "He's actually perfect . . ."

"What happened to 'brain-dead meatheads,'" Dean teases.

"Oh hush," I say. "That was then; this is now."

"That was all of thirty seconds ago," says Alicia, laughing.

"Anyway, I thought you had a rule about not obsessing over straight guys?"

"Just because he's a soccer player doesn't mean he's straight, Alicia, jeez. Besides, there's one important difference between you and me."

"And what's that?"

"You never pay enough attention to a person's shoes."

"A person's *shoes*?" she exclaims. "What's that got to do with anything?"

Dean grins. "Look. Rainbow laces."

"Oh my God," Alicia gasps. "You mean he's gay?"

"To be confirmed," I say, looking him over for more clues, but it's hard to get a sense of his personality from a soccer uniform.

"Well, there's one way to find out," Dean says. "Let's just go over and say hey."

"What? No! Have you seen how hot he is?"

"All the more reason to talk to him," Dean replies. "Come on! He's the new kid, he's cute, and he's potentially queer—he needs to meet the Woodside gays. We can tell him about the Queer Club."

"Okay, but just . . . not yet, all right? I need to fix my hair, and I need a better outfit. I have to convince him I'm not a total loser . . ."

"Maxine," Dean says warningly. "What have I told you . . ."

"I know, I know," I say. "Just not yet, okay?"

"Fine. But tomorrow, then?"

"Okay," I say, but deep down I know there's no way that's going to happen. Boys like me don't talk to boys like him.

He's a solid ten—an eleven, in fact. I'm barely even a six.

Chapter Thirteen

I wake to the sound of breaking glass, the crashing sound piercing through my hangover. Despite what I told Darius, I guess I drank a little more than I realized, which is exactly why I should *never* play Never Have I Ever. I open my eyes and there's Oliver—sweet, gentle Oliver—dropping bottles into a garbage bag as he attempts to put his house back together again.

"Hey," I say groggily. Oliver turns to face me.

"Hey, sleepyhead. I hope the sofa wasn't too uncomfortable? I thought it'd be easier to let you sleep here than trying to get you upstairs."

I've got a blanket with a colorful dinosaur print thrown over me. Adorable, considering that Oliver is seventeen and doesn't have any siblings.

"Slept like a baby," I say, sitting up and rubbing my eyes.

I'd gotten back just as Oliver was kicking everyone out of the house. The last thing I remember was sitting down on the sofa. I guess I must've passed straight out.

"Wow, this place is really trashed." It's amazing how much mess a few dozen teenagers can make if they really set their minds to it.

"Just a little," Oliver replies. "But what's a party without a little drama?"

He has a serious black eye, the purple bruise really setting in now.

"Does it hurt?" I say. "Your eye, I mean? It's all my fault. I'm sorry."

"It's not too bad actually. Makes me look like a bad boy, don't you think?" He grins widely as he says that, and, with those dimples, Oliver Cheng couldn't be a bad boy if his life depended on it.

"I had a chat with Thomas," he adds.

"Oh God," I say. "Can we just not talk about him right now?"

"Okay," he replies. "I get that it's a sensitive subject."

"Another time," I say. "Anyway, can I help?" I push myself to my feet.

"Please. If you could just gather up the empty glasses?"

"Sure," I say, scanning the dozens of "glasses" that litter the room. "Was somebody really drinking out of this?" I hold up a vase that's half filled with a brownish-yellow liquid I can only hope is cider.

"Things got a little bit wilder than anticipated . . ." He laughs.

"Teenagers and alcohol," I say. "What did you think was going to happen?"

"It never got like this back in London . . ."

"Ah well, there you go," I say. "You're not in Kansas anymore, Oliver. Us country bumpkins know how to throw a party."

"And trash a house," he adds. "My parents are gonna kill me."

"They're not back for a few days, right? We'll make it look good as new."

"And that?" he says, pointing through to the kitchen where I can see one of the windows has an enormous crack running right down the middle.

"Ah . . ." I say. "I don't think I can help with that. What happened?"

"A particularly energetic game of Duck, Duck, Goose . . ."

"And who broke the window?"

"That would be the goose," he says, pointing to himself. At least he can see the funny side. If this were my house, I'd be hyperventilating right about now.

"Want some music?" Oliver asks, taking out his phone and fiddling with it until the soft tones of Frank Ocean begin to fill the house. The perfect soundtrack for a cleanup job.

If it wasn't for the hangover still pounding away behind my eyes, it would actually be quite relaxing pottering around as the two of us try to straighten out the house. Oliver attempts to sing along sometimes, and there's something endearing about the way he confidently belts out the lyrics despite being so terribly off-key.

"Did you hear anything from Alicia?" he asks. "I texted her this morning, but she hasn't replied."

I pick up my phone to check. I'd sent her a few messages last night, but I haven't heard back either.

"She's probably just sleeping off the hangover," I say.

"And is everything all right with you guys?"

"Well . . ." I begin. I instinctively want to do the very British thing of saying everything's fine, but I know he'll see right through that. "Not really actually. It's complicated. I mean, I guess I always thought being in a relationship would be easy. All cute dates and being hashtag couple goals on Instagram."

"We've all been sold the Disney happily-ever-after," Oliver says. "Impossible romance. All those princesses waiting around for true love's kiss? Not real life, though, is it? Relationships take work, not magic."

"You make it sound so hard . . ."

"Ah, see, that's where you misunderstand me," he says with a smile. "Committing to someone? Making the decision to put the work in? That *is* romantic. You've just gotta ask yourself whether you love the person enough to do it."

I don't answer that. I don't even know *how* to answer that. It's hard to be honest about my feelings when I don't even understand them. What does honesty even mean when I'm torn between two realities? There's Straight Max and Gay Max, and they're both telling me such conflicting things, it's hard to distinguish which feelings are mine and which have been borrowed. So everything I say ends up feeling like a half-truth or a lie.

What I do know is true, though, is that Alicia means the world to me. All the memories we've shared and all the incredible times we've spent together. Maybe I haven't been good to her in this world, and maybe it's time to fix that.

"You're right," I finally say. "I've still got some stuff to figure out, but I think you might be onto something . . ."

"Well," he says, "not to roll out the gay-best-friend talking-to again, but don't take too long, okay? It's not fair to keep her waiting."

I sigh. "I know. But it's not like I signed up for any of this."

"You did, though," he says. "That's what a relationship is, Max. Life can't always be a fairy tale."

"But I never asked for a relationship . . ." I start to say, but then immediately realize that's not true. This is *exactly* what I asked for.

I wish I could have what you have, Alicia. I wish I could be one of the normal kids.

Life can't always be a fairy tale, Oliver says, but mine is sure as hell starting to feel like one. Except it's one of those cruel Brothers Grimm versions Mr. Grayson had us read freshman year. They never had a happy ending. Even true love's kiss can't save me now because I'm too straight to accept one from Prince Charming.

Or am I?

I look up at Oliver then, and I know it sounds ludicrous, but is it possible that a kiss from him could actually save me? Nothing else makes sense in this world, and I *had* always fantasized about him being my prince . . .

"I should probably take a shower," he says, sniffing his armpit. Really regal behavior. Prince Charming indeed.

"Actually, Oliver?" I say, stopping him as he heads for the stairs.

"Yeah?" he replies, and there's something about his gentle demeanor that makes me feel I could tell him anything. Like, I could say that the sky isn't blue, and he'd just smile and tell me that's an interesting way to look at it.

"Do you think we could talk a bit more?" I ask, my gaze trailing away. It suddenly feels impossible to look at him. "There's something I need to get off my chest."

"Sure," he says, sitting down on the sofa and gathering the dinosaur blanket around him. He taps the seat next to him. "Talk to Uncle Oliver."

"Well," I say, sitting down and pulling the other end of the blanket around my legs so that the two of us are now cocooned by some very friendly-looking stegosauruses, "it's kind of hard for me to say this out loud. Like, I don't even know where to start . . ."

"Maybe try the beginning?"

"I don't even know where that is anymore," I say with a sigh. "I don't know who I *am* anymore." I pause, waiting for a reaction from him, but he just nods like he's listening. "I mean, I'm still Max," I continue. "I go to Woodside—those things are still true . . ."

"So what's different?"

I think of all the feelings that have been bubbling away over the past few days. Maybe he *will* understand.

"Well"—I struggle with the words—"I'm not exactly . . . straight."

"Okay," Oliver says.

He doesn't seem all that surprised, to be honest. I expected a gasp or something, but he just sits there with that ever-inquisitive look.

"So, like, you've been having some gay thoughts, you mean?"

"Well, no, that's exactly the point. I haven't been having any gay thoughts at all. Not lately anyway." Oliver cocks his head and looks a little confused. "I mean, look," I say, pulling up my search history and holding out my phone to him.

"'*Brazilian babes foot job*,'" Oliver reads aloud, and he sounds more confused than ever. "Are you trying to tell me you have a foot fetish, Max?"

"What?" I say, flipping the phone around. "No! Not that! But look," I continue, scrolling through so he can see it. "It's all girls. All of it."

"So you're *not* gay?"

"Not anymore."

"So you *were* having gay thoughts, but now you're not?"

"Exactly! Three days ago, I was gay, but now I'm completely straight."

Oliver puffs out his breath. "Max . . ." he begins.

"Look, I know this sounds crazy, but I just need you to listen, okay?"

"Sure," he says. "I'm listening, Max. Whatever it is, you can tell me."

"Do you believe in the supernatural?"

"Like ghosts and things? Vampires and aliens and all that?"

"Well, not exactly," I say. "But things that don't make any sense. Things that go against what we know to be true. Things you can't quite explain?"

"Sure. I mean, magic is just science we haven't figured out yet, right?"

"Right!" I say. "So what about a parallel universe? Do you think that's possible? That there could be multiple versions of the same reality all happening at the same time?"

"I guess so, but what does that have to do with—"

"I know it sounds insane, but I think I've slipped into an alternate reality," I say in a rush. "I used to be gay. Like *really* gay. Like Billy Porter at the Met Gala gay."

"Right," Oliver says cautiously. "I'm not sure I understand, but—"

"Everything was fine until I got into a huge fight with my friends," I say, speaking faster and faster now because I know that if I stop I won't be able to start again. "I told them I wished I could be 'normal.' That I wished I could be just like one of the straight boys. And then I woke up the next day—and I was."

"Okay . . ." Oliver blinks. I can tell he's struggling to believe me, but at least he's trying. "And the fight? What was the fight about?"

"Well," I say, looking down at my lap, "it was about . . . you."

"Me?" He sounds shocked.

"In the real world, we weren't friends," I say. "We both went to Woodside, but we barely knew each other. We'd hardly even spoken."

"I find that difficult to believe, Max," he says with a smile. "Alternate realities? Sure. But a world where the two of us aren't besties? That I don't buy for a second."

"But it's true," I say gloomily. "We weren't friends because I liked you so much that I couldn't even bring myself to talk to you. I liked you, Oliver. I *really* liked you."

"Oh," he says. "Like . . . a crush?"

"I guess. And I thought if maybe we could . . ." I break off. This is too hard.

"Go on . . . ?" Oliver prompts, reaching over to take one of my hands in his.

"I thought that now maybe you could be my Prince Charming. That if maybe we could . . . kiss . . . it might break the spell and things would go back to normal?"

"Oh," he says, his hand going still in mine. "I don't know, Max."

"No, forget it. It's stupid," I say quickly, pulling away from him.

"It's not stupid," he says, trying to catch hold of my hand again. "It's just that I've never kissed anyone before, and this isn't exactly how I expected my first kiss to go. I always wanted it to be special, you know?"

"You've really never kissed anyone?" I say, amazed. "But you drank. In Never Have I Ever, I mean."

"It's a game, Max. I lied," he says with a shrug. "And it's not the only thing I lied about either. You're not the only one who has secrets, you know."

"But what about all the boys who leave comments on your Instagram?"

"Oh, you noticed those, huh?" He laughs softly. "Like I said, I always wanted it to be special. Besides, you have a girlfriend. We can't do that to Alicia."

"No, you're right," I say.

"Sorry, Max," he says. "Maybe if things were different . . ."

"It's fine," I say.

I don't know why I suggested it in the first place. This isn't a fairy tale; it's real life, and a kiss from Oliver isn't going to solve anything. "All right, I guess we better get this place cleaned up . . ."

"But what about this alternate reality?" he says.

"Forget about it. It was just a theory, is all. I'll finish in here. You go and take that shower—you stink."

Chapter Fourteen

"I'm worried about Alicia," I say as Oliver and I leave English later that day. Mr. Grayson has told us to read *The Bloody Chamber* as homework, so we make our way to the library to find a couple of copies, even though Woodside library books are guaranteed to be battered within an inch of their life, missing a crucial page, or covered in dubious stains. Sometimes all three.

"Her dad wouldn't let anything happen to her. I'm sure she's just hanging," Oliver replies. Alicia hasn't shown up for school today and still hasn't replied to either of our messages. "Maybe just give her a little time?"

"Yeah, maybe," I say, but I'm not convinced. Everything that happened is my fault. I can't just wait around and hope that it all sorts itself out.

We push through the double doors into the library, where Oliver greets the librarian as if he's one of his closest friends. Imraan is a new graduate in his early twenties. He has sleek black hair, deep brown eyes, and a gentle, welcoming smile. He's always been a little quiet and reserved, and, although he's admittedly somebody I never paid all that much attention to in my old reality, I find it comforting that he's still here in this one, not taken by my Thanos snap.

"What happened to your eye?!" he gasps. "That's quite a shiner, Ollie."

"Long story," Oliver says with a big cheesy grin. "Anything new in?" He peers over at the books on the librarian's desk. He's clearly in his element. I've never seen somebody get quite so excited about a school library.

"They've just arrived. I saved this one for you." Imraan holds up a beautiful pink book with a white fist etched into the front. *How to Survive a Plague*. "It's about the HIV/AIDS epidemic. It's a tough read, but an inspiring one."

"Thanks," Oliver says, taking the book and reading the blurb. "I think I've heard of this actually . . ."

He carries on talking to Imraan, but I've already tuned them out because my eye has caught sight of something else. Another book on Imraan's desk that glimmers and sparkles just beyond my reach.

"What's that?" I interrupt them as I admire the cover, a vintage photograph of a young masculine person dressed in a long, flowing sequined gown. There's a look in their eyes, a glimmer buried there, that suggests they know the world isn't quite ready to accept them yet, but that it will be one day. *The History of Androgynous Fashion* is printed in bold type along the spine. "May I?"

"Be my guest," Imraan says, sliding the book across to me. "I think you may have converted another one here, Ollie."

"I'm as surprised as you are." Oliver grins as I pick up the book. I never really understood the point of a library when we have the entire internet quite literally at our fingertips, but it feels somehow like this book called out to me.

"Can I take it out?" I say, flicking through the pages of people dressed in all manner of elaborate clothing. The photos go back decades, all the way through to modern day. It feels like a glimpse into a world I never even knew existed.

"Of course," Imraan says. "That's literally what they're here for."

"Taking out a book that isn't part of the assignment?" Oliver laughs. "Who are you and what have you done with my best friend?"

"I just like the pictures," I say, tucking the book under my arm.

"Okay," Oliver says. "I'll take this one too." He holds up the book Imraan just gave him. "And we need two copies of *The Bloody Chamber* by Angela Carter."

"Let me guess—Mr. Grayson?" Imraan says, coming out from behind his desk and leading us through the dusty stacks. "He's obsessed with fairy tales, that man. Like, totally obsessed. You've gotta hand it to him, though: he likes pushing boundaries. He got in a lot of trouble for trying to put *Erotic Fairy Tales* on the syllabus back when I was still a student."

"Sounds like my kind of book," I joke. "Does that have pictures as well?"

Imraan chuckles. "Not quite, and we don't have it either. It's very graphic. Cinderella's prince has a foot fetish. The things he does to that glass slipper . . ."

"Max has a foot fetish!" Oliver blurts out. "*Brazilian babes foot—*"

"Oh my God, I do *not* have a foot fetish!"

"Whatever you say, Max. But I've seen his search history," he whispers to Imraan, who laughs as he pulls two copies of *The Bloody Chamber* from a shelf. One has already lost its front cover.

"I'm not judging. Whatever floats your boat and all that," he says, handing us the books. "Sorry they're so battered. I remember reading this, like, ten years ago. We're in desperate need of some new copies, but budgets and all that . . ."

"Thanks, Immy," Oliver says. "We're used to it by now. Besides, a battered book is a well-loved book, right?"

"Right," Imraan says. "Happy reading, boys."

Oliver has soccer practice, so I swing by the common room just to see if Alicia has shown her face. Dean's already missing from my life; the last thing I need is for her to disappear as well. I guess everyone has already gone home, though, because the place is completely deserted. Except for Thomas.

"Max!" he calls, but I turn on my heel and head straight for the door.

"Max, come on, wait," he says, following me. "Just for a minute, please?"

"What do you want?" I growl, coming to a halt. If I could have disappeared anyone, it should have been him. A much better way to spend a wish.

"I just wanted to apologize," he says. "About last night, about everything."

"Leave me alone," I say dismissively, moving toward the door again. "You should be apologizing to Oliver; it's his face you busted. Shouldn't you be at practice anyway?"

"This is more important," Thomas says. "And I already apologized to him. Last night, before I left, I told him everything. He was pretty upset to hear what I used to be like . . . but you were right, Max. I did used to be a bully."

He pauses for a moment as if he's really accepting that for the first time. "What I did was awful, and I should never have dragged you into it. I've always felt guilty, but I guess I thought everyone had forgotten. That we'd all moved on."

"It's not something you easily forget," I say. "That kind of bullying sticks with you. It isn't something that just goes away."

"I know," he says. "And I should have listened to you. I shouldn't have done it. I think I just felt insecure. He was always taking the spotlight; everything always had to be about him. I guess I just wanted to take him down a peg. It was wrong, I know that now, but we were just kids, Max . . ."

"Him?" I say. "Who are you talking about?"

Thomas rubs his hand across his face. "That's the thing that's been really bothering me," he says. "The worst thing. I can't even remember his name. It was ten years ago. I'd almost managed to forget about it until you brought it up last night. Now all that guilt has come rushing back."

And that's when it hits me, and I feel a sinking hollowness as I try to process what he means.

"Dean," I say. "You're talking about Dean."

"Yeah, that's it."

Thomas's crocodile tears come thick and fast then, but I'm not buying it.

"What did you do to him?" I snarl, the hollowness beginning to fill with rage. "Where is he?"

"I don't know," he says. "After he dropped out of school, we never heard from him again."

"People don't just disappear, Thomas!"

He's really sobbing now. It's almost believable.

"I didn't mean to really hurt him. I never thought that everyone else would join in."

"Join in with what?" I say. "What are you talking about?"

"It was me who started the rumor," he says. "That he was gay. It was just supposed to be a joke, but then it got out of control. You remember—gay boy, that's what we all called him. It sounds so stupid now, but—"

"What do you mean, I remember?" I demand.

What I remember is how Dean had stood up to Thomas when he'd used those words against me. How he'd saved me, protected me. Surely I would have done the same for him?

Thomas looks at me in confusion with his red-rimmed eyes. "You were there, Max. You joined in. Everyone did."

For an instant, I can't breathe.

"No," I say finally. "No. I would never do that."

"It was a long time ago," he says, putting a hand on my shoulder. "We were just kids, Max—"

"I don't accept that!" I shove him off me. "You're a liar!"

"Max, wait!" he cries as I go for the door, but I don't even look back.

I break into a run and keep running until I'm out of the school. My heart hammers against my rib cage, but I don't stop until I reach home. I burst through the front door and run upstairs, straight to the photo on my desk, snatching it up and praying that it can't be true.

But it is. And it was right there in front of me the whole time. Our first-grade class photo. I've looked at it pretty much every day for my entire life—Dean and me front and center, pulling the focus away from everyone else. But in this photo, it's not us two at all. It's me and Thomas grinning into the camera, arms wrapped around each other like we're the best friends in the world. And there, in the back where you can barely see him, is Dean.

Except it isn't the same Dean I knew. He seems smaller somehow, in plain clothes, his trademark grin wiped from his face. He's the only person in the photo who isn't smiling, and, as I stare at it, it's almost as if it comes to life. I can feel his anguish because I know exactly what he's been through and what that's like. I can hear the kids tormenting him, and what's worse is that I can hear myself joining in with them too.

"Hey, Mr. B," Oliver's voice says from downstairs. "Is Max here?"

"Yeah, he is, but he's not feeling so great," Dad replies. "Probably best to let him rest, but I'll tell him you stopped by?"

"Please," he says. "Tell him we're worried about him."

"I will," Dad says. "And, Ollie?"

"Yeah, Mr. B?"

"Thanks for always being there for him."

"What are friends for?" Oliver says.

I hear the front door click shut, and Dad's footsteps slowly climb the stairs. Mum's been out all afternoon, so I just made up a lie about feeling sick again when Dad came home from work early to find me holed up in my room.

My phone pings. Oliver again. He's sent about a thousand texts this afternoon, but I haven't looked at any of them. I don't deserve his friendship, or anyone's for that matter. Thomas tried to message too, but I blocked him. He can absolutely go fuck himself.

I put my phone on silent and flip it over, burying my head in the pillow and letting the guilt eat away at me. I deserve it: Dean is out there somewhere, his life ruined, all because of me and my own stupid selfishness. I imagine him in some terrible school, in some awful town, being bullied by people who don't accept him for who he is. How could I be a part of that? I should have been there for him, just like he was there for me.

"Max?" Dad says, opening my door. "Ollie was just looking for you. I told him you're sick, but I don't think you are, are you?"

"Huh?" I say, refusing to look up and face him.

"You might be able to fool your mother," he says, "but it's not going to work on me." He comes to sit on the end of my bed. "I know there's something bothering you, something you're not telling us . . ."

"It's nothing," I say. "Please just leave me alone, Dad."

"Well then, I wouldn't be doing my job now, would I?" he says gently. "It's okay to ask for help sometimes, Max. Whatever it is you're going through, you can tell me. You can tell Mum. We'll always be here for you."

"But how can I, Dad?" I turn to face him now. "I mean, seriously? How am I supposed to do that when you're always fighting? I just don't get it. If you're not happy, then why don't you just . . ."

"Yeah?" he says, but I can't bring myself to finish that sentence. I don't think any kid should ever have to finish that sentence.

"I just want us all to be happy again. I want you *both* to be happy."

"Like when you were younger?" he says, but that's not what I meant at all. I meant like in the other world. They were happier there. We all were.

There's silence for a few moments as Dad thinks about that. I can tell he doesn't know what else to say.

"Do you remember the time you lost your balloon?"

"Huh?" I say. "What's that got to do with it?"

"We were at the fairground. You can't have been any older than four or five. You let go of your balloon, and it went soaring off into the atmosphere. You wanted me to get a ladder to go up into the sky and get it." He gives a soft, nostalgic laugh. "You cried and cried, and I would have done anything to get you that balloon back."

"But you couldn't."

"I couldn't," he repeats. "I can't always fix things for you, Max, but no matter what happens I will always be here for you. Your mum too. No matter what."

"I know. And I appreciate it. But I think I just want to be alone right now."

"Okay, champ," he says, touching my hair and heading for the door. "I'll be downstairs if you need me."

Two Years Ago

"He's *sooo* gorgeous."

Alicia is eyeing up Zach Taylor, who's sitting with some of the other juniors at the end of the boardwalk. They're the year above us, and impossibly attractive. It's like all the hottest guys in school banded together to form a Hot Guys Club and now just sit around all day being hot. It's infuriating how much I'm into them. I'm pretty sure they're all straight, though, so I make a point of not paying them any attention. I've seen enough Netflix shows to know what devastation comes from falling for a straight guy. I'm not about to put myself through *that*.

"Perhaps you've finally found your muse?" Dean teases, tapping the blank page in Alicia's sketchbook.

We're in Woodside Park, sitting on a grassy bank by the side of the lake, sweltering. It's one of those summer days so warm that when the wind blows it feels like somebody is blasting a hairdryer in your face.

"Maybe you could paint him *like one of your French girls*? Or perhaps carve him out of marble?"

"It's like he's *already* been carved out of marble." She's practically drooling. "You know he's captain of the soccer team? What more could a girl want?"

"Decency? Kindness?" I check them off on my fingers. "The ability to count to ten?"

"He *can* count to ten," she says, rolling her eyes.

"And that's the benchmark, is it?" says Dean, laughing.

"Oh, whatever," she says. "You can't pretend the two of you aren't into him. Don't think I haven't caught you staring."

"The difference is we know it's *never* gonna happen," I retort. "So we're not gonna waste our time on him."

"Wiser words never spoken!" Dean says. "Proud of you, Maxine."

I grin. Best friend or not, it's still nice to hear him say it.

Zach stands, and we all watch as he takes a running jump from the boardwalk and backflips into the lake. He disappears beneath the water for a moment before reappearing with his swim shorts in his hand. I hear myself gulp.

"Suddenly I need to be in that water," Alicia says, and, despite our previous objections, Dean and I both mutter, "Me too."

"Hey!" Shanna calls, coming down the grassy bank toward us, breaking our deeply hormonal trance. "I didn't know you guys were coming?"

"Every kid in Woodside's here," Dean says dryly. "Gabi not with you?"

"She's gone to get into her swimsuit," Shanna says, nodding toward the changing hut. "She's never worn one in public before, so be cool about it, yeah?"

"As if we wouldn't!" Dean says, putting on an exaggerated expression of offense.

"I know you wouldn't, but just . . . Max, I'm looking at you."

"Me?!" I say indignantly. "Why me?"

"I take full responsibility for him," Alicia interjects firmly. "He won't say anything stupid on my watch. Promise."

"Oh my God." I roll my eyes. "Since when was I such a liability?"

Dean laughs. "Since literally always. I can't believe this is news to you."

"All right, well, I'm gonna go check on her," Shanna says. "Do you mind if we sit with you guys?"

"It can be the unofficial Queer Club field trip," Dean replies with his easy smile.

"Perfect," Shanna says.

She heads off down to the changing hut, crossing paths with Poppy Palmer, who has just changed into a *tiny* red swimsuit that conjures up images of *Baywatch*.

"There goes trouble," Alicia says, watching Double P as she makes her way over to flirt with some of the boys from Grove Hill.

"Ugh," Dean says. "I can't stand those kids. I don't get what she sees in them. They're all so entitled and up themselves. I mean, look at those ridiculously tiny designer Speedos. They're barely holding them in . . ."

"I dunno, Dean, it kinda sounds like you're into them . . ."

"Oh, as if," he shoots back, but he's *definitely* staring at one of the bigger guys.

"They can't be all bad," Alicia says. "Not all rich kids are assholes."

"I dunno," Dean says. "I heard they have a massage room at Grove Hill for when the students are feeling stressed. Talk about privileged."

"That is absolutely not true," she says with a snort. "There's no way that's true."

"Whatever," says Dean. "I can't imagine anything worse than going there. I'd rather rewatch the film adaptation of *Cats*."

"How did they cast Judi Dench, Idris Elba, *and* Ian McKellen," I say, "and *still* make it bad?"

"I never actually saw it," Alicia says.

"Consider yourself lucky!" says Dean, and that's when Gabi and Shanna emerge from the changing hut. They're in matching polka-dot swimsuits now, and it's actually adorable, Gabi in pink and Shanna in blue.

"Those two should be a couple," Alicia says. We were all thinking it.

"You're so right," says Dean. "I really wish they were." And, as if by magic, we watch Gabi reach out and take Shanna by the hand.

Alicia turns to us, jaw dropping. "Did you actually just wish that into existence?"

"One of my many talents," Dean says, lying back on the grass, satisfied. "You know," he continues, "I've been thinking about Gabi's name change. Mrs. A made that so much easier for her than it might have been. I've been thinking about maybe doing it too . . ."

Alicia shoots me a surprised look. "Like, you think you might be trans?"

"No, no," Dean says. "I'm definitely cis. It's just . . . I've been carrying around a white man's name for all these years now. But it's Mum who raised me, not *him*. Dean Kellar? I think I'd rather be Jackson."

"Jackson Kellar?" I say.

"*Dean Jackson*, you absolute clown," Alicia says to me. "He's going to take his mum's name."

"*Ohhhh*," I say. Then, "Oh! That's amazing!"

"Yeah, she's the one who raised me. Why should I go by Dad's name?"

"So, Dean Jackson, then?"

"Dean Jackson." He smiles. "Has more of a *theatrical* ring to it, don't you think?"

"I love it," says Alicia.

Our special moment is interrupted then by the rest of the Hot Boys Club cheering loudly. We look over to see them all tearing off their swimsuits and jumping into the lake.

"You know," Alicia says, picking up her Polaroid camera, "I think I might have finally found my inspiration after all."

"I don't think you can photograph them without their consent . . ."

"You're an idiot, Max," she replies, flipping the camera around selfie-style and snapping a photo of the three of us.

Chapter Fifteen

The beeping alarm clock drags me out of my dream and back into my waking nightmare.

"Not today, Satan! Not today!" I moan, grabbing the alarm clock from the bedside table and hurling it against the wall. The case shatters, but the clock somehow keeps beeping.

"ARGHHHHHHHH!" I yell, getting up to yank the plug from the wall. Then I rip the posters down from the walls. Fuck these busty *Baywatch* babes—and fuck Zac Efron as well. Being straight is officially the worst thing that can happen to a person. I can't believe I used to be jealous of *this*.

I'm no longer going to tolerate this recurring simulation of hell. If I have to be stuck here, I'm gonna do it *my* way. I'm still me, I'm still Max, and I'm still going to be *queer*, even if it means I have to do that while being *straight*.

I pull open my wardrobe and flick through my clothes until I find a faded yellow T-shirt that's ever so slightly too small. Rummaging through my desk drawer, I grab a pair of scissors, a needle, and a spool of white thread. I roughly cut the T-shirt across the middle, fold the jagged edges under, and stitch it into a very high crop. I pull it over my body. It's tight on my chest and arms, making me look more ripped than I am, and just loose enough around my middle to expose what pass for my abs. It's messy, and the yellow clashes a little with my striking blue nails, but otherwise it works.

I pull on a pair of ripped denim jeans and a pair of bright yellow high-tops and face myself in the mirror. The crop top, the nail polish, the jeans that show off my ass. It's my own small act of queer rebellion. All that's really missing is a rainbow bracelet, and then I might actually feel like myself again.

Dressing like this requires an empowering soundtrack, though. You can't just step out of the house with your tail between your legs; you have to own the space. Dominate it. Show the world you're proud of who you are and that you aren't going to back down for anyone. Dean didn't creep into that auditorium in full drag; he kicked open those double doors and made the audience his bitch.

I find a pair of oversized white headphones and pull them on, drowning out the outside world with "Dangerous Woman" by Miss Grande, my go-to song for empowerment. Nobody can fuck with you when Ariana's blasting in your ears. I rush down the stairs and out of the house, settling into my stride as I head to school. A few people do a double take as they see me. A boy in a crop top was never exactly run-of-the-mill for Woodside, and in a world where they haven't had seventeen years of Dean Jackson? It's completely unheard of.

I try to channel Dean's energy as I step into school but, try as I might to keep my head raised high, the sea of judgmental students threatens to overwhelm me. I turn Ariana up louder to drown them out, but the looks on their faces say it all. The same people who'd once complimented Gay Max on his extravagantly camp outfits are now silently staring with horror.

"What on earth is he wearing?" I lip-read one of the girls from the junior class. Several of the soccer boys are openly laughing. Others turn away, like they're embarrassed on my behalf.

My stride begins to falter, my tail drops between my legs, and my once proud power walk shrinks to a timid scurry.

And, just when I think things can't get any worse, I run straight into Mr. Johnson. Literally.

"Slow down, Baker!" He's carrying a bag full of basketballs that almost gets away from him. "And what's this in aid of?" he says, looking me up and down. "Comic relief?"

"What do you mean?" I say, trying to hold it together. That's the thing about people like Mr. Johnson: you can't let them see your weakness.

"This . . . clown getup," he says. "Is it for charity or something?"

"No," I reply, gritting my teeth. "I just thought I'd try something new."

"And you're aware we have a dress code, right? Where's the rest of your clothes? This is totally inappropriate."

"But the girls are allowed to wear crop tops and—"

"And are you a girl, Baker? Are you a transgender?"

"A transgender . . ." I bite back some words I'll regret. "No, but—"

"Then go home and change," he says. "And take off that nail polish while you're at it. This is a place of learning, not one of your Ron Paul's *Drag Shows.*"

"It's *Drag RACE*," I say. "And Ron Paul is a right-wing politician."

Mr. Johnson looks bamboozled. "He's a drag queen *and* a right-wing politician . . . ?"

"They're two different people!" I exclaim. "And I'm not changing!"

He looks at me like he's going to explode, but that's when Mrs. A appears behind him. Thank God for that. Here comes the queer cavalry.

"What's going on?" she asks, trying to disguise her puzzlement as she looks me up and down. This *must* be a look if even Mrs. A is shocked by it.

"Apparently I'm violating the dress code," I say bitterly, looking Mr. Johnson dead in the eye as I do. "But I can wear whatever I want. Tell him."

"Look," he says, "I turned a blind eye to Cheng wearing his rainbow laces, but this is a step too far."

"A blind eye?!" I shout. "If Oliver heard you say that—"

"All right, listen!" Mrs. A says. "We're not getting into an argument over this. If you have a problem with the dress code, Max, you can come and see me, and we'll discuss it. But right now Mr. Johnson is correct. If we start bending the rules for one person, we have to bend them for everyone."

"What?" I say, disbelieving. "So you're taking *his* side?"

"I'm not taking anyone's side, Max. But we have to go through the appropriate channels. That's how this works. That's how change happens."

"But this is blatant homophobia!"

Some of the students in the corridor have stopped to listen now. Good—I want an audience for this.

"Max . . ." she says, clearly trying to stay calm. "You can't just throw around words like *homophobia* simply because you don't get your own way."

"He's not even gay," Mr. Johnson says with a smirk that makes me want to lunge at him. "Everyone knows he's dating the Williams girl."

"So what?!" I say. "Gay, straight, whatever. Everyone should be able to dress how they want. This isn't the 1950s, for Christ's sake."

"And I agree with you," Mrs. A says, still with that infuriating calm. "But now isn't the time to argue this. Come and see me on Monday, and we can talk some more, okay?"

"Nah, fuck that," I snap. "You're supposed to be on our side! I can't believe you're siding with this bigot!"

"Excuse me?!" Mr. Johnson booms. "Who do you think you're talking to?"

"Go fuck yourself," I snarl with all the venom I can muster, turning back in the opposite direction.

"Max!" Mrs. A yells, but it only makes me walk faster. "Max, come back!"

I think I hear Mr. Johnson yelling something about me being suspended, but I really don't care anymore. Go ahead, suspend me. As if being barred from school will make any difference in this hell. I turn the corner and keep moving, pushing my way through the corridors until they're both out of earshot.

I turn another corner, and another, and find myself outside the library. I don't know what I'm doing; it's like I came here on autopilot. The place is empty; it's too early for Imraan to be at his desk. It's just me, alone, with the dusty old books. I take a deep breath and try to swallow my anger, but in that moment it's like all my emotions come at once. Everything I've been trying to bottle up, all of it comes pouring out of me. Tears fill my eyes, and, as I gasp for breath, I let them spill down my cheeks.

"Max?"

The voice is gentle, and I look across the stacks to see Oliver peering out at me. "What's wrong?"

I open my mouth to speak, but nothing comes.

"It's all right," he says, setting some books down on a nearby shelf so he can wrap his arms around me.

"I don't know what to do," I say. "I just don't know what to do."

"Don't worry," he says. "We'll figure it out, yeah?" He squeezes me a little tighter, and I let my hands find him to hug him back.

"I can't do it," I say, my tears staining his T-shirt. "I can't pretend anymore."

"It's all right, Max," Oliver says. "Just breathe." And, as I feel his chest slowly rising and falling, I try to match my breath to his.

"There has to be a way out of this, Oliver," I say, pulling away so I can look at him. His eyes are deep and understanding, his hands still firmly gripping me, steadying me, and stopping me from coming completely undone. "I just need to reverse the spell, find a way to undo it. There has to be a way . . . there just has to—"

"Max," Oliver says softly. "Just stop, okay? It's all right." And, for the briefest moment, the whole world comes to a standstill as he leans in and gently kisses me.

The lights in the library seem to dim and flicker, like we're in the raging eye of a storm. I close my eyes and inhale as I feel his lips against mine. This is the moment I've waited for, longed for, the moment that will set the world right. But . . . it doesn't. There's no magic, no fire; it's just his mouth awkwardly pushed up against mine.

"So?" he says, leaning back and looking at me hesitantly. "Did it work?"

Once again, I don't think, just speak.

"I don't feel anything," I say. "I don't feel anything at all."

"Oh," he says, his gaze flicking down to the floor, his hands releasing me and dropping down to his sides. "I just thought that maybe . . ." His voice cracks as he stammers over the words.

"Wait," I say, and take his hand in mine. He looks up hopefully, and I stare deep into his eyes, willing that spark I once felt to reappear, to reignite those feelings I had for him. But though I know he's the boy I used to dream about, and he's standing right in front of me, no matter how hard I try to find him, it's like he's just not there.

"Nothing?"

"Nothing." I let go of his hand and shake my head.

"Okay," he says, and he sounds genuinely sad. "I just thought that maybe this was what you needed to accept it . . ."

"Huh?"

Oliver shakes his head. "All this stuff about alternate dimensions . . . I thought that was just your way of dealing with . . . feeling something."

"Dealing with it? No, Oliver, it's true, all of it! I thought you understood . . ."

"I thought I understood you too," he says ruefully. "I knew you were having a hard time, but I thought you . . . I thought we . . ."

And that's when I finally see something buried in his eyes. Not the spark I'd hoped for, but the slowly fading hope of a boy with a broken heart.

Oh God. What have I done?

"Wait, maybe we just didn't do it right?" I blurt and lean in to try to kiss him again.

"Max?!" another voice gasps, and I turn to see Alicia in the doorway. "What are you doing?" she says, and that same look in Oliver's eyes is now mirrored in hers.

"It's not what it looks like!" I cry, but she's already gone. "Alicia!"

I run out into the corridor, trying to catch hold of her arm.

"Don't touch me," she says furiously, shrugging me off as she keeps moving.

"Alicia, please," I say. "It isn't what you—"

"Just stop, Max. Do you really think I'm that stupid?" she says, whirling on me. "I heard you had a huge argument with Mr. Johnson so I came to check on you because I was worried, but instead I find you trying to make out with my best friend."

"I know it looks bad," I say, "but you have to listen to me . . ."

"I don't have to do anything, Max!" she screams, and then falls silent as the tears start to come. "I just don't know why you felt you had to lie to me. I would have listened, Max. I would have understood. If you're gay, bisexual, whatever this is, it's fine. I just wish you'd told me."

"But I'm . . . not," I say helplessly. "Well, not really . . ."

"Don't lie to me, Max!" she says. "It's so obvious. First the nail polish, then the clothes, and now Ollie. I should have seen it coming— the two of you are inseparable. It's like you want to spend every waking moment together."

"But I'm not attracted to him! I was once, but I'm not anymore."

"Oh, save it, Max!" she snaps. "You're obviously in love with him."

"But I'm *not*," I say. "I'm telling you the truth."

"Whatever, Max," she says. "Just leave me alone, okay?"

"Alicia, plea—"

"Leave me alone!" she screams with such rage that it leaves me frozen to the spot.

I watch her disappear down the corridor, and I want to go after her, but I don't. There's no point. We're over. There's no coming back from this.

Chapter Sixteen

Oliver's gone. I hoped I'd find him waiting in the library when I got back, ready to comfort me again with that big idiotic grin. But the stacks are empty, and there's just Imraan at his desk, sorting through a box of books.

"Where's Oliver?" I ask, trying to disguise the shakiness in my voice. Imraan shrugs. "He ran out just as I arrived," he says. "He left those behind," he adds, nodding toward a stack of books on his desk.

I pick up the books and flick through them. *The History of Androgynous Fashion. Costumes Through the Ages. Fashion that Changed the World.* I don't think Oliver was checking these books out for himself. I think he was picking them up for me. And this is how I've repaid him. By shattering his heart.

"You make a cute couple, you know?" Imraan says.

"Oh, we're not together." It feels like salt in a fresh wound.

"Oh sorry," he says. "I shouldn't have assumed."

"It's fine. I can see where you might have gotten that impression," I reply, gesturing to my outfit. Wearing it doesn't bring me joy now. It just feels like I'm playing pretend.

"Well, it's just nice to see that Woodside has become so accepting," he says. "It wasn't always that way, you know? I wasn't out when I was a student here. Even Mrs. A wasn't out to the students back then."

"Really?" I say.

It's hard to imagine a time when Mrs. A wasn't out and proud. I glance over to the collection of LGBT+ books on one of the display shelves. I've never noticed them before, but then I'm hardly a regular in the school library. "This was you then?"

Imraan nods. "My little contribution to the cause. Maybe they'll find their way into the hands of the right kid and help a little, but even if not, at least they make the library a bit more colorful." He points to the pile of books Oliver picked out. "Do you want me to put those back for you?"

"I think I'll hold on to them actually," I say, opening one of the books. It's filled with extravagant outfits and it's like each photograph speaks to me.

I'm touched that Oliver went out of his way to pick these out for me. It feels like he knows me better than I know myself. He deserves so much more than this. So does Alicia. And Dean. It seems all of Woodside would be a lot happier without me.

I riffle through the pages until I land on a picture of a handsome Black dancer dressed in a skin-tone sequined bodysuit. I think of Dean and how much he'd love to wear something like this, to take to the stage in something so elegant. I don't know where he is right now, but, if there's one thing I'm sure of, it's that he's still performing. There could be a million and one different realities, and Dean would be onstage in all of them. Nothing could stamp out that spark, certainly not Thomas Mulbridge.

"Hey, guys," I hear somebody say and turn to see a person I don't immediately recognize. It isn't until Imraan uses her deadname that I realize it's Gabi. He doesn't say it with malice, of course—it's Imraan after all—but just hearing it said out loud makes me wince.

"Hey . . . *friend*," I say.

I refuse to use her deadname, but it's clear Gabi's not out in this world, so I can't use her real name either. Her hair is cropped short, and she's wearing ripped pale blue jeans and a giant white hoodie that's at least three sizes too big. It's shocking to see her like this, but, after thinking I'd disappeared her, it's really good just to lay eyes on her at all. As I look closer, though, I see that her sense of style may be diluted, but there's still a distinct femininity there. Subtle enough for the average person not to notice, but androgynous in its own way. It's simple, but the more I look at her the more I realize its brilliance.

"I just came to return these," Gabi says, unzipping her backpack and passing a stack of graphic novels to Imraan. The ones on the top aren't anything to raise an eyebrow, but I notice a copy of *My Trans Teen Misadventure* buried in the middle. I wonder if she even read the others at all, or if they were just part of her clever camouflage. I remember those days too well.

I notice the pins on her backpack then. They're mostly just decorative—a Pac-Man and a Totoro and a whole collection of Pokémon—but there are political ones too. One that says PRO-CHOICE, another declaring her a PROUD ALLY, and even one that says BLACK TRANS LIVES MATTER. Gabi may not be out in this world, but it doesn't stop her from being vocal about what she believes in. It wouldn't surprise me if she was quietly out to some of her closest friends.

"Checking out anything new?" Imraan asks, and I see her eyes flash briefly toward the Pride display before she zips her backpack shut and shakes her head. I wish there was a way to tell her that I love her for who she is, but I don't know how to do that until she decides she's ready to come out to us.

"What's that?" I say, noticing a shimmering rose-gold bracelet as it slips out from underneath the sleeve of her hoodie.

"It's nothing," she says, instinctively pulling her cuff down to cover it.

"It's really pretty," I quickly add. "It suits you."

"Agreed," Imraan says.

"Oh," Gabi replies, smiling hesitantly. "Well . . . thanks."

"Where'd you get it from?"

"I borrowed it," she says, pulling her sleeve back so we can see it properly. "From my mum actually. And when I say 'borrowed' . . ."

"Took it without permission?" Imraan says, laughing.

"Maybe, yeah." She smiles a little more confidently now. "Thanks, guys."

"Don't mention it," I say, and she looks us up and down for a moment as if assessing us before giving us an appreciative nod.

"Well, see ya, then," she says, raising her hand with a little wave and heading back the way she came.

She still seems pretty confident in who she is, just a bit shy, and that makes me wonder why she never came out in this world. Then I think of Dean and the Queer Club, and all the queer people she was surrounded by there. Perhaps that gave her the courage to come out, and her doing so inspired Dean to change his name in turn. It's not so much that she needed him or he needed her—they both needed to find each other.

And that's when the pieces finally click into place. If Gabi never changed her name in this reality, then Dean wouldn't have either! I pull out my phone, but there's no signal down here.

"Imraan!" I say excitedly. "Is there a computer I can use?"

"Yeah, there's one in the back," he says, nodding to a machine that looks like it's literally from the nineties.

I rush over and search again for theater productions, this time starring Dean Kellar.

Bingo! A high-school production of *Mean Girls* with Dean Kellar playing Regina George in drag. There's no picture, but it *has* to be him. It's quite literally got his name written all over it. I scan the page for the venue.

GROVE HILL PRIVATE SCHOOL. WOODSIDE.

He's been right here this whole time. My heart is racing as I click through for more details. I know where the show is, but when is it? Have I already missed it? Finally, on the booking page, I find the date— October 27 at 6 p.m.

The performance is tonight.

Grove Hill is miles away from Woodside Academy, and as I make the long journey that evening, I realize that must be why Marcy moved away from Brimsby Road. She'd do anything for her son, even if that meant leaving behind the home she'd always known and loved. Dean had always made it clear how much he hated the idea of Grove Hill, though, so I can only imagine the torment he must have been put through to make him decide to go there. The torment I helped put him through.

Believing I'd somehow wished Dean out of existence was easier than facing this reality, but at least now I can try to fix it. I'd spent the best part of three hours earlier drafting apology messages to Oliver and Alicia, but everything just came up short. I've never been good with words; it was always Dean who helped me to express myself.

Straight Expectations

The show was completely sold out online, so I've deliberately shown up late, hoping I can sneak in once everyone else has taken their seats. Grove Hill is said to have tighter security than Downing Street, but their impenetrable cordon in fact turns out to be a couple of bored juniors by the front gate. Two blond, privileged muscle boys who look like they've been lifted straight from the sort of video Gay Max would have been watching under the duvet after everyone else had gone to bed. You just know they're called Garrett and Chad. They're dressed in their pristine Grove Hill uniforms—burgundy blazers with garish yellow stitching. For a school with a lot of money, they sure have very little taste.

"I heard she hooked up with Seb in the bike sheds," Garrett says as I approach.

I knew I'd stand out in my crop top, so I went home and changed into something a little more preppy—a tight blue polo with chinos and boat shoes. I look like a rich kid with absolutely no style. I'll blend in just fine.

"Yah, right! Sebastian's a total virgin," Chad says scornfully, then straightens up as he sees me. "Good evening," he says. "Have you got your ticket?"

"Yeah, it's here somewhere," I say, patting my pockets. "I'm running so late. The show hasn't started yet, has it?"

"It started half an hour ago," Garrett says, checking his tacky Rolex.

"I think I forgot my ticket," I say. "Oh God, Kayleigh is going to kill me."

"You know Kayleigh?" Chad asks. "Kayleigh Adams? In the chorus?"

Of *course* there's a Kayleigh. There always going to be a Kayleigh.

"Wait, are *you* the boyfriend she keeps talking about?" Garrett says.

"Oh, uh, yeah, that's me."

First Alicia, now Kayleigh. Why the hell not?

"Oh my God, she told us about what happened on her dad's yacht! We were DYING. What if he'd walked in on you?" Chad brays. "Honestly, dude, serious bro points for that one. Respect."

"Thanks," I say. I'm now one ridiculous anecdote away from completely exposing myself as a fraud. "Anyway, I better get inside. The last time I was late for one of her shows she was moody with me for weeks . . ."

"Girls, right?" Garrett says, laughing.

"Go ahead," Chad adds, stepping aside to let me past. And, with a dash of good old-fashioned misogyny, I'm inside. Like taking candy from a pair of incredibly posh babies.

Tall, perfectly manicured hedges hide the school from the outside world, but, once you're through the gates, even I have to admit it's something quite special. The main building is almost entirely made of glass, every corridor has floor-to-ceiling windows, and—unlike the ones at Woodside—none of them are broken. Spotlights dot the pristine flower beds, and an elaborate sprinkler system makes a gentle spritzing sound as it irrigates the lush gardens. Seems unnecessary when it rains here six times a week, but that's rich people for you. The whole place looks more like one of those edgy modern art museums than a place to educate kids.

Inside, more Garretts and Chads direct me to the auditorium. I can hear the music blasting before I even open the doors, and, when I quietly slip inside, I'm blown away by how fancy and high-tech it all is. You could fit Woodside's studio theater in here four times over. Hundreds of cascading seats curve around the enormous stage beneath a huge lighting rig. I always thought we had a pretty decent setup at Woodside but seeing this makes me realize how much we're really missing.

The set looks like something from a West End show. The whole stage is lit in soft pink, with rose-gold lockers on either side, and a huge banner that reads: WELCOME TO NORTH SHORE HIGH.

I recognize the song they're performing instantly—"Where Do You Belong?"—and realize we're just a couple minutes away from Regina George's big entrance. There aren't any free seats, so I stand in the shadows by the doors, my heart pounding as I wait for my best friend to appear.

When we were younger, Dean and I had made up our own choreography for the entire show, lip-syncing away in our bedrooms. I'd always been Cady, and Dean had always been Regina—insisted on it in fact—and, if nothing else, I'm glad he at least now gets to live out that fantasy on a real stage.

The girl playing Cady belts through the end of the song. Her performance is impeccable, pitch-perfect on every note, with a voice to bring the house down. I will grant she may have a better vibrato than I do. She's so good I almost don't hear the doors quietly open beside me. I turn to look, and my heart actually stops because there he is. My best friend. Dean.

I want to grab him and hug him, let him know how much I've missed him, tell him how sorry I am for ruining his life in this world and for the stupid things I said to him in mine. But I can't spoil this moment and take his grand entrance away from him.

He looks *incredible.* He's in full drag, one of the best looks I've ever seen him create, his whole body adorned with pink sequins, face painted with a striking cut crease. He has a Burn Book in one hand and a stack of singed pages in the other. He glances in my direction, and I'm filled with terror that he'll recognize me as one of the kids who used to bully him. We make eye contact for a moment, but then he winks, places a finger to his lips, and smiles.

I'm a complete stranger. He doesn't remember me at all.

The song starts, and Regina comes to life. The spotlight snaps through the audience to find her, and I realize I'm caught in it too. I try to move out of the way, but Dean slinks around to stop me in my tracks as he sings his opening line.

Everyone in the audience is looking at us as he takes my hands and puts them on his fake breasts, gasping with feigned outrage as he does so. Truly embodying the spirit of Regina, he elicits a huge laugh out of my embarrassment and instantly becomes the most popular person in the room.

He struts away, taking the spotlight with him and leaving me and everyone else in the shadows, exactly as he did in his show-stopping performance in *Little Shop*. He'd been the star then, and he's still the star now. The ensemble is phenomenally talented, but they pale in comparison to Dean.

My eyes are fixed on him, and I'm sure that's true of every other person in the room. Every note, every move, every expression—everything is perfect, from the second the spotlight finds him until the moment he leaves the stage. I find it hard to believe that this is happening in a school just across town. This was here the whole time, right at his fingertips, and he turned it down for what? To hang out with me and Alicia at Woodside? Maybe he's better off here.

I watch the whole show in silent awe. I keep thinking about how much I wish Oliver and Alicia were here, and then feeling that pain all over again when I remember how badly I've fucked things up.

Pink confetti canons explode as the show reaches its finale, putting our little green party poppers to shame. The whole room is raining pink and white confetti, the set doesn't collapse, and Dean is standing, tall and proud, center stage, with the rest of the cast around him.

The entire audience is on their feet, and I'm clapping along with them as Dean jumps down from the stage, and someone in the front row catches him. Except it's not just "someone": it's someone I *recognize*. It's Kedar, and he's grinning from ear to ear as he lifts Dean up in his enormous arms and spins him around. Kedar's boyfriend—the one who couldn't come to Oliver's party because he had a show to rehearse for—was Dean all along. I'm totally shaken.

The two of them share a kiss, and I truly don't remember the last time I saw Dean this happy.

Some of their friends run over to join them then, all highly fashionable, a few of them proudly and visibly queer. He has everything he could ever want here; this is all he could've dreamed of and more. I stand at the back of the auditorium as the crowd begins to empty out, waiting for the right moment to approach him, but the longer I stand there, the more I struggle with the words.

"Hey, I'm from an alternate universe where we're best friends. Do you want to maybe leave this perfect school and come back to Woodside Academy with me?"

It isn't going to work. I came here to rescue him, but, as I stand and watch him laughing with his boyfriend and his friends, I realize there's nothing to rescue him from.

As Dean detaches himself from his friends and heads backstage, he takes one look back out into the auditorium and sees me standing there. To him, I'm just a stranger, and it's best for everyone that it stays that way. He's better off here without me. I give him a little wave, and he waves back with a grin before disappearing backstage.

Goodbye, Dean, I say to myself as I make my way out of the school. I may have made a mess of everything else, but he's the one good thing in all of this. The sooner I accept that, the sooner I can move on.

This whole time I've been feeling sorry for myself, waiting for somebody to wave a magic wand and make everything better. But, if there's one thing Dean taught me, it's that you have to fix your shit yourself. I'm the only person responsible for the mistakes I've made, and it's time to start righting some wrongs.

Chapter Seventeen

"I was wondering when you'd show up. You're lucky I don't slam this door in your face."

Darius looks absolutely furious. Right now I think the only thing that's stopping him from twisting my head off like a wine cork is the fact that I got caught in a downpour on the way over and currently look like a drowned rat. I think it gains me a grain of sympathy.

"I know," I say. "And I'd deserve it, but I want to make things right."

Darius takes a long look at me, assessing, weighing me up, trying to decide if I'm worth even one more moment of his daughter's time.

"I'd like to tell you to get lost. But you did the right thing by calling me the other night," he finally says. "Not a lot of kids would have done that."

"It was the right thing to do," I say. He doesn't react, his face remaining stern, unaffected.

"You can go up and knock." Begrudgingly, he stands aside. "But I don't think she'll let you in. She told me what you did, Max."

"Thanks, Mr. Williams," I say, stepping in out of the rain.

"I have to say, I might have expected this from you," he says, "but not from Ollie. Going behind her back like that?"

I shake my head. "It wasn't his fault," I say.

"I know *exactly* whose fault it was," Darius says, looking me up and down. "Five minutes. That's it."

I head up the stairs before he can change his mind and knock on the door of Alicia's attic room. I hear her fumbling around for a moment, and then she opens the door just a crack.

"You got past my guard dog, then," she says flatly. "I never thought he'd let you in."

"I didn't think he would either. Maybe he does have a softer side after all."

Her face doesn't ease.

"Here." She disappears for a moment and then hands me an oversized hoodie from her wardrobe. "It's yours anyway."

"Thanks," I say, peeling off my wet polo and putting on the warm sweatshirt. "I'm really sorry. About before. About everything."

"I don't want your apology, Max," she says with a sigh. "I just want you to be honest with me. What is this really about?"

"Truthfully?" I say, hesitating. "I'm still trying to figure that out. I do know that I'm sorry, though. For putting you through this."

She opens the door a touch wider. "The signs were always there. I should have realized the second you asked me to paint your nails. What world was I living in?"

"Straight guys can wear nail polish too," I say. "You were being a good friend. A supportive girlfriend. There's *nothing* wrong with that."

"But you're not, though, are you? Straight, I mean."

I don't answer that. I don't even know *how* to answer that.

"I think maybe there was a part of me that always knew," she continues. "Like I've been lying to myself this whole time, believing what I wanted to. And I've been thinking that maybe I've been holding you back? Maybe I should've let you go a long time ago, let you figure this out without distraction."

"No," I say firmly. "It was *me* who was the distraction. You're one of the most talented people I know. You're an artist, Alicia. Just look how talented you are!" I take my phone out and open up her Instagram, scrolling back to the work she used to showcase. "*This* is what you should be focusing on. Not boys. Certainly not me."

"Well, now you're starting to sound like my father," she says. "I don't know. Maybe you're right, Max. I just really wanted us to work."

"I know," I say. "And I'm sorry. I really am."

"I'll be okay," she says, offering a slightly warmer smile now.

"And I want to talk to you about Oliver," I say. "It wasn't his fault, you know. Genuinely. I should never have dragged him into this."

"You're right," she says. "You shouldn't have. That really wasn't fair, Max."

"I'm going to go apologize and make things right. But, if you see him first, will you tell him how sorry I am?"

"Why don't you tell him yourself?" she says, opening the door to reveal Oliver sitting on the bed.

"Oliver!" I say, and he gives me a little broken smile. His eyes are red and puffy from crying, the black one swollen even more now. I sit on the bed beside him. "I'm so sorry, Oliver," I say. "I don't know what I can do to fix this. But I'm going to."

"I really thought you liked me, Max," Oliver says weakly. "I knew you were with Alicia, and I shouldn't have kissed you, but I really did think you liked me."

"I know," I say. "And I thought maybe I did too, but things aren't that simple. I should have just figured this out on my own, I shouldn't have dragged either of you into it."

"Well, that's where you're wrong," Alicia says, sitting down on Oliver's other side. "You don't have to go through anything by yourself. We're friends, right? We're supposed to figure things out together."

"You mean we still are? Friends, I mean?"

"Well, I think that's up to Ollie."

Oliver hesitates for a moment, and then puts one arm around each of us. "Yes," he says. "That goes without saying, doesn't it? Of course we're still friends. Always have been. Always will be."

Mum and Dad are in the kitchen when I get home. Things are still raw with Oliver and Alicia, but I think it's going to be okay. It's late now, and the yelling that usually fills this house has come to a stop. Mum and Dad are sitting in silence, a half-empty bottle of wine between them.

"Max?" Mum calls. "Is that you? Have you got a few minutes?"

Her voice is calm and gentle. I think about retreating up to my room, but I know it's finally time to face them head-on. I can't explain everything, but I have to tell them my truth, in words they'll understand.

"Hey, Mum," I say, lingering in the kitchen doorway. "Dad . . ."

They both turn to look at me, and it's like all the pain they've been clinging to dissipates. Whatever hurt they were feeling doesn't seem to matter anymore because they're unified, in this moment, in their shared concern for their son.

"There's something we want to talk to you about," Dad says, nodding to the empty seat at the table. "We've been thinking about what you said yesterday, Max. Everything you said. And you were right. It's about time we start being honest with each other."

"Okay . . ." I say, sitting down.

I know exactly where this is going. The conversation is so familiar that it feels as if they're reading from a script. Like we're on a predestined course, and, no matter what I say or do, there's only one ending. I know it's for the best, though, because I've been through it before. I take a deep breath and brace myself.

"I think you know that your father and I have been unhappy for a while now," Mum says. "We've been trying to make things work, really trying . . . but it's clear now that they aren't, and we don't think it's fair to keep putting you through this."

"And obviously this has nothing to do with you," Dad adds quickly. "If anything, you were the one keeping this family together. We thought things would be better if we were both here, together, but I think it's time to accept that's not working. Something has to change."

"So . . ." Mum says, "your dad and I are thinking about taking some time apart. We'll always be a family, that won't ever change, but we think maybe a trial separation might be better for everyone."

They pause then and look at me, for permission to take this next step. I hadn't handled this moment so well the first time around, but now I've seen both the consequences of them staying together, and how things could be so much better if they go their separate ways.

"I know you haven't been happy," I say. "And I agree this hasn't been good for any of us. So I think you should do what you feel is right."

Dad gives me a sad little smile. "You're sure?"

"I'm sure," I say. "I just want you both to be happy."

"Okay," Dad says. "We'll figure this out together, all right?"

I nod. "Whatever you need."

"How did we ever raise such a sensible young man?" Mum says with a short laugh. "Thank you for understanding, Max."

"It's okay," I say, and I know this has to be my moment.

"There's something I want to talk about too actually." My voice is quivering already.

"Oh yeah? What is it, Max?" Dad asks, and it's like I'm twelve years old all over again, bracing myself to come out to them. Only this time

I don't know what I want to say, how to put what I've experienced into words. How, in spite of all of these straight feelings, I still feel like I'm gay, deep down in my core. I don't want to lie to them anymore, but I'm stuck in a place where whatever I say can only be half true.

"I'm . . ." I start, but the words catch in my throat. Like something is stopping me from saying it out loud. "I . . ."

"It's okay, Max," Mum says as if she can read my thoughts. "You don't have to say anything."

She comes over and wraps her arms around me, and, slowly but surely, I feel the weight begin to lift. The weight of two worlds bearing down on me, the weight of pretending and trying to fit in, the weight of trying to understand so many things that deep down I know I can't.

I feel Dad's hand on my shoulder then, squeezing, saying nothing, but letting me know that he supports me, no matter what. And that's when I realize Mum's right. I don't need to tell them anything. I don't need to label myself as either gay or straight because, whatever I say, I know that they'll be here for me.

The moonlight pours through my bedroom window, shining on the bare patches of wall where I ripped down the posters. I go into the wardrobe and take out the yellow-and-blue varsity jacket. Putting it on makes me feel safe, and it makes me feel like I'm home. I stand in front of the mirror, and, for the first time in as long as I can remember, free of the expectations of everyone around me, I really see myself. Not Gay Max, not Straight Max, just Max. The person I always was and the person I was always meant to be.

I open the official Instagram account for Grove Hill. Their most recent picture, posted just a couple of hours ago, is of Dean and two of his costars. The caption reads "Meet the Plastics" with a lipstick emoji. Kayleigh Adams and Isabella Gutierrez have been tagged, but Dean hasn't. I guess his no-social-media rule held fast in this world too.

I read some of the comments. All of them are positive. Kedar-Mukiwa06 has written "OBSESSED" with a dozen fire emojis. It's the top comment with over a hundred likes. I add a like from me as well. Somebody has written "#CoupleGoals" underneath, and so I like that too.

I want to write something, but everything I can think to say feels far too personal for a public account, so I find Dean's Grove Hill student email instead.

From: Max Baker <Max.Baker@woodside.ac.uk>

Date: October 27, 2023 at 11:11 pm

To: Dean Kellar <Dean.Kellar@grovehill.edu>

Subject: A boy destined for a career on the stage . . .

Dean,

I hope you don't remember me, but I just wanted to say how incredible you were tonight. Back in elementary school, my friends and I bullied you, and I have to tell you how sorry I am—we should never have tried to dim your light. You deserve the world, Dean, and if I had just one wish it would be for you to be happy.

Please don't feel the need to reply. I just wanted you to know that you're amazing.

Sending broken legs always,
Maxwell Timothy Baker

Straight Expectations

I hit send and put down my phone, lying back on my bed, the varsity jacket still snugly wrapped around me. I think of Dean, clutching my bare wrist as I imagine lazing around in his room, gossiping about nothing in particular. I think of him until my eyes grow heavy, and, as my two worlds converge and drift apart, I'm back at Brimsby Road, playing video games as if the last few days never happened at all. And, for a few hours, I'm happy, blissful in my inability to tell reality from a dream.

Chapter Eighteen

I wake to the sound of Dad cheerfully whistling as he makes breakfast. Not his famous pancakes today, though, because the fire alarm is beeping and the smell of fresh blueberries and maple syrup has been replaced with the tang of burning toast. It's almost like he's no longer trying to overcompensate by fattening me up on sweet treats.

I hear him calling Mum's name then, and that's when I realize and rush for the door and down the stairs, wearing nothing but my Calvins. As I burst into the kitchen, I see Mum by the sink and somebody else at the breakfast bar.

Dad doesn't burn toast.

"Chris!"

I practically rip his arm off as I pull him into a hug. It's probably a bit weird for him to be hugged by his girlfriend's half-naked son, but I don't care because as annoying as he is, I've actually missed him, and if he's back then hopefully everything else is back to normal too.

"Who's my best friend?" I demand.

"Um . . . me?" he says with a confused smile as I release him from the hug.

"No, you idiot, my actual best friend, like at school?"

"Dean?"

"Dean!" I exclaim. "And you're dating Mum!"

"Yeah . . . ?" he says with a laugh. "Are you feeling okay, Max?"

"More than okay! I'm great," I say. "You haven't been working on a secret construction project to tear down Brimsby Road, have you?"

"Not that I'm aware of. *I think your son's on drugs,*" he says to Mum in a fake whisper.

I grin. "The only thing I'm high on is life."

Mum snorts. "Did that boy you like kiss you or something?"

"Something like that," I say. "Hang on to this one, Mum; he's a keeper."

I kiss her on the cheek and fly back upstairs to find my phone and check the date. Apparently it's Tuesday, which means time has stood still while I've been galivanting through Straight World. That means last night was the night of the argument, the night I messed everything up. There are no messages from Dean or Alicia, but I'm not surprised. After what happened I wouldn't want to talk to me either. I can fix it, though—I can fix all of this—I just need to take it one step at a time.

I message Dad.

> Hey Dad—how's work?

Great! he replies almost instantly. Do you want to see my new tie?

He sends a photo through without waiting for a reply. Koala bears in sombreros. It might be culturally insensitive if it made literally any sense at all.

Love it! I type back, and I actually mean it. It may be tacky, but it has Dad written all over it. If he loves it, I love it too.

> Time to grab a coffee before school?

> Is this just because you want free coffee?

> Guilty. You free?

> I'll have to check with the boss . . . Oh wait, that's me.

> You're such a loser. Meet you at Starbucks?

> No, wait there, I'll pick you up.

I lie down on my bed and spread out like a starfish. I can't explain it, but the air feels lighter; the bed feels softer; everything's just *better*. I look up and see that KJ Apa is on the back of my door again and . . . it's official, I'm *gay*—capital G-A-Y! How could I have ever been so stupid to want to wish away any of *this*?

"What can I get you?"

"A double espresso," Dad tells the barista (who is rocking a super-tight T-shirt that does *wonders* for his pecs). "And a venti skinny . . ." He looks at me helplessly. He can never remember it.

"A venti iced skinny white mocha," I say. "And hold the cream. I've gotta fit into a corset this weekend."

"A corset?" Dad says.

I laugh. "Never you mind." The barista seems amused by this exchange.

"Name?" he asks.

"Bryan Cranston," Dad replies.

"What?" I say.

"He plays the lead in *Breaking Bad*."

"That's not how you play the game," I say. The barista looks really confused. "I'm sorry about him. It's *Max*. Just put *Max*."

"All right, Max," he says with a wink, and Dad taps his phone to pay.

"Why is it wrong?"

"It just is," I say as we wait for our drinks. "Anyway, there's something I want to ask you."

"Oh yeah?"

"I know you quit your job and started your own business, but why? What prompted you?"

It's the one thing that I still don't understand about my little trip through Straight World. Why did he never quit his job there?

"You really don't know?" Dad grins incredulously. "I can't believe I never told you this. It was you, Max. I wanted to be more like you."

"You what?" I shake my head. This makes no sense at all.

"I was under all this pressure at work but didn't want you or your mum to know. I absolutely hated that job. Loathed it. And then one Friday I got home from work, and you came thundering out of the closet. Twelve years old and ready to take on the whole world. You didn't care about the people that might bully you or the things that might make your life harder. The next day you had your nails painted and your whole wardrobe switched. You didn't wait around for anyone to give you permission: you just did it, and that was that."

"But what does that have to do with you quitting your job?"

Dad laughs. "Isn't it obvious? I was so proud of you, Max. I couldn't believe my twelve-year-old son had more balls than I did. And so on Monday I walked back into the office and quit. If my son could do whatever he wanted, then I sure as hell could too."

"That's a great story," I say as our drinks are placed on the counter. One for Max and, mortifyingly, one for Bryan Cranston. "But there's no way it's true."

"It is," he replies, sipping his drink. "Ask your mother. I swear on your life."

"You swear on *my* life?" I laugh. "I don't think that's how it works."

"It does when you're a parent, Max."

"Well, you're welcome," I say as we head toward the exit. "You're so lucky to have a gay son."

"Just not so lucky you have such expensive taste . . . Speaking of which, did you decide what you want to do this weekend?"

"Yeah, actually. I thought maybe we could go to the soccer game for a change? Apparently Chris *knows a guy*, and he can get us all cheap tickets."

"Okay, who are you and what have you done with my son?" Dad laughs. "What happened to '*gays don't like sports*'?"

"Well, I like boys in shorts, so there will be something there we can all enjoy. Besides, I'm starting to think that soccer isn't such a straight sport after all." I think of Oliver and Kedar then, and of all the queer people that don't perhaps fit the same stereotypes that I do. Maybe there are even gays out there who *gasp* prefer their coffee hot? And you know what? I support their right to drink their coffee at whatever temperature they choose.

"Well, as long as you're sure?" Dad says.

"Yeah," I say. "But you have to buy me a hot dog."

"Two foot-longs coming right up," he says without a hint of irony. Honestly, straight men. "Do you want a lift?"

"Nah, I can walk from here," I reply. And then I do something I haven't done in a long time and go in for a hug. "Love you, Dad."

"Love you too, Max," he says. "Love you too."

I want to see Dean more than anything, but something tells me that a text apology won't cut it, so I concoct a plan and message Alicia instead.

I'm so sorry about last night, I type as I head the rest of the way to school. I was so totally out of order. Can you meet me after first period?

I see the two check marks appear to confirm that she's read it, and then she tortures me by leaving me hanging for five agonizing minutes. It's what I deserve. I'm genuinely surprised she replies at all.

> You were such a dick, Max. You should be apologizing to Dean, not me.

> I know, I want to make it up to him though, can you please meet me?

> Fine. See you after class then.

Full stop. No emoji. No kiss. Brutal.

It's so good to be back in my own clothes. Apart from having a core part of my identity switched off, the worst thing about Straight World was not having my real-world stuff. I'm wearing a white crop top and my favorite varsity jacket, the red one with the gorgeous cream sleeves, and it feels *so damn good*. I walk with a spring in my step, the jeans lifting my ass as I walk. I couldn't be happier in my own skin. I need to sort my nails out, though—the nude look is *not* working—but there's only one person who can fix that.

I head into the main corridor, and that's when it starts happening all over again. That feeling of losing control as my emotions are flipped. Except this time it doesn't feel like a bad thing as Oliver turns the corner up ahead of me.

It's impossible to look anywhere else but at him. His messy hair, his dimpled cheeks, his pristine skin and sparkling, unblackened eyes. It suddenly feels absolutely inconceivable that there could ever have been a world in which I didn't have a thing for Oliver Cheng. He's so hot the air around him positively sizzles.

"Max!" he calls as he spots me, and I feel like a deer caught in headlights as I remember that this Oliver and I are not best friends. *This* Oliver ignored my Insta message last night—the *real* last night— so why would he approach me now? This isn't how ghosting works. He's supposed to awkwardly turn in the other direction or suddenly be so terribly busy on his phone that he can pretend he hasn't seen me. If he's not going to address the elephant in the corridor, I guess I'm going to have to.

"Oliver, hey!" I say. "Listen, I'm really sorry about last night. I know you were just looking for a friend, and I shouldn't have—"

"Oh God, no! I should be the one apologizing," he interrupts. "I started to write back, but my parents confiscated my phone literally mid-message."

"Shut up," I say. "You're actually joking?!"

"Nope," he replies, turning his pockets out to show that they are indeed empty.

"Well, I know how that feels! What did you do to deserve such a cruel and unusual punishment?"

"Too much screen time apparently," he says, and then jokily does the jerk-off gesture, and my mind goes to all kinds of places it shouldn't. "They said I was clearly addicted because I was messaging you when I *should* have been listening to their stupid house rules for while they're away."

"No drinking, no parties . . ."

"And no boys in my bed," he says. "The fact that they so obviously don't trust me only makes me want to break their rules even more. Especially the last one."

"Oh gosh, well . . ." I say, clearing my throat. Oliver just grins, clearly amused that he's got me flustered.

"I really enjoyed hanging out with you yesterday," he says. "*Loads of fun*," he teases, reminding me of the cringeworthy content of my message.

"So you're just openly mocking me now?"

"It was cute," he says, his cheeks dimpling.

Shut *up*. He did *not* just call me cute. I know Oliver was into me in Straight World but that doesn't mean he likes me here too, right? Like, what if he was only into Straight Max? What if Gay Max isn't his type? I'm blushing now, and I don't know what to say. But weirdly it looks like he's blushing a bit too.

"So I was wondering . . ." he says haltingly, "if maybe you might like to go to the dance with me?"

"To the dance . . . ?" I gulp. "With . . . you?"

"Yeah," he says. "If you don't already have a date, that is?"

"I'd love to," I say in a rush, but then I think of Dean, and how he'd been so excited for us to go with Alicia. "But it's our last year, I've been going together with my friends for so long. It's our little tradition. I don't wanna break that."

"Oh," Oliver says. He looks a little put out. "Well, okay, no worries. But maybe we could hang out sometime?"

"Well . . . how about now?" I say. "I'm heading to the library to pick up some books. Maybe you'd like to come with?"

His face lights up with a big dorky smile. "I thought you weren't into books. You said you weren't much of a reader?"

"I wasn't," I say. "But then a new friend got me into it."

"Since yesterday?"

"You'd be surprised. Besides, the librarian is really cute."

"Immy?" He laughs. "You don't have a crush on Immy?!"

"Don't go getting jealous," I tease. "I'm not your property, Oliver. We haven't even been on a date yet."

"So you'd like to, then? Go on a date, I mean?"

"Sure."

The simple confidence with which I say it surprises me. My mind would usually be in overdrive right about now, but I'm actually starting to feel pretty relaxed around Oliver. There's something about the way he smiles so easily that lets me know it's okay to just be myself. I don't feel like I have to impress him anymore. "We could try the new pizza place?"

"Well, that depends," he says. "What's your position on Hawaiian? Because I'm a firm believer that it's God Tier, and I won't tolerate any pineapple slander."

I laugh. "Fine with me. As far as I'm concerned, there's no such thing as bad pizza, as long as it's not veggie. I love a meaty topping."

"A 'meaty topping' . . ." Oliver looks at me, deadpan. "Good to know."

"No, that's not . . . I—I didn't mean . . ." I stammer. "I'm not saying I want . . . I mean, I've never . . . I haven't quite figured that out yet."

"Oh my God," Oliver says, laughing. "Slow your roll, Max. Let's wait until after the first date, yeah? How about Thursday night?"

"Okay," I say. "Thursday night sounds great."

"This better be good," Alicia says, sitting down next to me on the bank by the soccer field.

The grass is still slightly dewy as a gentle haze rolls over. It's nice seeing her with my own eyes again. It's as if the rose-tinted glasses of straightness have been taken off, and somehow it only makes me like her more. In a strictly homosexual, platonic way, of course. I'm glad my heterosexual feelings are now firmly relegated to the past.

"Thanks for coming," I say. "I'm really sorry about last night. Sometimes I get so wrapped up in my own feelings that I kind of forget about everyone else. That's not an excuse, though—I know I shouldn't have said the things I did. But I really didn't mean it."

"You did mean it a little bit, though, right?" she replies. "That stuff about you missing out on the high-school experience. I never really thought about it that way. It's okay to open up about these things, you know? Otherwise you end up bottling it up and then ripping your friends' heads off. I didn't know you were struggling, Max. I thought you were happy. Proud, even."

"I am," I say. "I guess I just got so focused on the things I was missing out on that I forgot to appreciate the things I already have. Woodside isn't so bad, especially not with you and Dean here. I'm not sure what I'd do without you."

"All right, well, don't get sappy on me," Alicia says with a grin. "Save that energy for Dean. He's the one who needs to hear it."

"Is he okay?"

"You've really messed him up, Max," she says. "Like, *really*."

"I'll fix it. I promise. But I was wondering if maybe you could help me?"

"Help you?" she says. "I mean . . . sure. What do you need?"

"Here," I say, taking a copy of *The History of Androgynous Fashion* out of my bag. "I need your help with this."

Dean has a free period this afternoon, and I know exactly where to find him. I knock twice on the door to the drama department before entering.

"Hey, Max," Mrs. A says, looking up from the stack of homework she's marking. "Dean's in the back." She gestures at the door that leads through to the haunted grotto.

"Thanks," I say. "Oh, and Mrs. A?"

"Max?"

"I just wanted to say thanks. For everything you do for us, all the queer kids. It's nice knowing we always have you in our corner."

"Oh," she says, smiling gently. "Well, I don't know about all that. Caring about kids is part of a teacher's job description."

"You should tell that to Mr. Johnson," I remark. Mrs. A frowns.

"I just mean all the extra work you put in. Into the show. Into us. I want you to know that it doesn't go unnoticed."

"Well, I don't do things by halves, Max. And you kids are all right. Despite the fact you're giving me grays." She bounces her curly hair with her hands, and I grin.

"Sorry about those," I say. "I know I'm responsible for half of them."

"And Dean Jackson the other half," she replies. "Go on in and see him."

"Did he say something about what happened?"

"He came in here wearing a T-shirt and sweatpants, no nail polish, asking me if he should tone it down."

"Fuck," I say. "That's my fault."

"Language!"

"Sorry. But you're not mad at me?"

"Max, I'm Switzerland—perpetually neutral. I'm too old to get wrapped up in teenage drama. Just go and straighten things out."

"Will do, thanks," I say. "Oh, and Mrs. A? There is one more thing . . ."

"Oh God, what now?" Mrs. A says, taking off her glasses.

"I was thinking about next year's show. I know I won't be here, but I have a suggestion . . ."

"We've been through this, Max. I'm not having any of the boys take their shirts off. I don't care if you think it 'makes the show more authentic.' This is a school, not a strip club. Honestly, it's like you want to get me sacked."

I laugh. "It's not that," I say. "Though I still don't understand how you can do *Rocky Horror* without *someone* wearing the gold hot pants . . ."

"Max," she says firmly, "you're going to be the death of me. But go on then, let's hear it. What's the suggestion?"

"Well . . ." I say. "There's this musical. I don't know if you've heard of it, but some of the seniors love it."

"It's not *Mean Girls*, is it?" She looks exhausted by the very thought. "And let me guess, you want Aaron Samuels to be topless and Regina George to be played in drag?"

"You know *Mean Girls*?"

"*Mean Girls* is *my* generation, not yours. How old do you think I am?"

"Well, it's not *Mean Girls*," I say. "Although that would be pretty sick. It's called *Hadestown* . . ."

"Oh," Mrs. A says, surprised. "Well, yes, actually, I have heard of that one." She tries her best to conceal her smile. "Not a bad idea."

"So you'll do it? Maybe Dean and I will come back to watch?"

"The students pick the show. You know that, Max. But maybe I can throw it into the mix."

"Thanks, Mrs. A. You're a real one," I say.

"I know, Max. You're a real one too—a real pain in my neck. Now go and make up with Dean."

Dean is sitting on the floor in the corner of the haunted grotto, script in hand, silently mouthing the words to himself. I want to rush over and pull him into a hug—I really thought I'd lost him—but I can tell something isn't right. He looks different, smaller somehow, as if the light has been knocked out of him.

He's not wearing any makeup, his clothes are plain, and his colorless nails are blinding. The only time I've ever seen him with a bare nail is in the brief transitional period where he takes off one color to replace it with another.

"Mind if I come in?" I say timidly from the doorway. Dean glances up briefly before looking back down at his script.

He shrugs. "I guess." He might not *want* to see me, but I have to make this right.

"Look, I was wrong," I say. "About all of it, about everything. I should never have said any of it. I was out of order. I was being a dick."

Dean doesn't say anything; he just sits there. He's still turning the pages of the script, but I can tell he's just pretending to read it now. I go over and sit down opposite him.

"Dean, I'm sorry," I say. "I'm really, truly sorry. I know I can't ever take those words back, but you have to know that I didn't mean them. I love you exactly the way you are. You taught me to love those things about myself too."

I pause for a moment, giving him a chance to speak.

"It's for my stupid audition," he finally says.

"Huh?" I say, and he lifts up the script.

"I've been thinking," he goes on. "What if you were right last night? Maybe I should tone it down. Because what if they don't like campy, over-the-top Dean Jackson? These are serious schools, Max, not some cabaret club. They want class, elegance, not some wannabe drag queen."

These thoughts are all my fault. Dean told me never to doubt myself, but now, because of me, he's doing exactly that. I can't believe I did this. I can't believe I let myself turn into everything I hate.

"My whole life I've been putting on this show," he continues. "Everything larger than life, everything extravagant. But what if it's all a facade? Something to hide behind because I know I'm not good enough and never will be."

He tosses the script aside, and that's when he finally cracks. Fierce, unbreakable Dean Jackson. I haven't seen him cry since we were kids.

"But that's not true," I say. "You're not putting on an act—you're not putting on any of this. I know you, Dean, and this is who you've always been. Who you were always meant to be. You were parading around in heels since before you could tie your shoelaces! You're going to drama school, Dean, not in spite of who you are but *because* of it. And if they don't take you then fuck 'em. You shouldn't change for anyone. Not for them, certainly not for me."

"Do you really mean that?" he asks, making eye contact for the first time.

"Of course," I say. "I'm not sure of a lot of things, but I'm certain about this. I would be completely lost without you, Dean. You've taught me everything. How to be brave. How to be a good ally. The only thing you haven't taught me is how to do my nails. I've no idea what I'm going to do about them when you go off to your fancy drama school. I'll have to visit you just to get them painted."

Dean lets out a soft laugh, stifled by his tears.

"Speaking of which," I say, reaching out to hold up his bare nails, "what on earth are we going to do with these?"

"I don't know what I was thinking," he exclaims with some of his old sass. "Get this queer some nail polish, *stat*! I'm about to go into withdrawal. I'm five minutes away from huffing from the bottle just to feel something."

"Here," I say, holding out a bottle of glittery purple polish.

"'*Unicorn Trampocalypse*'?" He squints as he reads the label.

"Alicia had it with her. Maybe you could do mine as well?"

Dean purses his lips. "Only if you promise you're not going to throw another temper tantrum. I'm not wasting my time if you're just gonna take it off again."

"I promise," I say, then slip off my backpack. "There's something I want to show you. Something else I need your help with."

"*Two* helps?" He rolls his eyes. "Aren't you supposed to be the one apologizing?"

"Just wait," I say. "Here." I hand him a large black art folder.

"Oh . . ." he says, opening it and looking at the contents. "Max, I'm speechless. Did you really do these?"

"I had Alicia's help," I say. "And they need more work, but yeah . . ."

Dean stares down at the collage of three elaborate costumes. They're made from clippings from various fashion magazines and are a celebration of gender expression and androgyny. They're rough around the edges because we did them in such a rush, but I'm so happy with the way they turned out.

"Max . . . they're stunning," he says. "But what are they for? I mean . . . what is this?"

"Well," I say, "you've always told me that one day I'll find my passion. One that isn't boys. And I think maybe this is it."

"So, like, a designer?" he asks. "That's what you wanna be?"

"I think maybe more like a stylist," I say. "I don't know, I haven't figured that out yet, but I guess I never realized how much clothes mean to me—putting together a look, pushing boundaries, all of it . . ."

"Well, these are amazing, Max. I'd look incredible in *that*," he says, tapping one of the three costumes.

"Well, good, because that one's for you," I say. "They're for the three of us to wear at the Leavers' Ball next year. If you want to, anyway. I'll have to source the pieces, but I've already got some ideas, and—"

"Max, I'd love to."

"I know I haven't been a great friend to either of you," I say, a little more somber now. "Both of you do so much for me, and I guess I realize now that I never really gave much back. I'll make a million paper lanterns, I'll run lines with you till the end of time if that's what it takes."

"We run lines plenty," he says. "And you do realize Alicia didn't actually need you to make those lanterns, right? That's not what we need from you, Max."

"It's not?"

"I guess sometimes it feels like you don't listen to what I'm actually saying. I know you mean well when you say I don't need to worry about my auditions, but I do need to. I need to because I'm not white. Alicia gets that because she has to think about that too. When she says I'm a shoo-in, she says it with the understanding that the game is rigged. But when you say it, Max? Honestly it just sort of comes across like you're not really listening."

"But you are a shoo-in! You're so good at what you do—you both are!"

"Because we have to be. You get that, right? We have to be better because we're not running in the same race as the rest of you."

"I guess I never thought about it like that," I say. "How come you never said any of this before?"

"Well, did you ask?"

"I suppose not," I say. "I hear you. I'm sorry. I'll do better."

"Listen," Dean says, a little cheerier now. "You've got your own problems to deal with. You're an effeminate crop top–wearing gay boy.

Life's not always gonna be easy. But that doesn't mean you can forget about the rest of us."

"How could I ever forget you?" I say with a smile now.

"What gave you this big epiphany, anyway? Like, where did this all come from?"

"Would you believe me if I said I slipped into a parallel universe where I was straight? Like, fully heterosexual? And I was *still* obsessed with fashion?"

"Ha!" Dean barks. "Max, if there were a *million* parallel universes, you'd still be a raging gay boy in all of them."

"I'll have you know I was as straight as they come!"

"A soccer jock?" he says, one eyebrow raised.

"Well, no, actually. I was still really bad at sports . . ." I admit, and he laughs.

"And, speaking of being a massive gay boy, did Oliver message you back? I'm sorry for winding you up about it before. I know you really like him . . ."

"It's okay," I say with a shrug. "Alicia was right. He is just a boy . . . A boy who's taking me on a date!"

Dean actually squeals.

"Shut up! He is *not*!"

"He is!" I say. "He came right up to me this morning and asked me out like it was nothing. Oliver Cheng asking *me* on a date. Can you actually imagine?"

"I'm happy for you, Max."

"That's Maxine to you," I say, and he grins broadly. Dean's smile reminds me of how happy he looked onstage at the end of *Mean Girls*, and I know there's something I have to ask.

"Dean . . . ?" I say. "Do you think you made the right decision? Coming here to Woodside?"

"What do you mean?"

"You could have gone to Grove Hill. Do you think you would have been better off there?"

"Nah," he says. "I took one glance at their fancy-pants theater and knew it wasn't for me. That place is soulless."

"You really mean that?" I say.

"Yeah," he replies dismissively. "Their sets are impressive, but they're all hired in—they don't have that magic Woodside family feel. Alicia's sets were what made *Legally Blonde* and *Little Shop*. You can't buy that, Max. Besides, a professional set wouldn't have come crashing down around me, now would it? That's why Woodside is special. Because we somehow get it *right*, even when things go wrong."

"So you're sure you prefer it here?"

"I wouldn't have chosen it if I didn't think it was the right place."

"So you didn't come here just because of me?"

Dean snorts. "I know you think the whole world revolves around you, Maxine, but I'm here to tell you it doesn't. Not even in a world where you've lost your gay card. Now tell me: were we still friends in this world where you were a raging macho straight boy?"

"Oh," I say. "I mean . . . what do you think?"

He grins. "I knew it. Even heterosexuality couldn't keep you from me. Friends?" he says, offering his hand.

"*Best* friends," I say, slapping his hand away and pulling him into a hug.

Chapter Nineteen

"Why *Rick*?" Oliver asks, reading my cup as I hand him his venti iced vanilla latte.

The wait has been unbearable, but it's finally happening. It's Thursday, and it's date night, and I think I may actually burst. The sun is just beginning to set, and it gives the world that warm autumn glow as Oliver leads me across the soccer field. I don't know where we're going, though. Pizza is in the *other* direction.

"Read yours," I say. "It's cheesy, I know, but I was trying to be romantic."

"Romantic?" He sounds confused as he reads the word *Morty* written on his cup.

"Well, they're a gay couple, right?"

Oliver laughs. "I think maybe you're a bit confused. You've never actually watched *Rick and Morty*, have you? Rick is Morty's *grandfather*. They're not a couple, Maxxie."

"They're not?" I gasp. "Wait, who am I thinking of?"

"I have literally no idea . . . Ten out of ten for effort, though."

I'm a bit embarrassed, but at least he's laughing. At least he already seems to be having a good time. That's better than the awkward silence I dreaded might happen.

"Where are we going anyway?" I ask as we turn and start heading toward the back of the school.

"Just wait," he says, leading me through one of the doors and into a dusty old stairwell. It's a part of the school I've never been in before, and, by the looks of it, no one else has either.

"Come on, Gramps," he teases, bouncing up the steps two at a time as I follow behind him.

"What's going on?" I ask, already out of breath. We've only managed two flights, and it looks like there's about eight more till we hit the top.

"Just trust me," he says, turning back with a smile that sparks my second wind.

I really don't know why we're back at school, though. I've fantasized about my first date a thousand times—restaurant dates and activity dates and cute cinema dates with a hole in the bottom of the popcorn—and run through every single scenario and yet never imagined *this*.

"Are you at least going to tell me what's in the basket?"

"Nope!" he says, the wicker basket swinging by his side as he effortlessly bounds up yet another flight of stairs.

He laughs. "Come on," he says, noticing I'm struggling now. "Last flight." He offers me his hand and drags me up. "Ta-da!" In front of us is a very old and rusty steel door with a huge padlock.

"Oliver, this could be the start of a horror movie . . ." I say. "What are we doing up here?"

He reaches into his pocket and holds out a small key. "See for yourself."

"This is the part where the audience is screaming at me not to be so stupid. You realize that, right?" I take the key and undo the padlock. "Please do not murder me, Oliver Cheng."

That could be the title of the movie. Not words I ever thought I'd be saying, and yet here we are. The padlock pops open, I unfasten the chain, and the door creaks open to reveal an extremely dark storage cupboard. There's nothing inside but some deflated soccer balls, a folded-up tennis net, and some really old gymnastics equipment.

"Okay, this is a tad presumptuous," I say with a grin. "I'm not going to bang you in the storage cupboard, Oliver."

"You're not?" he says with fake puppy-dog eyes. "But I brought condoms. And a basket full of lube. You can't disappoint me after we climbed all this way."

"Very funny," I say. "But if not for sex, and if not for murder, really, what are we doing here? You're not expecting me to play sports, are you?"

"You mean you don't like sports?" He puts on an expression of horror. "But you dress *so* sporty!"

"I'm practically a jock. I know, it's a surprise to everyone."

"Well," he says, "that's not it either. Look."

He steps into the cupboard and moves some of the sports equipment aside to reveal a second door at the back. He pushes it open, and a glimmer of the sunset shines in from outside.

"Though we can just stay in the cupboard and have sex if you prefer?" he adds, biting his lip. I know he's only teasing, but Mother May I?

"How do you have a key for this place, anyway?"

"Mr. Johnson sent me up here to get some extra balls a few weeks ago and forgot to ask for it back." He shrugs. "Finders keepers, I guess?"

"That's not how it works," I say. "You can't just rob a bank and shout 'finders keepers' as you jump into the getaway car."

He grins. "Sure I can. Come on."

He leads me through the outer door onto the rooftop. The lilac sky is dashed with pinks and oranges, and you can see out over all of Woodside. I may have lived here my whole life, but I've never actually seen it, not like this, anyway—from the namesake woodland near my house all the way down to Brimsby Road at the bottom. You can even see Grove Hill way off in the distance.

"I can't believe this view has been up here this whole time," I say softly. "Like, why do they never show us this? It should be part of day one orientation!"

"I'm not sure they want freshmen hanging out on the rooftop, Max. Besides, I don't think half the teachers even know this is here." Oliver takes a long sip of his coffee. "It's better that it's a secret anyway, don't ya think?"

"I'm not very good with secrets," I reply. "Come on, tell me what's in the basket! There's food, right, not just contraceptives?"

"Patience!" he says, laughing, but I can't stand it anymore. I grab the basket and hold it just out of his reach.

"You can either tell me," I say, "or I'm going to find out for myself." Oliver narrows his eyes at me. "You wouldn't dare."

"Wouldn't I?" I say, lifting the lid a fraction.

"Nope," he says. "You wouldn't. In fact . . ." He snatches the basket back. "Forget the basket—we don't need it anyway."

He holds it over the side of the building and flips it upside down. The lid falls open and . . . absolutely nothing falls out.

"It's empty?" I say, confused, as he hands it back to me. I look for a secret hidden compartment or *something*, but there's literally nothing inside. "I don't get it."

"I told you," he says. "It's a surprise." He takes his phone out and looks at it. "There's not long now anyway."

"You got your phone back, then?" I say as he tucks it back into his pocket.

"I told my parents I had a date, my *first* date . . ."

"And that actually worked?"

"I think everyone's a romantic deep down," he says. "And, speaking of which, I think we're about two minutes away from the magic."

"Magic?" I echo.

I've had just about enough magic over the last week, but somehow that doesn't seem to matter when it's Oliver that's offering. We stand side by side, looking down over the soccer field. There's a lone fox slinking across the grass, but otherwise it's perfectly still. There's no sound but the gentle evening breeze.

"Watch," he says as the sun begins to disappear below the horizon and, one by one, the floodlights make a shuttering sound as they come to life. The field is illuminated, and everything else disappears into velvet shadow.

"Pretty," Oliver says as I take it all in, but, when I turn to face him, I see he's not looking at the view at all. "Maxwell Timothy Baker," he continues in a soft voice.

"You know my full name?"

"Max T. Baker?" he says, throwing in the hand gesture. "*Everyone* at Woodside knows your full name."

"Because you've all got filthy minds?"

"Something tells me yours isn't squeaky clean either." Oliver laughs just as his phone starts buzzing in his pocket.

"He's here."

"Who's here?" I say. Who on earth has he asked along on *our* date?

"Look," he says, pointing, and I can see somebody cycling across the soccer field, the floodlights catching in their reflectors. They stop in the middle and look around like they're confused. That's when I realize it's the pizza guy.

"Up here!" Oliver yells, so loud it actually makes me jump. "Just a second!" he adds, disappearing for a moment to retrieve one of the large ropes that are supposed to be used for gymnastics. He wraps the rope around the handle of the basket and then carefully lowers it down the side of the building.

"This is ridiculous," I say, helping him. "This is absolutely ridiculous."

He grins. "You say ridiculous, but I say *romantic*."

"He's definitely giving you one star for making him do this."

"Or five for making his job a bit more entertaining."

It's hard to tell from up here, but it does actually look like the delivery guy is laughing to himself as he loads two large pizza boxes into the basket. They don't exactly fit, but they're balanced just well enough for us to start slowly hoisting it back up again.

"Thank you!" Oliver yells as the delivery guy gives him a little wave and a thumbs-up before hopping on his bike again. "Definitely five stars," he says, beaming.

"Make sure you give him a big tip," I say, nudging him, but I do it a bit too hard because it makes him slip, and the basket bashes against the side of the wall.

"There goes your meaty topping!" Oliver gasps as one of the pizza boxes flips out of the basket, sending chunks of ham and pepperoni everywhere.

"Fuck," I say. "Sorry!"

"It's fine," he says. "I just hope you really do like Hawaiian?"

"Of course," I say. "Who doesn't love pineapple on pizza?"

"Exactly." We hoist the remaining pizza box over the side. "Success!" Oliver exclaims, opening the box and offering me a slice.

It smells incredible. It's one of those artisan types with sourdough crust, the toppings scattered liberally, cheese and sauce puddled together in a disgustingly delicious, gooey mess.

"Worth all the secrecy?" Oliver says, helping himself to a slice as I bite down into mine. I respond with an enthusiastic nod as the sauce dribbles down my chin. Not exactly a sexy look for a first date, but when the pizza is this good, I simply do not care. Even Oliver Cheng will have to take a back seat for a moment because, for all his charm, pizza is still my first love.

While we eat, Oliver tells me about the books he's reading, things at home, and his friends back in London. I just happily sit and listen, dipping my crusts in the garlic sauce until there's nothing but crumbs left in the pizza box. The perfect date. Nothing could be better than this.

"Wait," Oliver says suddenly, cutting himself off mid-sentence. "Did you hear that?"

"Huh?" I say. "Did I hear what?"

"Someone's coming," he says, jumping to his feet, and as I listen a little more closely, I can hear the faint sound of footsteps echoing in the stairwell.

"Quick," Oliver says, forcing the pizza box inside the basket and pushing it into my hands. He tosses the rope back into the storeroom and then grabs me and pulls me into the little space just behind the door. My back is pushed up against his chest, and I can feel his warm breath on my neck.

"Hello?" a voice calls, and I immediately recognize it as everyone's least favorite teacher. "Is there someone up here?" Mr. Johnson calls.

"Fuck, fuck, fuck," I whisper, but then Oliver's hands find my arms, and as he gently holds me, I feel my body slowly untense.

"Shh," he whispers as we hear Mr. Johnson pushing his way through the storeroom. We freeze as he comes into view. If he looks behind the door, we're done for.

"Anyone up here?" he calls again, and I can hear both my and Oliver's hearts thundering in my eardrums. "Stupid teenagers," he mutters to himself as he goes back inside and closes the door behind him.

"Phew," I say, dropping the basket once I'm sure he's out of earshot.

I turn to face Oliver; our eyes meet and both of us go dead silent. He looks down at my lips and then back up at my eyes, and I know that this is it. The moment. We're finally going to kiss. His hand pulls at the sleeve of my jacket, as if inviting me to do it, and then just as I lean forward there's a noise that makes Oliver's eyes grow wide with horror.

Mr. Johnson just clicked the padlock shut.

"Fuck!" Oliver says, scrambling past me to push on the outer door, but it's no use. He returns, coyly scratching at the back of his neck. "I think we might be stuck."

"Oh my God," I say, but I'm only concerned for about half a second, and then I just start to laugh. "Well, at least this will make for a good story, right?" Trapped on a rooftop with Oliver Cheng. A boy can only dream!

"We could get the delivery guy back?" he suggests, pulling out his phone again. "Order some more pizza, throw down the key?"

"You've made that man's job hard enough already," I say with a laugh.

"He *definitely* gave me five stars."

"Let me try Alicia," I say, taking my own phone out to call her. "I think she's still in the theater, getting things set up for the Monster Ball."

"Max!" she answers after a single ring. "Why are you *calling* me? Send me a text or a voice note like a normal person."

"Hey," I say, putting the phone on speaker. "You still in the theater?"

"Yeah, why?" she says. "And, oh my God, how was your date?! Did you tell him about the locker room thing?"

"He's still here, and you're on speaker," I say, turning bright red.

"Oh . . ." she says. "Hey, Ollie."

"Hey," he says, laughing. "What's this about a locker room?"

"Well," she begins, "Max has this recurring dream where you and him are in the locker room and then—"

"THAT'S NOT WHY WE'RE CALLING!" I interrupt. I hear some laughter from the other end of the phone. "Wait, you're not alone?"

"Oh, it's just Rachel and a few others . . ."

"It's okay, Max," says a voice I don't recognize. "I fantasize about the boys' locker room too!"

"Oh my God," I say. Oliver is laughing even harder now.

"Well anyway," I continue, "what would you say if I told you we'd managed to get ourselves in a bit of trouble . . . ?"

"Oh God, what have you done now, Max?"

"Nothing," I reply. "But we're maybe kind of . . . stuck."

"Please tell me you didn't mistake the lube for superglue," she says. "Because you two are on your own with that one . . ."

"Alicia!" I laugh. "Stop saying words! Just listen! You know the old building down by the soccer field? The one that literally nobody ever goes in?"

"Yeah?"

"Well, if we throw you a key, how fast do you think you can get here?"

"Oh my God, Max," she says. "You're such an idiot."

"It's my fault actually," Oliver confesses. "Coach locked us up on the roof."

"Then you're a pair of idiots," Alicia says. "You're a match made in heaven actually. I don't know why you didn't start dating sooner. I'll be there in five minutes, so put your clothes back on, okay?"

"I'm not making any promises," Oliver teases. "Oh, Max!" he moans. "Not with Alicia still on the phone! Oh, Max! Stop it!"

And, even though I know he's just joking, it still manages to turn me on.

Chapter Twenty

"And you definitely didn't bang on top of the crash mats?" Dean says, arching an eyebrow as he leans against his locker at the end of the following day.

The main corridor is decorated for Halloween now—nothing flashy, just a few pumpkins and paper ghosts, but still there's a definite festive buzz in the air, and everyone is in good spirits.

"No!" I laugh. "I'm telling you, we didn't even kiss!" We're sipping on the last of our iced coffees, slow, gentle sips because we have to make them last all afternoon. His cup says *Bert* and mine says *Ernie.*

"Well, why not?" he demands. "It's literally *all* you've talked about this year, and now he's dangling the opportunity right in front of you, and you don't seize it with both hands?"

"Oh, believe me, if he was dangling it in front of me, I'd definitely seize it with both hands," I say with a smirk, and Dean recoils, clutching a set of imaginary pearls. "Besides," I say, "it wasn't the right time."

"Oh, come on, Maxine! I swear to God, if you don't kiss him at the dance later, I am actually going to grab your heads and force your faces together."

"Please do. I still can't believe we actually went on a date. Me and Oliver Cheng. An actual date, like real-life heterosexuals!"

"You are too cute, Max," Dean says as I open my locker and a folded note falls out. "A message from lover boy?"

"*'Happy Monster Ball! Can't wait to see how hot you look tonight,'*" I read aloud with a smile stapled to my lips. "*'I hope you like my costume too . . .'*"

"Oliver?" Dean says, but, as I look down to the name at the bottom, my heart begins to sink. Bad butterflies. Oh my God, not again.

"*'Love, PP xo.'*"

Dean gasps. "Double P? Surely not?" he says, snatching the note out of my hand and reading it himself. "Oh my God, Max, Poppy Palmer is your secret admirer!"

"Oh God, don't," I say with a groan. "Surely she knows I'm gay, right?"

Dean laughs. "Everyone knows you're gay, Max. Maybe she just wants what she knows she can't have. That's a thing, right?"

"Urgh," I say. "I don't know. I just don't want to deal with this right now."

"Then don't," Dean says, tearing the note in two. "You're free to ignore it, Max. You don't have to make a big deal out of it."

"But what if she, like, tries to make out with me?"

"Then just tell her you're dating Oliver. She's a big girl; she can handle it. You don't owe her anything, you know? Consent 101."

"Yeah?" I say. "You're really sure it'll be that simple?"

"I'm sure, Max. Just try to forget about it. Let's not even mention her . . ."

"Hey, guys," Rachel says, approaching us. "Have you seen Simon?"

"Not since third period," I say. "Why?"

"He asked me to meet him here . . ." she says, and just as she speaks, we hear music start to play over the loudspeakers. It's the "Monster Mash."

"Oh my God," I say. "Not this. Dean, we need to leave *now.*"

"Why?" he asks. "What's going on?"

"Just trust me," I say. "Or we're going to be permanently traumatized."

"The 'Monster Mash'?" Alicia says. "That literally doesn't even make sense. And why the need for a big promposal? Like, obviously they were going together. They've been a couple for *months.*"

"Thank you! That's what *I* said!" I've never felt so vindicated.

We're in Alicia's room later that day, putting the finishing touches on our outfits. Dean is helping Alicia fasten the back of her long, flowing black dress.

"Well, speaking of couples, Max has a secret admirer!" he says, then cackles loudly. Honestly, he's literally had one drink. "And it's a girl! Poppy Palmer!"

"Oh my God!" I say, adjusting the black-feathered wings that match perfectly with my long-line mesh vest. The two of them agreed to let me coordinate our outfits for the Monster Ball, so I've styled us all as fallen angels. "What happened to not bringing it up again? What happened to not making a big deal out of it?"

"We can't keep it from Alicia, though!" Dean says.

He's wearing a long, split-thigh skirt with a corset laced tightly around his middle. His upper chest is exposed, and with some careful contouring we've made him look even more muscled than he already is. A little masc, a little fem, Dean Jackson to a T.

"He's right," Alicia says. "You can't! What happened? Spill!"

"There's nothing to tell," I say with a sigh. "I just got a love note in my locker. I'd show you, but Dean ripped it up."

"From Poppy?" Alicia says. "You must be mistaken! She would have told me if she had a thing for you. And *surely* she knows you're gay? I mean, *everyone* knows you're gay, Max . . ."

"That's what I said!" I say. "But it was signed Double P."

Alicia shakes her head. "God, you think you know someone . . ."

"Guess I really am just that irresistible, huh?"

She laughs. "Yeah, I'm *sure* that's what it is! Here, what do you think?"

Alicia turns around slowly so I can get the full view of her outfit. She's painted her skin to look cracked and broken, with twisting black veins running along the surface. Her hands are gloved, her waist cinched, her braids styled into an updo, her wings ruffling in the air as she twirls.

"Ariana, Lana, and Miley could never!" I say. "You look incredible."

"You look pretty great yourself," she says. "Bound to give Ollie a hard-on."

"You sure it's not too much?" I look at myself in the mirror a little self-consciously. "I don't look too . . . slutty?"

"No, Max," she replies, smoothing out my feathers. "And what have I told you about using that word?"

"I'm reclaiming it!"

"You can't reclaim a word rooted in misogyny," she scolds, but then her face softens again and she gives me a little smile. "Don't worry, you look perfect."

"Almost perfect," Dean interjects. "It's just missing one thing. I know it doesn't go with the rest of the look, but I thought you might like to wear this?"

He goes over to the chest of drawers and takes out the friendship bracelet I'd ripped off on the night of the argument. I had no idea that he'd held on to it.

"Dean . . ." I say, and I feel my voice catch in my throat. "This will . . . totally clash with everything. But I wouldn't be caught dead without it." I hold out my wrist. "Here, lay it on me."

"You know all your wishes are supposed to come true when you break one of those?" Alicia says. "Good job you didn't wish for something stupid, Max."

"Yeah," I reply. "*Thank God for that.*"

"All right, make a wish, then," Dean says, pulling the bracelet tight.

"You know what? I think I'd rather not. You may have been right before—things are pretty great just as they are. I wouldn't change them for the world."

"All right, fun police," Alicia says, rolling her eyes.

"Don't say the *P* word!" Dean gasps, and the pair of them laugh.

"Well, I think you're wasting a perfectly good wish," says Alicia. "Do you know what I'd wish for? I'd wish that—"

"I can't bear it any longer! Can I please come in?" It's Darius, knocking on the door. "Please let me see!"

Alicia laughs. "All right, come in," and he practically bursts into the room.

"Wow," he says. "Wow, wow, wow."

His nails are painted now—Dean's handiwork, of course—and they actually look good on him. Two coats of gleaming black polish to match ours.

"Our honorary fourth angel," I say. "And you're *sure* you're not gonna take that polish off for the gym tomorrow? You promise?"

"Are you joking?" Darius says. "I wouldn't dream of it."

"What will your clients say?"

"You really think they'd dare say anything?" he says with a smirk. "If you boys can walk around proudly showing off your nails, so can I."

"Proud of you, Daddy," Alicia says.

"And I'm proud of you, baby girl," he replies. "And now—your carriage awaits." He pretends to wave a magic wand. "You shall go to the ball!"

"Hold your horses," Alicia's mum says in her warm American accent, filing into the room behind him. I don't get to see her all that much, but she really is the spitting image of Alicia. "I thought I'd drive them, actually."

"What about work?" Alicia says. "I know you're busy with your clients, and—"

"The clients can wait," she says. "I'm never too busy for you."

"I don't think I have enough time to paint your nails as well," Dean says. "As much as I'd love to."

"Already done 'em," she says with a wink, presenting her jet-black nails.

"Well, you can drive, Shonda, but I'm riding shotgun," Darius says. "As long as you three don't mind squeezing in the back?"

"Pressed up against these two?" I say. "Can't imagine anything worse."

"All right, fine," Alicia says, playfully rolling her eyes. "But no manspreading. And I'm not sitting in the middle."

"So this is it, then?" Alicia says as we stand outside the auditorium, me and Dean linking arms with her. "Our last Monster Ball."

"I guess we better make it count," I say, waving to her parents who are refusing to drive away. The giant softies want to see their little girl go in.

Alicia smiles. "Absolutely. You ready, then?" she says, pushing open the double doors and revealing the masterpiece within.

The music hits us before anything else, Kim Petras's unique brand of Halloween anthems blasting through the sound system. The entrance is filled with realistic cardboard trees, their branches twisting to give the appearance of a haunted forest. My and Oliver's lanterns hang among the branches, fairy lights leading us through to the warm glow of the dance floor. Expertly carved pumpkins lie scattered around the room, and *RUN!* and *TURN BACK!* have been painted in bloodred writing on the boughs of some of the trees. It's the perfect balance between cute and spooky.

Mrs. A comes over to greet us. She's dressed like Winifred Sanderson, and the resemblance is uncanny.

"*I smell children!*" she says, projecting her voice. "*On All Hallows' Eve, when the moon is round, a virgin will summon us from under the ground!*"

"Uh, why did you look at me when you said *virgin*?" I say.

"And why are you dressed as Barbra Streisand?" Dean adds.

"You two have to ruin everything, don't you? It's a special skill you've developed."

"Ignore them," Alicia says. "I think you look great."

"Well, thank you, Alicia." She smiles. "And so do you. All of you. I'm loving the attention to detail. Now can you promise me you don't have any alcohol hidden in those costumes? I'm not going to have to frisk you?"

"Oh, we already stashed the alcohol in the haunted grotto," I say with a mischievous wink. "There's a bottle of rum inside the beanbag."

"That's a joke, right?" She pinches the bridge of her nose. "Please tell me that's a joke, Max . . ."

"Would we lie to you?" I smile innocently.

"Well, no. I think that's the issue, isn't it . . . ?"

"He's joking, I promise," Alicia says, her fingers crossed behind her back.

Gabi and Shanna appear behind Mrs. A. They've dressed up as the other two Sanderson Sisters, and their costumes are absolutely flawless.

"Oh my God," Dean gasps. "The lesbians have synced up their outfits!"

"Who do you think put her up to it?" Gabi says proudly.

"And we're going viral!" Shanna adds, showing us the TikTok of the three of them on her phone. They can't have taken it more than an hour ago. "We're even on LADbible," she says happily, reading the title of the article. "'*Lesbian couple convince their lesbian teacher to dress up with them for Halloween.*'"

"You're joking!" I say, snatching the phone out of her hand. "This is iconic! The lesbians have actually gone viral!"

Alicia laughs. "Can you all stop saying 'lesbians'?"

"Lesbians," I repeat. "Lesbians, lesbians, lesbians. Come on, say it with me—don't be homophobic," I tease, and she swipes at me.

"More people are arriving!" Gabi says. "Shall we?"

"Come on, then." Mrs. A smiles. "Behave yourself, kids, and happy Monster Ball," she adds as they move on to greet the next set of students.

"*On All Hallows' Eve, when the moon is round, a virgin will summon us from under the ground!*"

Dean guffaws. "What just happened? Literally, what just happened?"

"Only at Woodside," Alicia says, laughing too. "All right, you know the drill. Max, grab us some punch and then meet us in the haunted grotto."

"You're the boss," I say, giving her a little salute as I head off toward the punch bowl.

The table is decorated with fake cobwebs and plastic spiders, bowls of gummy worms, sugar mice, and a four-tier cake stand loaded with chocolate skulls. There's a jack-o'-lantern with *Monster Ball 2023* carved into it too, and two giant cauldrons filled with glittering green-and-purple punch.

"Hey, Max," someone says from behind me as I bite into one of the sugar mice. I turn around to see Thomas Mulbridge. He's dressed as a scarecrow, his clothing stuffed with straw that must be beyond uncomfortable

"Oh . . . hey . . ."

He's the last person I want to talk to. I've still not forgiven him for bullying Dean out of school in Straight World. I know he's not *exactly* the same person, and maybe I shouldn't hold him accountable for something he *technically* hasn't done, but real-world Thomas is hardly any better, so I feel no guilt in continuing to categorize him as a douche.

"Nice outfit," he says, reaching for my feathers.

"Don't touch the wings!" I say, sidestepping away from him.

"Oh sorry," he says, withdrawing his hand. "How are you doing, anyway? I heard you and Oliver finally went on a date."

"Yeah," I say, slurping on a gummy worm. "Why, did he say something?"

"Just that he had a good time," he replies, and I can't help but smile. It's hard to hate even Thomas when he's delivering such good news. "It's cute, you and him," he adds, and he sounds like he actually means it.

"Well, it's just one date," I say. "It's not like we're boyfriends or anything."

"Yeah, I know. I just think you'd be good together, that's all."

"You said that about me and Dean," I say, filling three cups with punch.

"Yeah, well, this time I actually mean it."

"Well, thanks," I say. "I think so too. Just don't tell him I said that."

"I won't—don't worry," he says, grinning. "Anyway, I was thinking that maybe, with the two of you dating, you and me can finally be friends?"

"Friends?" I say, surprised. "You know, you've not always been that nice to me."

"Oh . . ." he says, and he sounds a little taken aback. "When we were kids, you mean? I was a bit of a dick back then, but you know I'm sorry for all that."

"How am I supposed to know that when you've never actually said it?"

"I haven't?" he says, shifting awkwardly. "Well, I'm sorry. I mean, obviously. Of course I am."

"Well, it's about four thousand years too late."

"I know, but I'm not really sure what else to say."

"Just forget about it," I say dismissively, picking up the filled cups and turning back to the party. "Have a good night," I add half-heartedly, and leave him standing there by the punch bowl.

I can tell he's a bit pissed off by my response, but it's not my job to make him feel better. If he's got guilt, that's on him. I'm here to have a good time, not to relive childhood trauma, and that's what I remind myself of as I let Queen Petras put a swing in my hips and stride toward the haunted grotto.

I spot Mr. Johnson standing in the corner and deliberately swerve in his direction. He's completely unironically dressed himself as a PE teacher.

"What do you think of my costume?" I ask, shaking my wings at him, more skin on show than is probably appropriate. Mesh vests are definitely not in the school dress code.

"It's not to my taste," he says bluntly, arms folded.

"Perhaps you don't have any taste?" I say, shaking my ass a little as I walk away from him. I can practically feel his eyes burning into the back of my head. Outrageously petty and probably not a good idea to poke the bear, but that felt good. Really good in fact. That definitely felt like a win.

"Hey, Max . . ."

"Poppy!" I exclaim, practically running straight into her. She's dressed as a cavegirl, a very revealing leopard-print toga wrapped tenuously around her body. Oh God, Double P has barely concealed her double Ds. I remember the note then. *I hope you like my costume too . . .*

She's not the only one with skin on show, though. At least we have that in common.

"Great costume," she says, reaching for my feathers. Why does everyone want to touch my feathers?

"Thanks," I say. "I'm glad I bumped into you actually. I've been meaning to talk to you . . ."

"Oh yeah?" she says, twiddling her tousled hair.

"It's just that . . . Well . . . Look, I'm really flattered, but you're not exactly my type, you know? Maybe in . . . another world, if things were different?"

Poppy frowns. "Max, what are you talking about?"

"I got your note," I say. "In my locker. And it was really sweet, honestly. Like, totally romantic—who doesn't want a secret admirer? But I just can't be that person for you. I'm sorry."

"What note? Max, I didn't write any note."

"You don't need to be embarrassed," I say. "It's fine."

"No, really, it wasn't me," she says, sounding a little offended now. "Can I see it?"

"Dean ripped it up."

"Convenient . . ." She rolls her eyes. "Look, Max, I don't know what this is, but I'm not interested, okay? Aren't you gay anyway? Rumor has it you've blown half the soccer team."

"What? Half the soccer team?! It's just one player! Singular! And we haven't even kissed much less gotten to third base!"

"Well, whatever. I don't wanna be a part of your little game. See you later," she says, pushing past me.

Wow, rude much? Maybe Dean was right, and I should have just ignored it, but at least I've set the record straight.

"Got the punch?" Dean says as I reach the grotto. I hold up the cups. Simon Pike and Rachel Kwan are in there too. Promposal successful, they've dressed as what I can only assume is supposed to be Bonnie and Clyde. They're slumped on a beanbag, looking somewhat disheveled. It seems like we've disturbed a rather intense makeout session.

"Can I just get in here a moment . . . ?" Alicia says uncomfortably, kneeling down and awkwardly trying to unzip the beanbag underneath them.

"I was wondering what was digging into my back," says Simon, laughing as Alicia pulls out the large bottle of rum she'd promised Mrs. A was entirely fictional.

"I'd offer you some, but I don't have any more cups," I say, taking the rum from Alicia and topping up our drinks.

"Don't worry about it," Rachel says, lifting up a tiny silver hip flask. "We brought our own."

Amateurs, I think. *That won't last five minutes . . .*

"Shall we leave these lovebirds to it?" Dean suggests, tucking the bottle of rum back underneath them.

"Yeah, see you later," Alicia says, leading us back out into the party.

We stand on the stage and watch the dance floor fill with eager students.

I sigh. "I can't believe this is all coming to an end . . ."

"Dramatic much?" Alicia says. "We've still got almost a whole year. Save your tearful farewell for the Leavers' Ball, Max!"

Dean laughs. "It's kinda crazy, though, to think that this time next year we'll all be somewhere else. Do you think we'll stay friends?"

"How dare you suggest otherwise!" Alicia says. "Of *course* we will. Unless you ditch us as soon as you're a West End superstar?" She raises an eyebrow. "Although you better not because Max still needs you to paint his nails. Lord knows he can't do them himself."

"I'll be at the stage door every night, clutching a bottle of polish!"

"*Stage door?*" Alicia splutters. "I'm expecting a pair of front-row seats!"

"Make it three!" I say. "We'll need one for Oliver . . ."

"Wow, you went a whole five minutes without mentioning him," Alicia says. "Speaking of which, did you tell him you have a thing for Spider-Man?"

"Huh? I might have mentioned Tom Holland once or twice. Why?"

"Look over there," she says. "By the entrance."

And there he is, the boy who lives rent-free in my fantasies, Oliver Cheng in a tightly fitted Spider-Man suit that leaves *nothing* to the imagination. He's not wearing the mask, though, and his floppy hair and dimples are fully visible as he walks into the room, his face lighting up among the paper lanterns as he takes in Alicia's work.

"My God," I say. "I really must be dreaming . . ."

"About him firing his web shooter all over you?" Dean grins.

"Actually, I was thinking more along the lines of a super-romantic upside-down spidey-kiss."

Alicia snorts. "You're actually a thirteen-year-old girl, you know that, Max?"

"What?" I smile innocently. "I'm just being honest."

Dean laughs. "Come on," he says, grabbing me by the arm. "Let's go say hello before Max bursts a blood vessel or something."

"Hey, Max," Oliver says as we approach. "Hey, Dean, Alicia. You guys look amazing," he says, reaching out for my wings. I don't bat him away. Thomas and Poppy can keep their hands off, but Oliver can touch whatever he wants.

"You look good too." I grin dopily, the rest of the world ceasing to exist.

"Did you get my note?" he asks, beaming.

"Huh?" I say. "What do you mean, your note?"

"The one I put in your locker."

"What?!" I say. "But you signed it Double P."

"Yeah?" he says, gesturing to his outfit. "Peter Parker."

Oh my GOD.

Dean is straight-up cackling now. "Max thought it was from Poppy! Poppy Palmer!"

"What?" Oliver laughs. "I don't think you're her type, Max . . . Isn't she dating one of the Grove Hill boys? Some guy called Chad? Or was it Garrett?"

"Oh God," I say out loud now. "Oh God, oh God, oh God . . ."

"What's the big deal?" Alicia asks. "You didn't say anything, did you?"

"I *may* have tried to let her down easy," I say. All of them are laughing now. "I should probably apologize, right?"

"Just leave it," Dean says. "Honestly, Max, before you make things worse."

"So the note was from you?" I say, my eyes meeting Oliver's.

"Yeah," he says, blushing a little. "Dean told me you'd always wanted a guy to slip little notes in your locker. I probably should have signed it with my real name, but I thought it'd be cute to hint at who I was gonna dress as . . ."

"It really is cute," I say. "And you look great."

"Thanks. And wow, this place is incredible, Alicia. I can't believe you really did all this. In a single week?"

"Well, I couldn't have done it without you," she says. "Thanks for helping."

Oliver shakes his head. "I made maybe three lanterns? I think that wonky-looking one up there is one of mine."

"Well, it was a team effort," Alicia says modestly.

"Thanks again for rescuing us the other night, by the way," Oliver says.

"Anytime. Honestly, if Mr. Johnson had caught you—"

"It would still have been worth it," I interrupt.

"I'm sure it would. Right, come on, Dean—refills!"

"Oh, but mine's still half full . . ."

"No it's not," Alicia says, taking it out of his hand and downing it. "See you boys later." She gives us a little wave and practically drags Dean away.

"Sorry about them," I say, my cheeks hot with embarrassment. "They seem to think they still need to play Cupid."

"I think it's nice," he says. "Thomas is the same."

"What do you mean?"

"It's silly really," he says, blushing. "I'd wanted to ask you out for ages. I was too nervous to go to the Queer Club, but Thomas convinced me. Said he'd come with, to give me a chance to talk to you . . . But then Mr. Johnson arrived and—"

"Totally cockblocked you!"

He laughs. "Exactly! And then, just before *Little Shop*, Thomas insisted I go and talk to you, but I panicked and tripped over my own feet."

"I thought it was me that walked into you!"

"I guess we're both a little clumsy?"

"Just a little," I say with a smile. "But wait . . . So Thomas was trying to set us up this whole time? But he thought Dean and I were a couple."

"Oh," Oliver says. "Actually, that was *me*. I wasn't sure if you guys were friends, or more than that, so I asked Thomas to find out . . ."

"And I called him homophobic for asking." I slap my face with my palm.

"Yeah, he told me that," Oliver says. "But it's cool—don't worry about it."

"I really had no idea . . ." I say, scanning the room for Thomas. He's still standing on his own by the punch bowl, awkwardly sipping his drink. I think back to all the times I've been rude to him. *Once a homophobe, always a homophobe* . . . At the time, I thought he deserved it, but maybe he really has changed. Maybe he does deserve a second chance.

"So . . . do you wanna go check out the haunted grotto?" Oliver asks.

"The makeout room, you mean?" I raise one eyebrow.

"I don't know *what* you're talking about," he says innocently.

"I'd love to," I say, laughing, "but Simon and Rachel are in there, and they look sort of . . . *busy*. So maybe we could go say hey to Thomas first?"

"Sure," Oliver says, electricity filling the air as he takes my hand in his. It feels like the world moves in slow motion as we make our way across the room. I clock a few of the other kids noticing us holding hands and whispering to each other. I know it's silly, but I actually sort of love it.

"Hey, guys," Thomas says as we approach. "It's going well, then?" He grins, nodding to our hands. Oliver's feels warm and clammy in mine, but I don't want to ever let go.

"I like to think so," Oliver says. "Cool costume," he adds, adjusting some of the straw that's come loose from Thomas's oversized hat. "Isn't it uncomfortable, though?"

"It's SO itchy," Thomas admits. "This was definitely a mistake."

"You can change at mine later if you want," Oliver says. "You're still coming to the after-party, right?"

"I mean, if you guys want me there?" he says, looking at me now.

"Yes," I say, and I mean it. "I think we're long overdue for a catch-up."

He smiles at that, and something in his eyes says thank you.

"That reminds me actually," I say to Oliver. "Do you have room for two or three more?"

"I mean, we've already invited half the school," he says. "A few more isn't going to make a difference. Why? Who did you have in mind?"

Chapter Twenty-One

"Never have I ever . . . masturbated at school."

I grin, looking directly at Oliver. Who knows whether he committed the same deed as he did in Straight World, but I've been dying to find out. We're packed into his living room, and it honestly feels like the entire school is here.

"Oh my God . . ." He laughs, turning bright red as he takes a sip of his drink. "How did you know about that? I haven't told anyone . . ."

"Just a hunch," I say, but then Simon takes a drink as well. And so does Rachel. And Alicia.

"All of you?!" I say, disbelieving. "I cannot be the only one who hasn't jerked off at school. Since when were you all this horny?"

"We're teenagers," says Alicia with a shrug. "I'm quite surprised you haven't actually, Max. Masturbating in places you shouldn't is usually your MO."

"What's that supposed to mean?"

"That field full of cows?"

"Okay, but that was one time and—"

"Your grandma's house."

"Okay, but . . ."

"That night at mine when you thought Dean and I were sleeping."

"Okay, I get it!" How have they managed to turn this back on me? "But *all* of you? At school? Where? When? I have so many questions."

"The haunted grotto," Simon and Rachel say in unison.

"God, I hope you washed your hands," I say. Simon is holding Oliver's *Toy Story* cup. That poor Hamm . . . "And what about you, Alicia?"

"The supply room at the back of the art class," she says, a little too proudly. "Nobody ever really goes in there."

"And here's us thinking you were staying late because you were working."

"We were working. Zach and I used to work ourselves *to the bone*."

"Okay, gross," I say. "You're all perverts. I can't believe I thought I was the one that was depraved."

"Not very sex positive of you, Maxwell," Rachel teases. "But aren't you forgetting someone? Come on, Ollie, where was it? Spill."

Please say the boys' locker room. Please . . .

"Okay, I have this place . . ." he says slowly. "A secret place that nobody really knows about . . ."

He looks at me then and *actually* winks.

"The roof!" Alicia blurts out, slapping her thighs with glee. "It's where he took Max on their date!"

"And here's me thinking that was the most romantic evening ever, when you actually just took me to your own private wank parlor?"

"You really thought it was romantic?" Oliver grins.

"Well . . . yeah . . . I *did*. But that's not really the point . . ."

"Aww," he says, grinning even wider now. "Glad you had a nice time."

"In the private wank parlor," Alicia adds. "Just so we're all clear."

And that's when the doorbell rings.

"Hold that thought," Oliver says, opening the door to a girl I instantly recognize as Laci. It's like she read my mind because she really does look like Gwen Stacy, and she's leaned into that by dressing up as Spider-Gwen to match Oliver's Spider-Twink. I guess me, Dean, and Alicia aren't the only ones who coordinate our outfits for Halloween. It is Queer Christmas after all.

"I'm so glad you're here!" Oliver cries, lifting her into the air and spinning her around, her feet sending my drink flying out of my hand. Vodka cranberry splashes all over the furniture, but nobody saw it happen so if anyone asks it wasn't me. "I've missed you so much."

"I missed you too," she says. "Sorry I'm so late. I got detention again, and then the train took forever. Where is Woodside anyway? Like, literally, where in the country is this? Are we north? South? I'm pretty sure I've never even seen it on a map . . ."

"Oh, never mind that," Oliver says. "You're here now—that's what matters."

"This is a sweet step up," Laci says, looking around the room. "I knew your parents had *money*, but this is something else. You gonna give me the tour, then? Where's this boyfriend you won't shut up about?"

"Oh, we're not boyfriends." He blushes, stepping aside to introduce me. "But yeah, this is Max," he says. "Max, Laci."

"I've heard so much about you," I say, going in to hug her.

"You too. I thought you'd be a bit better looking, though. The way Oliver has been banging on about you, I thought you'd at least be a six . . ."

"Oh, uh, well . . ." I genuinely don't know what to say to that.

"I'm fucking with you," she says, laughing. "Ah, come on, you must know you're out of his league, right? If you want me to be your wing-gal, I can help find you someone better. One of these straight boys must be at least a *little* curious. What about him?"

"That's Thomas," says Oliver. "He's my best friend."

"I thought that was me?" Laci gasps. "Replaced me already, have you, Ollie?" She smiles over at Thomas. *Hey, Tom,* she mouths with a seductive wave, and he freezes like a deer in headlights.

"All right, let me give you the tour," Oliver says, leading her up the stairs. He puts his arm around her, proud to show off his best friend.

Alicia and I go through to the kitchen to find Dean.

"Stop moving!" Dean laughs as he tries to pick the last of the straw out of Thomas's clothing.

"Stop tickling, then!" Thomas protests, squirming. "I think I definitely win the prize for the worst costume."

"Who wins best, then?" Dean asks, straightening his corset.

"My vote is for Oliver," I say.

"Of course," Alicia says, rolling her eyes playfully. "Sorry, Max, if you're just gonna think with your penis, you don't get a vote."

"What! I think it's a good costume!"

"It's a Spider-Man costume off Amazon, Max," Dean says. "Literally just putting more money in Jeff's pockets . . ."

"Jeff?" Alicia echoes. "Are we really just casually referring to Bezos as 'Jeff' now? Like he's some bloke who works down at Sainsbury's?"

"Fine," Dean says. "He's just putting money in *Jeffrey's* pockets, then."

"You make a good point," I say. "It's really bad to spend money in such a place. Now remind me, where exactly did you get our wings from again?"

"Oh, um . . . a unique, independent, highly ethical store . . ." Dean says.

"Mm-hmm. And what was it called?"

"Oh . . . uh . . . it was, um . . . Was that the doorbell?"

The bell actually *does* ring then, and Dean seems incredibly proud of himself. I look over to see Oliver answering the door to Kedar and a couple of his friends. Right on time.

Oliver catches my eye and gives me a wink. I smile back. Dean Jackson isn't the only one who can play Cupid . . .

Kedar gives Oliver a little bro fist bump as his friends file into the house and start making their introductions. I immediately recognize the two who had been there with him at *Mean Girls*. They're both decked out in sequins and glitter, one wearing a top that reads FUCK THE CIS-TEM in silver lettering, and the other a pair of sparkling platforms that lift them at least eight inches off the ground.

"But seriously, Max," Alicia says, "if you couldn't vote for Oliver, then who? You're supposed to be the fashion guy now!"

"Fine," I concede. "I'd have to give it to Dean, then. I know I styled him, so I'm kind of just voting for myself, but look at him!"

"*Moi*? Really?" Dean says, feigning surprise. "In my wings that were definitely not purchased from Jeffrey?"

"Really," I say, laughing. "You look totally hot. I think that guy over there was just checking you out." I nod toward Kedar.

"Huh?" Dean says, looking over.

"Not the guy in the white top?" Alicia says. "Who even *is* that?"

"I think he plays soccer with Oliver?" I say, playing dumb. "Kedar, I think his name is."

"Oh, he is *ca-yoot*," Alicia says in a singsong voice, looking him up and down. Dean doesn't say anything; he's just staring, speechless for once.

"He's totally checking you out," I say, and this time it's true. He really is. The two of them make awkward eye contact and then coyly look away. "You should go talk to him!"

"No way!" Dean says. "Look at those shoulders! He's like a fifteen out of ten!"

"Oh, how the tables have turned," I say with a grin. "You made me talk to Oliver. I think it's time to practice what you preach."

"That was different!" Dean protests. "Oliver was quite clearly into you."

"And Kedar's quite clearly into you!" I shoot back. "He's literally staring at you *right now*."

"Okay, fine," he says. "I'll talk to him. But, just for the record, I hate you."

"Love you too," I say as Alicia, Thomas, and I watch him nervously go over and strike up a conversation. Fierce Dean Jackson reduced to a nervous wreck. I never thought I'd see the day.

"How did you know?" Alicia asks, looking at me suspiciously.

"Know what?"

"That he'd be into Dean. You planned this, didn't you?"

"No." I smile innocently. "Course not. How could I have?"

Alicia shakes her head. "Just when I think I've figured you out, Max, you still manage to surprise me."

I grin. "Gotta keep you on your toes."

Kedar and Dean are laughing now, and Dean has been so bold as to flirtatiously touch his arm.

"Well," she says, "we've clearly gotta get you a bow and arrow to match those wings."

"So I can fire it straight through Oliver's heart?"

"Oh, I think that's already taken care of." She nods over to Oliver, who is smiling in our direction. "He's so totally smitten, Max."

"You think so?"

"I know so," she says. "Now go make some babies or whatever it is gay people do when they're in love."

"I'll send you some websites where you can see for yourself," I reply. "I saw this one video where a guy took another guy's foot and—"

"Oh my God, Max!" Alicia splutters on her drink. "And here's me trying to convince my dad you're so sweet and innocent."

"I am both of those things," I say, leaving her with Thomas and going over to Laci and Oliver, who looks increasingly concerned about the number of people in his house. "Regretting it already?"

"Oh no, it's just . . ."

"Not like a London party?"

"Exactly," he says ruefully. "You took the words right out of my mouth. It's cool, though. One night can't hurt, right?"

"Right," I say, just as I hear a drunken voice from the kitchen suggesting a game of Duck, Duck, Goose. "But maybe we should put a stop to that?"

He laughs. "It's fine. Don't worry about it."

"Oliver and I were just talking," Laci says, "and we thought it might be fun if the two of you came up to London to see me sometime?"

"Oh yeah?" I say. "I mean, sure, I'd love that."

"We could go check out the London College of Fashion while we're there," Oliver says. "And I could show you that bookshop I've been telling you about?"

"You do have to bring me presents, though," Laci adds, perfectly deadpan.

"Presents? Like what?"

"Oh, I don't know." She smirks. "Something expensive? I can already see you have good taste." She gestures to my outfit. "Very well put together. You wanna be a stylist, right? I totally see that for you."

"Yeah, I mean, I think so," I say. "I'm still sort of figuring that out."

"Maybe you can give this one some tips?" She goes to mess Oliver's hair.

"I don't need tips!" he protests, dodging away from her.

"Mm-hmm, yeah, sure you don't," she says. "Well, anyway, I'm gonna go see if these Woodside kids know how to throw a party. Max, I think Ollie wanted to show you his room." She winks and squeezes his hand as she slips away.

"Your room?" I say, swallowing hard. I think I hear him swallow too.

"Uh, yeah, if you wanna see it?"

"I've been dying to see it actually . . ."

"Oh really?" He raises an eyebrow suggestively. "Come on then, as long as you promise to be on your best behavior."

"I'm absolutely not making that promise . . ."

"Oh well . . . even better." Oliver grins wickedly, leading me upstairs. "I don't let a lot of people in here, you know?" he says, hesitating for a moment at the door.

It's exactly as I remember it from Straight World—the rainbow bookcase, the Dragon Ball figurines, even the dinosaur blanket folded over his chair.

"It's cute," I say, smiling as I take it all in.

"*You're* cute," he says back, and then there's an awkward moment where we fumble and bump our heads as he tries to kiss me.

"Sorry," I say, but he doesn't say anything back, just stares at me like he really sees me, and for just a moment it feels as if the whole world comes to a standstill. Just like that moment in the library, the lights seem to dim and flicker and the rest of the world falls away until there's nothing left but the two of us. I'm so glad I get a second chance to do this, and to do it right, because this time there's no magic, and no expectations, nothing but us.

His hands slide up my arms and then, feeling the weight of his body against mine, we finally, *finally* kiss.

We may have done it in another world, at another time, but this is something different, something special, because I've truly never experienced *this*. I'm no longer searching for that spark in the darkness. This time my whole world ignites. Five drooling emojis, ten chili peppers, and as many eggplants as you can imagine. Kissing Oliver confirms that I literally could not be any more gay, and I know now that this is exactly where I was always supposed to be. Every single queer button is switched on and dialed up to a thousand. His lips are rough and sweet and addictive, all at the same time. It's every bit as good as I ever thought it could be.

I let his hands pull me in closer. "I thought maybe . . ." he begins, withdrawing a little before kissing me a second time.

"Yeah?" I say. There's a weightiness to my breath now.

"I thought maybe you might like to stay over?"

I furrow my brow. "But where would I sleep? Your parents' room?"

"Laci's in there," he says, pulling me even closer.

"I could crash on the sofa, then?"

"I was actually thinking we'd break the last of the house rules. No drinking . . . no parties . . . no boys in my bed."

"*Oh*," I say.

His fingers slip under the band of my underwear then, and I have to stop myself from letting out a gasp. My wish is finally coming true. I'm actually going to get a Friday-night sleepover with Oliver Cheng. "But . . . I didn't bring any pajamas."

"You still wear pajamas?" he says, laughing. "Cute, but . . . I think maybe you won't need them? I've got an old T-shirt you can wear, if you want."

"Well, let's see how it goes."

"All right," he says, kissing me again.

"Wait," I say.

"Are you okay?"

"Yeah. It's just . . . I know you always wanted this to be special. Your first kiss. Mine too . . ."

"Well, I think we're technically on our third now," he says, kissing me more softly. "And that one was the fourth . . ." He grins, his cheeks dimpling in the way that I love. "Besides, what could be more special than this?"

"I don't know," I say, suddenly nervous again. "I was thinking . . . maybe we should be . . ."

"Boyfriends?"

"Yeah." I smile. "So it's official, then?"

"It's official," he says with a gentle little nod, and as I stare into those beautiful eyes it's like I'm seeing him for the first time. Because for all the times I spent fantasizing about him, I never really saw him.

I see him now, though, and I realize he's not some perfect, unattainable thing to wish for. And he never was. In fact, he's just ordinary, friendly, plain old Oliver Cheng. And, for all our faults and all our flaws, maybe we are just a pair of normal kids after all.

Acknowledgments

I sat down opposite Ella Kahn, my wonderful agent, in the beginning of 2020 and told her that I wanted to write LGBT+ young adult (YA) fiction. I was nervous—all I'd heard from the industry was that "queer books don't sell"—but she was unbelievably supportive from the start. She believed in me, and the stories I wanted to tell, and that was all the encouragement I needed.

I already had an editor in mind—the wonderful Ben Horslen at Penguin Random House UK, a trailblazer within the world of children's fiction, and somebody who worked on some of my all-time favorite LGBT+ books. I knew it wouldn't be easy to get his eyes on my work, though, so together with the support of my agent, I spent the best part of a year working on a book entitled *The Gay Games*.

I worked round the clock and poured my heart and soul into it, hoping that it would be the novel that would land me my dream book deal. It wasn't. He turned us down, saying that he didn't believe the book was quite right. What he did say, however, was that he could see that I had enormous potential as an author of LGBT+ fiction, and he asked me if I had any other ideas instead.

Acknowledgments

I didn't—but of course I lied and said that I did, and as I frantically word-vomited my thoughts down into a Word document, the idea for *Straight Expectations* finally hit. A few months later, I had the first draft and a book deal, and I couldn't believe my luck. I still have to pinch myself even now.

I'm so unbelievably grateful to Ben, and the wider team at Penguin, for taking this chance on me. And they were absolutely right—this book is infinitely better than the one I first brought to them, and I'm so thankful that they helped me to realize that. Thank you to Laura Dean, Shreeta Shah, Emily Smyth, Charlotte Winston, James McParland, Alice Grigg, and everyone else who worked to make this book what it is. Thank you also to Simon Armstrong, who never officially got to work on this book, but has been quietly whispering suggestions in my ear the whole time. This book is all of theirs as much as it is mine. I'm so proud of what we've created, and I really hope that they are too.

I also have to say an enormous thank-you to all the queer YA authors who have inspired me up to this moment. I had the pleasure of working on the film adaptation of Becky Albertalli's wonderful queer romance *Simon vs. The Homo Sapiens Agenda* back in 2018, and that was a game changer for me. I believe the success of her work, as well as the work of countless other LGBT+ authors, really opened that door for me and made me realize how much I wanted to pursue writing my own queer YA. There are some subtle references to some of those authors hidden throughout this book— I'm not going to name-drop them all here, but they know who they are, and I hope they understand how much their support has meant to me.

I'm also delighted to say that this book is my first book that will be published simultaneously in the US. Thank you so much to Ardi Alspach and the team at Union Square for bringing Max, Dean, Oliver, and Alicia across the pond.

Acknowledgments

Thank you to Kevin Wada, the incredible queer artist who created the gorgeous illustrated cover. Seeing my characters brought to life brings me more joy than you can possibly realize.

Thank you to Helen Gould, Luxeria Celes, and Jason Kwan for taking the time to read the book and offer your crucially valuable feedback. The identities represented in this book are far more authentic than they would have been without your guidance. Your words and wisdom have been unbelievably valuable; there's a little piece of all of you in these pages.

Thank you also to all the queer teachers in my life—Dan, Haley, and Jon—and all the other wonderful LGBT+ teachers out there creating the safe spaces that kids so desperately need. Mrs. Ashford is all of you, she's the teacher I wish I had, and the teacher queer kids deserve. As for my own teachers? Thanks for inspiring Mr. Johnson. "Big fish, small pond?" I'm so delighted to prove you wrong.

Thank you to my wonderful readers, for continuing to support my writing and my career. It's thanks to you that I'm able to spend my days with characters that I love, and I couldn't be more grateful.

And finally, thank you to all the people who I've no doubt forgotten to thank—an LGBT+ book isn't created by a single person, it's created by a whole community. Thank you for being with me every step of the way; I couldn't have done it without you. Thank you, thank you, thank you.